KW-329-250

A. V. Denham taught in both London and Hong Kong before moving to Wales with her family. She joined the Women's Royal Voluntary Service and later trained for the emergency services. Denham enjoys travelling, gardening and is also interested in goldwork. She lives in Monmouth.

UNINTENDED CONSEQUENCES

In Burma, James and Carol Morgan meet Brian and Kimberley Pickering who protest against the Junta and are arrested. Interrogated by Military Intelligence as accessories, the Morgans are ultimately freed but ordered to take the Pickerings' children to Bangkok. Carol agrees to take the children home, but James refuses, abandons them and goes to Australia . . . At home, the children's uncle, Peter, is initially hostile and the children run away to London. And when Peter and Carol go looking for them, they are forced to share a hotel room. Now faced with unintended consequences, Carol must make a difficult choice . . .

Books by A. V. Denham
Published by The House of Ulverscroft:

THE STONE BOAT
SEEDS OF DESTRUCTION
THE GIRL WHO DISAPPEARED

A. V. DENHAM

UNINTENDED CONSEQUENCES

Complete and Unabridged

ULVERSCROFT
Leicester

First published in Great Britain in 2007 by
Robert Hale Limited
London

First Large Print Edition
published 2008
by arrangement with
Robert Hale Limited
London

The moral right of the author has been asserted

British Library CIP Data

Denham, A. V. (Angela Veronica), *1936 –*
Unintended consequences.—Large print ed.—
Ulverscroft large print series: general fiction
1. Political prisoners—Burma—Fiction 2. Runaway
children—Fiction 3. Uncles—Fiction 4. Abandoned
children—Fiction 5. Large type books
I. Title
823.9'2 [F]

ISBN 978–1–84782–249–9

Published by
F. A. Thorpe (Publishing)
Anstey, Leicestershire
Set by Words & Graphics Ltd.
Anstey, Leicestershire
Printed and bound in Great Britain by
T. J. International Ltd., Padstow, Cornwall

This book is printed on acid-free paper

For want of a nail the shoe was lost,
For want of a shoe the horse was lost,
For want of a horse the rider was lost,
For want of a rider the battle was lost,
For want of a battle the kingdom was lost,
And all for want of a horseshoe nail.

Trad.

1

'How long have you known the Pickerings, Carol?'

'I told you,' she said wearily, as she had said — how many times was it? — 'we only met them at the airport in Rangoon.'

'We call it Yangon and you lie.'

Sitting across the empty metal table from the man in olive green uniform, a member of Burma's Military Intelligence, Carol Morgan forced herself to remain calm. Despite his youth, and smooth, light brown skin, his dark, impenetrable eyes terrified her. His face was cold as he assessed her, with no hint of humanity or compassion.

'It is the truth.'

He sat back in the padded chair on the other side of the table and regarded her insultingly. 'You knew them before you came to Myanmar, Carol.' He understood very well that when he did not use this elderly woman's honorific it made her uncomfortable, possibly even more uneasy than the hard chair she had sat on for so long. That, along with the uncertainty of what was going to happen to her. 'Carol, if you confess, it will be so much easier for you.'

She began to understand how it was that, in the end, people who were interrogated for a long time confessed to things they had not done. 'I want to see the British Consul,' she said. She tried to sound convincingly firm. Even she could not hear confidence in her voice.

Once again he ignored her request. 'Why did you spend time with the Pickering family?'

'We didn't spend time together. Twice we were asked to give them a lift because their car had broken down.'

'I don't believe you. You had dinner together.'

'You have to believe me because it's true,' she cried despairingly. 'That evening . . . it only happened once . . . we wanted to see some Burmese dancing. The Pickerings were there, too. You can ask the guide. All our guides knew that we preferred to be on our own. Where is my husband? Where is James? Why have you not sent for the British Consul?'

He snarled. 'We ask the questions here. Not you.'

★ ★ ★

James and Carol Morgan were supposed to be flying out of Rangoon to Bangkok that evening. Alone for a moment in their room in the hotel by the airport, while James settled their bill, Carol was startled by the sudden appearance of two Burmese in military uniform who burst through the door. They insisted she accompany them, then unceremoniously hustled her out through the foyer and into a car. She went protesting, but no one came forward to offer assistance. Why should they, with the authority of a much-feared uniform forbidding anything more than a sympathetic glance from a solitary guest? The two young receptionists behind the desk merely averted their eyes from her predicament.

The steamy heat outside hit her like a hammer blow. There was a car already pulling away from the kerb and Carol thought she caught a glimpse of James's head through the rear window but all the windows were of smoked glass and she could not be sure.

'Find my husband. Tell the tour company,' she screamed, as a more senior hotel manager, dressed formally in a black suit, emerged through the imposing glass doors to hover several feet away from the official cars. Again she could not be sure, but she thought he merely shrugged.

The whole thing was a nightmare. One moment she was rearranging their luggage for the flight, the next she was thrust rudely into something totally beyond her comprehension. And she was on her own.

From the large, rambling building dating back to the colonial era, Carol surmised that she had been taken to police headquarters in Rangoon. Once inside she was manhandled to a small room on the top floor, with one window, heavily barred. There she was left. The only furniture was a table and two chairs. Only then did it occur to her that she had the dubious consolation of not being handcuffed.

'Have I been arrested?' she demanded of the man who appeared after a long interval. He was a larger man than most she had seen in Burma. Better fed? At that moment her indignation and terror were roughly equal.

'You are not under arrest yet,' he answered. 'We are merely detaining you for questioning. How long you remain here depends on your answers to my questions. Sit down.' His command of English was excellent.

Carol sat down, reluctantly.

'How long have you known the Pickerings?' So the interrogation began.

★ ★ ★

During the short intervals when her interrogator left the room, while she had waited for — whatever was to happen next — Carol thought back to what had been the start of the events which seemed to be culminating in such a frightening way.

It was a Friday afternoon in early September. Carol was making beetroot and ginger chutney in the kitchen of their Georgian house on the outskirts of Otterhaven, a village in the Welsh Marches, when the front door slammed and James Morgan announced his arrival in his usual fashion with the thump of his briefcase on the polished oak chest in the hall followed by the thud as his shoulder hit the kitchen door.

'Hi, I'm back,' he said, unnecessarily.

'How did your meeting go? Want a cup of tea?' responded his wife, not waiting for a reply to her first question. 'It'll take another ten minutes or so for the chutney to thicken but I can take a break as long as I watch it.'

'I'll put the kettle on.'

Tall for a Welshman, James Morgan reached across for the kettle which he half-filled then set on the hob next to the large pan in which the chutney bubbled. He was a man whose build was of the rugby-player kind, and although his body remained firm, his face betrayed a life well-lived. At fifty-nine, he had dark eyes with bushy eyebrows and abundant greying hair. He was well-dressed, as usual, in a dark business suit, pale blue shirt with a sober tie and well polished leather shoes.

As she passed him two mugs, Carol was aware of barely suppressed excitement. 'I wasn't expecting you so early today. You haven't forgotten we're going to the Hendersons tonight, have you?'

'Can't we cancel?'

'Not at this late stage — unless it's a crisis. Marion particularly wants us to meet a couple who've recently moved here.' Marion Henderson was Carol's best friend and her husband, Clive, was one of the few Otterhaven men James would acknowledge as his intellectual equal. 'Is there a crisis?' she asked cautiously, as James reached for the tea caddy.

'Not exactly a crisis,' he answered. 'Oh, leave the chutney and come and sit down. I've something to tell you.'

With no sense of foreboding, Carol gave the chutney another stir and left the pan to simmer gently. She wiped her hands on a cloth. Then she fetched the biscuit tin and sat down at the kitchen table opposite James. 'What's happened?'

'I've left the job. I'm unemployed. No work

to go to. Free. Well, there are a few loose ends to sort out but that's it. I'm finished for ever with the nine to five job.'

Carol blinked. Whatever she had expected it was not that.

'Close your mouth, dear,' he said fondly. 'Thought I'd surprise you. You are, aren't you? Surprised, I mean.'

Carol swallowed. She ran her fingers through her own short, greying hair which she had stopped tinting when she reached forty-four. She tucked the ends behind her ears. 'I don't understand,' she said huskily. 'How can you be unemployed? Only this morning you were enthusing about what you were going to set in motion next week, once today's meeting had . . . Oh, James, what happened at today's meeting?'

He told her, explaining the details carefully. Afterwards, Carol could recall practically nothing of what he said, so taken aback was she by his news.

James Morgan was an engineer who discovered in his early thirties an uncanny knack for solving problems of production which were sometimes, though not always, an engineering matter. Over the following fifteen years he had been head-hunted by a series of firms for whom he saved a great deal of money by troubleshooting for them. Then a smallish firm in Glamorgan in South Wales offered him a seat on the board and James, tempted by the salary, the challenge of carrying through the changes he was suggesting, not to mention the chance of returning to his roots, accepted. He and Carol and their son, the sixteen-year old Matthew, settled in Otterhaven where they had remained ever since — though Matthew was long since gone; firstly to university and then to a series of oil rigs, the most recent one off the coast of Aberdeen. With James on the board, the small firm had grown, had diversified with EU development money and was now one of the success stories of that depressed region. James had fully expected to be offered the chairmanship. This would have taken him to retirement and a more than satisfactory pension.

'Today has been something of a revelation,' he said, catching hold of Carol's hand as it rested by the biscuit tin.

'You can say that again,' she said, gently but firmly releasing her hand and taking another biscuit, thinking to hell with the fat and the sugar content. 'This morning . . . I thought . . . You were hinting there would be changes. I never guessed it would be this.'

'Nor did I.'

His smile disarmed her, though she was

aware of growing anger. 'I thought we discussed life-changes before we actually made them. I thought we didn't have secrets from each other. How could you decide on such a change of direction without mentioning anything to me first?'

'Because, as I said, it came as a revelation.'

'Revelation! Since when have you relied on revelation to come to any decision? You have always weighed facts and figures and known exactly what you wanted from life. How come this is different?'

'Carol, you know what I think about *Johns' Precision*. You know how much energy I've devoted to the firm. Actually, devoted is just the word for my feelings towards it and what we've achieved. This morning, when I went into the board meeting I knew what was going to happen; I knew that the other members of the board had accepted that, once again, we have to restructure. I knew I would be offered the chairmanship formally. When I left home this morning I fully intended to accept it and implement the new changes myself.'

'Then why didn't you? Why turn the offer down?'

'It wasn't what I wanted to do any more.'

'So you declined?'

'That's right. Restructuring inevitably means

job losses. I pointed out that a member of the board had to go as well as a percentage of the workforce. I suggested that the board member should be me.'

'But why? Why you, when you haven't got all that long before you retire? Have you been head-hunted again? Is that what all this is about? Have you another job to go to? Why haven't you told me any of this?'

'Because there's nothing to tell. No job, no plans. Well, that isn't strictly true. I do have plans, I think.'

'James, you are not making sense. What plans?' A feeling of intense dread was beginning to assail her. She wondered fleetingly if he might be ill. Mentally? Physically — the dreaded C-word? Theirs had been an uncomplicated life: more so since Matthew had got his degree and was established with a job. (Maybe Matthew was not quite established, since he wasn't yet married, which was perhaps a blessing in disguise. Carol wasn't too sure of the staying power of Matthew's live-in girlfriend.) At least Matthew was a source of pride rather than concern.

'You see,' James said, with a broad grin on his face, 'I suddenly realized I was bored.'

'Bored . . . '

'Carol, dear, you are parroting a bit, you know.'

'Pa . . . ' she began, and stopped. 'Well, I'm very sorry that my reaction to this stupendous news of yours is something of a disappointment,' she snapped. 'I'm trying to express interest, unconfined delight that you are doing what you want to do. If I am failing, you must forgive me . . . '

'Carol . . . '

She left the table hurriedly and went over to the Aga. I am not going to burst into tears, she thought, biting her lip as she dragged the chutney pan to the side of the hob and vigorously stirred the contents which she had a horrible feeling were about to stick to the bottom. They had not, but that was more by luck than her own care. With her back to James she said, 'We are due at the Hendersons at 7.30. We really can't cancel, you know.'

'Of course not,' he agreed amicably. 'Don't you want to know what my plans are?'

'You know I do, but I must get this potted before I change.'

'Are you afraid, Carol?'

She closed the lid of the hob and set the timer. 'Half-an-hour to cool, then I'll pot it,' she said. 'I'd better water the tubs now.' She continued, but instead, sat down again. 'Are

11

you ill, James? Is that really what all this is about?'

'Ill! Never felt better in my life. Don't be silly, woman. Of course I'm not ill. I said, I'm bored. Or I was, until this morning when I took voluntary retirement.'

'Vol . . . Well, I'm glad you aren't ill. You had me really worried for a moment.' Carol sighed. Then it had to be the D-word. 'Fine. You have plans. Might they possibly include me?'

He was looking at her as though he were totally mystified. 'Well, naturally they include you. You are my wife, after all. Ohh . . . ' he exclaimed, as enlightenment dawned. 'Come on, Carol, love, since when did you imagine I had a mistress? When do you think I've had the time or the energy to acquire the sort of mistress I'd leave you for?' He ended his protestations indignantly.

She smiled shakily. 'I don't know. But I find it difficult to accept that you've taken voluntary retirement simply because you're bored.'

'Do you? But that is how it is. I've twenty years or so of good living ahead of me before I can reasonably expect to have to cope with the infirmities of old age. We have twenty years. We have money to fund those years. I don't want to waste them.'

'So what are these plans.'
'I want to travel.'

★ ★ ★

'What do you know about the political affiliations of Brian Pickering, Carol?'

'I should like a bottle of water,' Carol said firmly to her interrogator, instead of answering yet another of his pointless questions. 'Please,' she added politely. It was no idle request, though she had made it to collect her thoughts. The room was not air conditioned and the window was closed. It was hot and airless and she was extremely thirsty.

Her interrogator took no notice of her request. 'How long have you known the Pickerings, Carol?'

'I don't know them.'

'That is nonsense. You have been in their company ever since you arrived in Myanmar.'

'I have not been in their company. We, James and I, met them for the first time at Yangon airport. Our guide asked us to give them a lift to their hotel as there was something wrong with their car.'

'We do not believe you.'

'Where is my husband? I should like to see him. I should also like to see someone from the British Consulate.'

Again her request was ignored.

'Where did you first meet Kimberley Pickering?'

'At Yangon airport.'

'When did you first meet Brian Pickering?'

Carol looked across the table at him steadily. It was probably the thirst, but her heartbeat was becoming uncomfortably erratic. 'At Yangon airport. When we arrived in Myanmar.'

'Do you have children, Carol?' Her interrogator changed the subject abruptly.

'I've already told you. I — we have a son. His name is Matthew.'

'Does Matthew know the children of Brian and Kimberley Pickering?'

'Hardly,' she said disdainfully. 'Matthew works in Aberdeen. In Scotland. The Pickering children are just children.'

'Perhaps he knows Brian Pickering?'

'I don't think so.'

The questioning continued for a long time though the questions were variations on the same theme: how long had she known the Pickerings? What dealings had she with them?

As the time passed Carol was becoming more and more agitated, which it was increasingly difficult to conceal. She suspected that not a lot passed this odious man. She wondered what would become of her

14

eventually — at the back of her mind was the word violence — how long it would be before the questioning became more forceful. Despite her thirst her body was drenched. She had nothing except the back of her hand to keep the sweat from her eyes or from trickling down the sides of her face and her neck, where it was collecting under her breasts and making her cotton bra uncomfortably sodden.

Finally she had had enough. 'I am not answering another question until you have brought me a bottle of water,' she declared, her voice considerably more resolute than she thought possible. 'I also want to know where my husband is and why I am here and by what right you have brought me here and are treating me like this. I have done nothing wrong. Absolutely nothing wrong. And neither has James.'

Her interrogator looked at her for a long moment. Then he smiled faintly, though it was a mere movement of his lips. 'You are a brave woman, Carol. Or, maybe, a foolish one.'

However, he rose, went to the door and knocked on it. It was opened immediately and he left the room.

★　★　★

15

Carol Morgan was fifty-seven. She had been born Carol Jones in Monmouth, a market town in South Wales. Her father was a dentist and they lived in a small town house with the surgery on the ground floor until William Jones had made enough money to take out a mortgage on a new house on the edge of town, keeping the surgery and installing a junior partner on the upper floors. Carol, an only child, won one of the places at what was then the local grammar school, a Haberdashers's school, where she did well — though not well enough to go to university, the places available being limited in those days. She acquired instead a secretarial qualification in Cardiff and returned home both to work for, and subsequently look after, her father as her mother had died when she was twenty-two.

This nurturing lasted only a short time. William Jones surprised his family (he had three sisters) by marrying again within nine months of widowhood, choosing a woman who was twelve years younger than himself, and a lot livelier than Carol's mother whose personality had always lacked confidence.

It was fortunate that Carol took after her father. She rallied from the shock of being ousted in her father's affections and, using money her mother had left her, found a job in Bristol and bought a small flat in the space of two weeks, while the honeymooners were still in Majorca. Mary, William's new wife, released from the prospect of being an active stepmother, took it upon herself to ensure that Carol had everything she needed for her new life, including a small car, and promised to feed her up on those weekends she decided to visit — monthly, Mary suggested in a tone of voice that made the invitation more of a decree.

Thus it was that Carol embarked on the challenges of independent living, job, friends, social life. Five years after her mother's death she met James Morgan. It was safe to say that until that Friday afternoon when he declared that he had unexpectedly taken voluntary retirement, Carol's life had followed a simple and unruffled course.

★   ★   ★

'I want to see something of the world,' James said, on that day when he gave up his job. 'I don't just mean a world cruise. Perish the thought. I want to wander a bit, stop where I feel like it, move on when I've seen enough.'

'I never took you for an ageing hippie,' said his wife. 'We've been to France, Italy,

Spain. I thought you enjoyed the holidays we've taken. You've always decided where we were to go.'

'Naturally I've enjoyed them. Perhaps they've been a bit too structured for my tastes.'

'When you've only got two weeks you have to structure your time.'

'Precisely my point. You know who I've envied all these years? The Hendersons and their long summer holidays.' Clive Henderson taught physics at the now independent boys' school in Monmouth. 'The way the whole family took off in their caravan and aimed for six weeks in the sun on the continent.'

'It wasn't always foolproof,' objected Carol. 'Marion admitted once that when they found a caravan park they actually liked, they often had to move on too soon because their pitch was already booked. Anyway, with three children who fought constantly there was never enough space. Or peace and quiet.'

'We usually managed peace and quiet, didn't we?'

'Sometimes I wondered if Matthew really liked our holidays.'

'He came with us, though, until he was seventeen. Carol, I don't want a series of holidays. I want to travel.'

'There's a difference?' Her back was turned as she potted the chutney, so she missed the

18

steely look he cast in her direction. 'I suppose you are going to write a book about it,' she remarked.

'I suppose nothing of the sort. Look, there are no plans. Not yet. I'm not thinking of taking off tomorrow, or the day after. I'm merely saying that I want a change of direction. There's good money coming with the voluntary redundancy. We can afford to spend some of it doing things we've not done before. I'll go back to consultancy work after a few months off. Top up the account. You know.'

'That's assuming you can get the work.'

'Carol, once it gets around that I'm available they'll be queuing up for my services.'

'I suppose there's nothing wrong with your confidence.' There was still an edge to her voice though the worry was fading from her eyes and she was half-smiling. 'You make it sound so simple.'

'It is. Believe me. Of course, it'll need a bit of planning. Guide books, that sort of thing.'

'Visas,' said Carol practically, but already just a modicum of excitement was creeping into her system.

'Passport and visas and practical travelling clothes and . . . '

'Locking up the house.'

'Selling it, more like.'

'Do you mean it, James? I'm not sure I like the sound of that.'

'I'm not suggesting we come back homeless. Just that we downsize. It makes sense.'

James and Carol had bought Windrush in Otterhaven because it was imposing yet its garden was manageable. The reception rooms were ideal for the sort of entertaining they both liked best — small dinner parties when they mixed diverse couples, or brought together their close friends. Only very occasionally were Carol and James required to host dinners on behalf of his firm. Carol was an accomplished cook who enjoyed the planning and achievement of a successful evening. But their house had five bedrooms — far too big for them once Matthew had gone (even though his room was still cluttered with his possessions).

'It's time to sell,' James declared now. 'We'll find something smaller in the centre of the village, somewhere we can shut up and leave for a few months without the fear of coming home to discover we've been burgled.'

'No one can guarantee that.'

'No, but it's safer having neighbours. I wouldn't want to leave Windrush without a house sitter.'

They were to be lucky. The Hendersons knew of a small terraced house that was due to come on the market soon. James made an offer which was accepted. Windrush itself sold without even being advertised, and it sold well.

★ ★ ★

Leaving everything that was familiar to travel had been the first of many surprises, Carol reflected, sitting on that hard chair somewhere in Rangoon, thirsty yet bathed in sweat, terrified at the prospect of torture to extract information that she did not have: pain inflicted deliberately. Carol didn't know how she would cope with pain. She'd only had gas and air in childbirth which suggested her pain tolerance was reasonably high (or that she had gone through an easy delivery?). But dwelling on the things men might do to her for the sake of hurting her was as frightening as the actual infliction of pain. Was that how it worked?

It had been so easy to change their lives. Frighteningly easy, even though Carol had a part-time job. Once she was married, Carol continued with secretarial work until she became pregnant. To begin with they were on the move regularly and this sort of work fitted their life style — and as she was extremely competent she never lacked for a job. Once Matthew came, Carol gave up work and never returned to it until he was at university.

Then, though James expressed his views about working wives, Carol told him she thought it was time she did some voluntary work, which it was less easy for him to deride. She explored various options and eventually approached the National Association for Citizens Advice. Working as a volunteer needed some training but this she found more interesting than onerous. She was good at this new work, too, after a few years becoming a paid part-time advice session supervisor. Home, James and the local CAB absorbed all her time and her energy.

★　★　★

'Where shall we go?' asked Carol, once the idea of travelling had sunk in, she had given in her notice to the CAB and she was becoming excited by the prospect of travelling.

'South East Asia. I thought Thailand, Burma, Cambodia, possibly Vietnam. We'll have to watch the heat and the monsoon season so I'd like to keep India for next time. Be home for the summer.'

'Sounds good to me.'

'We must ring Matthew tonight. Tell him what we plan.'

'He'll be so envious,' Matthew's father said with relish. 'As I was, when he took off on his gap year.'

'Not a year, James,' Carol said sharply. 'A month or so, you said. Be back here for the summer. That's all.'

'And that's what I meant. Promise you.'

2

On her hard chair, Carol shut her eyes as the door of the tiny room in the police headquarters in Rangoon was closed behind her interrogator. There was the ominous click of a turning key. She threw back her head, waiting for the thud of her heart to subside. Then she got up and stretched. The wooden chair was both small and very uncomfortable. Her legs felt numb.

Brian and Kimberley Pickering. James had been right about them. He had said they were an odd couple. Carol wondered what on earth they had done — for all this was obviously on their account. She supposed they must have taken part in some political demonstration, maybe handed out anti-Junta leaflets. James had told her in no uncertain terms that it was imperative they did nothing stupid when they were in Burma.

'What on earth do you mean by doing something stupid?'

'Such as suggesting that we disapprove of the politics of the Burmese government.'

'I don't really know anything about Burmese politics,' confessed Carol. 'I know more about the Khmer Rouge in Cambodia than what goes on in Burma.'

'Just as well. Anyway, we aren't going to risk trouble, are we?'

'Of course not, dear.'

Which conversation had the result that Carol made the effort to discover that Burma did, indeed, have a troubled history, particularly in recent years. An illegal regime run by a military junta refused to permit a democratically elected party to govern; tortured and killed its opponents and was exceptionally harsh in its treatment of minority groups. Daw Aung San Suu Kyi — known as 'The Lady' — who was in her seventeenth year of house arrest, spoke out against tourism on the grounds that foreign money was diverted to the Junta.

On reading this, Carol had experienced a momentary qualm: maybe South East Asia wasn't quite the travellers' idyll she had been led to believe? This was obviously what James had meant when he said they had to keep a low profile.

But they had been circumspect at all times. So Carol believed. So why were she and James involved with the authorities now? Why should the authorities think they had anything to do with the Pickerings?

After a while the door opened again. Her

interrogator and a woman entered.

Carol said immediately, 'I need to go to the toilet. Now. At once.'

The two Burmese looked at each other. The man shrugged. The woman said, 'You come with me.'

Carol followed the woman. By then the needs of her bladder were urgent. Interrogation was bad enough. She had an even greater horror of the humiliation she might suffer if she emptied her bladder involuntarily. Yet the desire not to seem cowed (and therefore guilty) was even more pressing. It was a footpad toilet she was taken to, as she had expected. The cubicle was fetid. Brown streaks stained the dirty white porcelain and its odour struck Carol forcibly as one that reeked of fear. Nevertheless, being offered even that as a concession was a minor victory, and the psychological effect was as immense a comfort as the physical relief.

On her return to the room, Carol saw that there was a small bottle of water on the table along with her passport and what appeared to be airline tickets. Her spirits lifted further. Torture, she thought now, was unlikely. At least, it was for her. For James? Her heart plummeted once more. 'What have you done with my husband?' she demanded, as she opened the water bottle.

'It is touching,' the man answered sarcastically. 'Both husband and wife so concerned about each other.'

The sarcasm was nothing. Her question had been answered, she thought, as she drank half the contents of the water bottle. James was most probably in the same building.

'Why are we here?' She screwed the top back on to the bottle.

The woman, who had been standing behind Carol, made a sudden movement. Carol could not prevent herself from flinching. Now she was certain that the appearance of their airline tickets was another form of torture after all.

'You are not here to be tortured, Carol,' the man said, smiling wolfishly, clearly amused by her fear. 'Though it would be as well if you remember that hard questioning is an option, if we arrest you. You are here to answer my questions. We shall begin again.'

How long had she known the Pickerings? Why had she and her husband come to Myanmar? What were her political affiliations?

'I am not interested in politics.'

'That is a lie. All men and women are interested in politics.'

'That may be so in Myanmar. It is not true in my country. There are many people who could not care less who governs us.'

At that, the woman interposed softly in Burmese. The man raised his eyebrows and commented in English, 'Then the British are more foolish than we give them credit for. But you are not one of them. You have a political agenda. That is why you have come to Myanmar. Confess that I am right, Carol.'

★ ★ ★

Christmas was spent in the new house with Matthew, who came alone, Rosa having declared she needed to stay in Scotland for her own family's celebration. The two would meet up for Hogmanay. Matthew had still not made up his mind whether to applaud his parents for their courage or pour scorn on their foolhardiness. Grudging admiration was, however, evident in his embrace as he said goodbye to them.

Carol and James arrived in South East Asia before the New Year. They spent three weeks in Thailand exploring first the frenetic city of Bangkok. Then they visited the ancient capital of Ayuthaya by rice barge before moving north to Chiang Mai and the Golden Triangle, where the borders of Thailand, Burma and Laos meet. There they did some easy trekking to hill tribe villages before reaching the border at Huay Xai from where they journeyed down the Mekong River to Luang Prabang in northern Laos.

Time took on an other-worldly meaning as they journeyed through misty mountains and lush green valleys to the enigmatic Plain of Jars, the sleepy cities of Luang Prabang and Vientiane. There were working elephants, gilded temples and ancient ruins, monks clad in saffron coloured robes, carrying alms bowls, and vibrant markets.

Laos was in many ways the honeymoon she had never had, Carol was to remember. James had taken her away for a weekend in Ludlow when they were married, insisting he could not spare the time for anything more. So for their first few weeks together they were essentially strangers to each other; daily finding themselves needing to negotiate their way through the relationship as though brokering a deal. In Laos their very familiarity meant that they could often voice each others thoughts; knew instantly what would please, amuse, irritate or bore. James was considerate of Carol's interest in the indigenous crafts, the weaving, silversmithing, carving in stone or wood. Carol herself never minded when James took off to find out how the local people lived and made their living, as though he could not quite shake off his fascination with market forces.

Carol was keeping a sporadic diary. Already the memories of the earlier weeks of their journey had become hazy. 'Was it in Angkor Wat that we saw monks training to become tour guides? What did we eat at that restaurant in Phnom Penh?' She wondered how much the young backpackers recalled of their time on the road (assuming they were not stoned out of their skulls). Was it just a kaleidoscope of heat and dust, sound and smell and colour, a total assault on the senses?

And then they reached Burma.

The problem with independent travel in South East Asia was that visa requirements and restricted zones were powerful restraints on the liberty to wander at will. At that time Burma — or Myanmar as the Junta had renamed it after the student rebellion in 1988 — could only be entered through Rangoon, now locally known as Yangon. The solution was for the Morgans to fly back to Bangkok and then on to Rangoon. Moreover, their visas were only valid for four weeks so that the dates for their visit had required advance planning.

They arrived in Rangoon in March, into an airport that had an imposing façade but inside was reminiscent of a previous generation. It was then that things began to go wrong.

Burma . . .

Carol and James's evening flight from Bangkok to Rangoon had been ninety minutes late. They were tired and irritable by the time they had completed the interminable wait for immigration formalities.

They were travelling light. Carol was actually amazed by how small a quantity of clothing it was necessary to possess. A suitcase remained in the luggage room of their hotel in Bangkok, containing a couple of thick sweaters and warm trousers, together with a few irresistible souvenirs. On this occasion one of their two small bags had been badly damaged. 'I said we should have taken the opportunity to buy something new in Bangkok,' grumbled James. 'Think of all those cases in the night market.'

'Well, we didn't,' sighed Carol wearily, 'and who's to say a new one wouldn't have been dropped, or squashed, or whatever. Let's find our guide and see if he knows where we can find a replacement.'

After much consideration, they had booked their accommodation in advance along with a car and a local driver. 'Travel in Burma is never going to be easy,' James had said. 'I guess for the sake of getting there we must just get used to being classed as a package tour of two.'

Ko Kyaw, a young Burman wearing a green checked *longyi*, with a pale green shirt, was suitably welcoming and helpful.

'Not a problem,' he said. 'We'll go to the market tomorrow.'

They emerged from the airport building into soggy heat, following two of the obligatory porters towards a line of elderly Japanese cars which James said, on seeing them, were made in Burma under licence. One of them was a people carrier. Standing by it disconsolately was a group of four, a man and woman and two teenage children.

'I need to ask you a favour,' Ko Kyaw said. 'These people are also on tour with my firm. Their car has broken down. Will you permit them to ride with you as far as their hotel?'

'Of course,' said Carol firmly, pre-empting James who, she could see, was about to remind the guide that they had paid for private transport. 'Shall we get in the back, James?'

In the car, with the family in front of them, Carol said brightly, 'We should introduce ourselves. I'm Carol and my husband is James.'

Almost reluctantly the woman said, 'I am Kimberley and my husband is Brian. Our daughter is called Jessica and this is our son, Daniel.'

'Dan,' said Dan firmly. 'I am twelve, and Jess is fourteen.'

Jessica gave her brother a violent nudge and glared.

'How do you do?' said Carol, smiling inwardly at the evidence that children — teenage girls — remained the same the whole world over.

From then on, though, the man and the woman were monosyllabic, the young people became increasingly sullen (probably exhausted, Carol decided charitably). Ko Kyaw made determined conversation during the hour-long drive from the airport to which Carol was the only one who made any response. They dropped the family off first.

'Well,' said James, as they arrived at a small boutique hotel near the centre of Rangoon, 'let's hope that's the last we see of them.'

Carol and James had become accustomed to organizing their days as they pleased while they were in Thailand and Laos and, to an extent, Cambodia, so they were not prepared to be dictated to by their Burmese guide. Ko Kyaw was told firmly that they would not be sightseeing at 8.30 a.m. on their first morning in Rangoon.

'This hotel has a pool,' said Carol delightedly. 'I'm going to use it tomorrow morning, and just lie in the shade afterwards.'

Though James insisted that wherever possible they would use good quality hotels in South East Asia rather than backpackers' hostels, on the whole they found themselves in modest accommodation. The Savoy was rather more up-market. It was late and they were both tired.

'It is best to visit the pagoda before it gets too hot,' pointed out Ko Kyaw reasonably. He intended taking them as soon as possible to the golden-roofed Shwedagon Pagoda which stands over-looking Rangoon on Singuttara Hill.

'Then we'll go the day after.'

'The day after we go to Twante on the ferry.'

'Then we'll do the market late tomorrow morning and the temple in the afternoon and stay until sunset.' It was a battle of wills which James was determined to win.

He said to Carol over breakfast, 'I think we are only going to see the places considered suitable for tourists. Still, after Laos and Cambodia I guess we can fill in the political background ourselves.'

'Do you mind the lack of freedom?'

'I think we have no choice, but I wouldn't miss this experience.'

Scott Market — renamed the Bogyoke Aung San Market — was crammed with stalls

34

selling rubies and a plethora of other precious stones (some undoubtedly of dubious worth). There were others selling the local *longyis* — a sarong worn by both men and women in a variety of silk and cotton — lacquerware, rattan-ware, embroidered wall hangings, brassware. It was stunning.

'There aren't too many buyers, though,' observed Carol shrewdly. 'I'll have to buy a flower-patterned *longyi* for myself. They are so elegant and the men look really good in the plainer stripes or checks.'

So they even haggled over a dark-red checked *longyi* for James while Carol chose a mid-blue one for herself, splashed with pink and white flowers and green leaves.

'I can't resist a ruby pendant either,' she declared. 'I think my dollars will stretch to something small.'

'Ruby or glass?' he teased her. 'But after we've found a case.' There was little selection. They came away with a large red and white striped plastic bag. 'I suppose it'll do until we get back to Bangkok,' said James dubiously.

'We could try somewhere else. Not too many Burmese need bags for travelling,' said Ko Kyaw apologetically. He had searched for two substantial straps to fasten the bag securely.

Non-committally James agreed that this

was probably so under the present regime. The guide glanced at him but made no reply. Carol realized immediately that they were in too public a place for the man to say anything that could be incriminating. She was cross that James had been so insensitive.

Later that afternoon (and wearing both her *longyi* and her ruby pendant), Carol and James met the guide again in the foyer to be taken to the Shwedagon Pagoda.

'There is another problem with the car that the other family is supposed to be using,' Ko Kyaw said. 'Would you mind if we take them to the pagoda. They have their own guide, just no car.'

James sighed heavily. Carol said immediately, 'What a nuisance for them. Of course we don't mind. Do we, James?'

'I hope the man has told everyone that we plan to stay at the pagoda until sunset,' said James, as their driver parked the car at the top of the hill.

'Not a problem,' said the other guide, a young woman in a yellow *longyi* in a batik design of reds and greens, with a plain yellow blouse. 'You are being very kind.' Gently she steered the family away from the Morgans. 'We shall be ready to leave only when you have seen enough.'

'Shoes and socks must be left here,' said

Ko Kyaw as they approached the precincts.

'Socks as well?' exclaimed Carol. Unlike the be-sandaled James, she was wearing trainers with socks as she had an aversion to grit between her toes. Elsewhere James had put socks on for pagoda-visiting.

'No socks.'

Carol sat on a stone step where she could remove her trainers and socks more comfortably — a disadvantage of one's later years was losing flexibility, she had come to understand — and afterwards she handed them over to a pagoda employee to be looked after.

Built over the shrine containing eight hairs of the Buddha, the Shwedagon Pagoda is considered one of Burma's holiest places, a huge bell-shaped stupa plated with solid gold and adorned with diamonds, rubies, sapphires, topaz and one enormous emerald. It is surrounded by smaller stupas, pavilions and administrative halls, sphinxes and the mythical lions called *chinthes*. Ko Kyaw told them the history of the pagoda and showed them the Bodhi trees and the Maha Gandha bell which was rescued from the Yangon River after a failed attempt by the British in 1825 to steal it.

Later, as they were guided to the western corner to view the setting sun, Dan and Jessica sidled up to Carol, having been hovering wordlessly just within her sight. She had not been thinking about them at all and now she felt guilty at the amount of time she and James spent at the pagoda. Jessica and Daniel were, after all, only children and might be expected to have a low threshold of boredom.

'We just want to wait for the sunset,' she told them diffidently. 'I hope you aren't too fed up with the whole business of sight-seeing. Though James and I have been travelling for several weeks, we are still besotted with pagodas and temple architecture.'

'Whatever,' Dan shrugged.

'What Dan means is we really don't mind,' said Jessica, giving her brother another sisterly nudge. She was a tall, willowy girl with a clear complexion and long, fair hair which she wore untied. When they first met, Jessica had been wearing jeans and a T-shirt. Now she was in a *longyi*, as was the whole family, the women wearing blouses which matched their flowered *longyis*, the men in checks. Daniel wore a white T-shirt with his and his father had a more formal coloured shirt. The outfit particularly suited the girl, showing off her already well developed figure. Carol guessed that though she was fourteen, like most fourteen-year-olds she was probably going on seventeen. Also, like her mother, Jessica wore no make-up.

'You are very lucky to be here in term time,' said Carol. She had been speculating as to how they had managed to get off school, though she was sure that the trip must be an education in itself.

'We don't go to school,' Jessica replied.

'Is that so?'

'Mum teaches us, mostly.'

'I see. Um, are you going to be in Burma for long?'

'Why don't you call it Myanmar?' asked Dan. 'We don't, but most people do what the Junta wants over the new names.'

'Quite so,' said Carol weakly. 'Would you prefer it if I did, too?'

'It might be safer.'

'How do you mean, 'safer'?'

'Dad says we have to be very careful. You know, you never can tell who is *Tatmadaw* or who is a member of the plain clothes police.'

'*Tatmadaw*, as in army?'

'Of course,' said Dan, a little scornfully. 'You do understand about the way the Junta spies on the people, don't you?'

Carol was about to say she thought it sounded far too James Bondish to be true — then she thought that Dan and his father were probably right. Besides, it wouldn't do to seem too unworldly in front of a boy of twelve.

'Daniel, Jessica. Come over here,' called Kimberley, from nearer the main stupa.

The children walked over to their mother, rebellion clear from the rigidity of their backs. Carol could see her scold them for bothering the adults. She smiled. The Pickerings were an interesting family, she thought, now that she knew they were not the same breed as most. The children might have some problem with their parents — which family didn't have its problems? — but they seemed well-behaved. That had been a perspicacious remark of Dan's. She would mention it to James when they were back at the hotel.

The sun went behind a large cloud. 'Sadly I think that is all we shall see of sunset tonight,' said their guide. 'When you are in Mandalay on Mandalay Hill you will see a fine sunset.'

'Let's go, then,' said James. 'I guess the kids are ready,' proving that he had not been oblivious to their conversation after all.

Back at the entrance to the pagoda, James and Carol collected their shoes. There were many visitors milling about, all having decided to leave at the same time, and Carol moved some way from James to be able to sit down, eventually perching on a corner of the pedestal of a pillar.

'Bad idea. Not with all these people around. I will see you tonight.'

The words were English, spoken urgently by a man. Carol frowned and straightened. She was sure she recognized Brian Pickering's voice.

'Best you say you go for a walk,' came a reply. 'You bring . . . '

You shouldn't listen to other people's conversations, Carol thought, getting to her feet. As she did so, the second man dropped his voice and she did not hear exactly what was being brought anyway. And none of her business, she thought, but as she looked back she saw she had been correct. It was Brian Pickering and he had been talking to a Burman. She shrugged, and went back to James.

As they reached the car, Brian bumped into her, stepping on one of her feet. He was a big man and though she was now shod, it hurt.

Carol waited for an apology, which was not forthcoming. A little devil inside her made her say, 'It must be very convenient to know local people in Rangoon.'

'It must, if you are in that position,' he said stiffly, after a pause. He looked at her, his face expressionless.

'I mean, think of actually being invited into someone's house,' she said, goading him. She

41

could have continued, but something in the man's eyes — was he now pleading for her discretion, or was he just defying her to contradict him? — persuaded Carol to add, 'Somehow I don't think that is going to happen to me, in Burma.'

Brian Pickering stood aside to let her get into the back of the car. 'As you say,' he said dismissively.

Oops, Carol thought. Peculiar man. He definitely had been speaking to a Burman. Then she thought, Oh, Lord. He hasn't brought anything contentious into the country, has he? Not when he has his family with him . . .

The Pickerings continued to turn up at unexpected moments. They were nowhere to be seen when James and Carol took the local ferry to Twante, a pottery town, where the two were bundled first into a trishaw and then into a horse-drawn wooden cart and bumped through the local market to a compound where, under primitive conditions, large pottery urns were being made. But that afternoon, the whole family was in the pavilion which housed the reclining Buddha at Kyaukhtatgyi. The children were making notes about the symbols on the soles of the Buddha's feet.

'Lurking,' said James darkly.

'Don't be silly, dear,' chided his wife, and smiled at Kimberley across the almost empty space in front of the enormous Buddha. The other woman merely nodded in response.

The Pickering were not in the Gem Museum which Carol insisted on seeing on her own, leaving James to wander the streets outside with his camera. It displayed a wealth of precious stones with a case of recent artwork in jewel-encrusted jade and over which she lingered.

The four Pickerings were at the restaurant overlooking the lake which James chose for an evening meal. 'Proves they are not immune to the good life,' he commented.

Carol sighed. James could be very tiresome when he became obsessed by a notion.

Two days later the Morgans reached Mandalay. This was very different from the more staid Rangoon; an assault on the nerves as their car battled motorbikes, bicycles, and ramshackle buses on their way to their hotel. There was litter everywhere and litter pickers, also beggar women at street corners.

The Pickerings had not been on their flight but the following day they came face to face with Brian Pickering as they emerged from a family-run gold leaf factory.

Carol was reeling from the shock of what she had just seen. She had been taken to a small, stone-vaulted cavern reached through a large, barnlike building full of all manner of antiquated machinery and what appeared to be rubbish heaps (but were probably anything but rubbish). Here there was an indefinable noise which increased to a loud clatter even before she reached the cavern. Inside it, down a flight of half-a-dozen stone steps, were eight or nine young women. They were pounding bamboo paper into thin sheets. These sheets were to be used for packaging the gold leaf, processed by the men in another room, which was sold to the Burmese to decorate whichever image of the Buddha they particularly venerated.

Carol could stand the noise for only a minute before she had to leave the cavern.

Their new guide had urged them to give the women a few kyats for having their photograph taken. 'They have families to feed,' he reminded them.

'As if having families to feed was reason for alms! The noise in there,' Carol said, aghast, as she handed kyats to the guide. 'Did you see those poor women? It's bad enough for the men in the front room, but the women must be deafened working in those conditions. How do they manage to look after their children with their hearing ruined?'

James shrugged. 'I daresay having a job at all keeps their families alive,' he pointed out pragmatically.

Carol knew he was probably right but she did not feel any better for acknowledging it.

However, for the first time Brian Pickering, who had heard Carol's protestations, addressed her spontaneously. 'Mandalay is full of family-run businesses. As James says, at least they have work, even if some of their profits go to the government.'

'You don't know that,' she observed sharply.

'It's an educated guess,' he shrugged. 'Did you buy anything?'

'Of course I did. Some of that money must go to the workers.'

He said nothing more but there was a glimmer of approval in his face as he said, 'You should be more careful of what you say in public.'

'Dan said that to me, too. I wasn't aware that I was being indiscreet.'

He sighed at her naïevety. 'You do know that spies of the Junta are everywhere?'

His condescension and the matter-of-fact way he spoke made her blink. 'I thought most people in Burma hated the Junta.'

'You may be right. On the other hand,

many people do what they have to do just to live, and keep their families safe.'

The impersonal menace of that shocked her. 'I suppose it's difficult to refuse even to inflict pain if your family's safety is at stake,' she commented softly. She was thinking of the genocide in Cambodia which had seemed so utterly inexplicable.

'Exactly so,' he agreed and began to turn away.

'Have you left the family at your hotel?' Carol asked.

'My wife is giving the children a maths lesson. We do not allow them total freedom from formal education, you know. Besides, neither of them is particularly interested in watching people work.'

'Of course not,' answered Carol hastily, who nevertheless found that a strange comment to make about a child.

'Do you not like these people?' asked their guide, when Brian Pickering was out of earshot.

'We have nothing against them,' said Carol circumspectly.

'We just prefer not to be with other tourists,' added James firmly. 'We did pay to have a personal guide.'

'Though as long as I get to see all the craft work, I have no objection to sharing our transport,' said Carol blithely, earning herself a glare from her husband.

'I suggest we should go and see the tapestry workers,' the guide said appeasingly.

3

James and Carol were staying at a small hotel away from the centre of the town. This hotel also had a pool. That evening, bathed despite the power cuts, which, they were told with a shrug, happened most evenings, they took a taxi across town to a restaurant where they were promised classical dancing. They were on their own in the large room for some time, though a harp player and a drummer emerged to play, incongruously, *Frère Jacques*. As their food was being served — uninspiring fare, though a perfectly acceptable Myanmar chicken curry with steamed rice — several more tables were filled. Among the new arrivals were the Pickerings. James glowered.

'Behave yourself,' hissed Carol. 'We don't have to socialize.'

'It'll look a bit odd if we don't.'

She was surprised, though, you never could tell with James, as he organized two tables to be joined together. Afterwards he said, 'I thought those children looked glum. I thought you would probably cheer them up.'

Carol was not sure if this was so, but she and Dan did have a giggle over the monkey dance. From what she could tell, the dancers were not top quality, and their costumes, though garish, were not elaborate (the shoes of one of the two male dancers had large holes in them) but they danced energetically and the female harpist was delightful.

'Where do you go from Mandalay?' James asked Kimberley at one point.

As he feared the answer was, 'Pagan.'

'Pagan. Of course. And then?'

'Back to Rangoon.'

'Then I suppose we shall see you among the pagodas. Do you visit the hill station tomorrow?'

'No,' said Kimberley. 'Relics of colonial times don't interest us.'

'I have a friend of a friend I want to meet,' said Brian, man to man to James, under cover of applause. 'Just me, you understand? He is a university student who hasn't been able to complete his course because he had two years in prison for dissent. I was given his address in London as he has the contacts I need to make on behalf of the Friendship House.'

'A house for friends? Should you be telling me this? Ah. I take it you'll be careful,' said James, who did not have a clue what the man was talking about and did not in the least care to ask.

Later, as they were undressing for bed, he

said to Carol, 'I suppose we'll run into the Pickerings in Pagan. You know, they worry me.'

'Why is that?'

'Nothing I can put my finger on. Except that Brian says he is meeting someone tomorrow. He mentioned something about a house for friends, whatever that might be. I'm sure he and Kimberley have a hidden agenda. I mean, who brings two kids to a place like Burma in the middle of term?'

'The children are educated at home. School doesn't come into it.'

'Then it should. If he's doing things the Junta wouldn't approve of he should have left his family at home not be using them as cover.'

'James. Do you mean that?'

'I don't know. Let's forget the Pickerings and just hope we don't run into them in Pagan.'

Pagan: spread over fifteen square miles on the east bank of the Irrawaddy river, and an ancient Burmese capital, its 13,000 religious buildings were once covered with inch-thick gold, according to Marco Polo. It was at the great Ananda Temple which housed four huge Buddhas that Carol ran into Dan Pickering. He was standing in front of one of the Buddhas, staring up into the golden face.

'Impressive, huh?' she asked softly.

'Spooky. Have you noticed that he smiles if you are far away or close to, but at this distance he just looks cross? As if he was judging you.'

'Trick of the light, I suppose,' she answered, thinking he sounded almost too overawed for a twelve year-old.

'I suppose so.'

'Nearly at the end of your trip. Have you enjoyed it?'

'Some of it. Too much hanging around, some days. Do you have a pool at your hotel?'

'We have, though I haven't really had time to use it.'

'You're lucky. Dad disapproves of hotels with pools in a poor country like Burma. It is poor. I hate seeing all those monks begging for their food every day.'

'But that's a tradition. You must have been told that's what Buddhist monks do. It's traditional that they live on the alms people give them daily. You see them all round South East Asia. They live a very disciplined life, eating their main meal by midday then having nothing further until early the following morning. The nuns, too.'

'Some of them are young children,' he protested. 'I mean, like, younger than me.'

'They don't become monks for ever at that

51

age. Both boys and young men become monks for a short time, the children just for a few weeks, to gain merit for themselves and their families. Our guide told me he became a monk for a couple of years when his university was closed by the Junta.'

Daniel instinctively looked over his shoulder and Carol thought he was going to chide her for being indiscreet. 'Children shouldn't have to beg,' he persisted instead.

But this really wasn't the place to go into the whys and wherefores of the Buddhist religion. 'James is waving at me. See you, Dan.'

* * *

Lake Inle was delightful, cooler than the Pagan plain, with flowers in abundance. They spent the day on the lake in a long-tailed boat, admiring the fishermen who manoeuvred their single oar with one leg. They glided between the fertile floating gardens formed from reeds and grasses which were anchored to the bottom with bamboo. And they bought silk from a family whose members wove the colourful stuff on ancient handlooms.

Carol arranged to visit Taunggyi to see the Shan State Museum while James had a massage, complaining of an old back strain.

After she had admired the ethnic costumes, Carol wandered through the market. It was reasonably well stocked, she noticed, though again there were few buyers. She came across a mother and small daughter selling *thanaka*, made from the bark of a small tree. As a cooling yellow paste, it is streaked across the forehead and cheeks — effectively a sunblock and worn by most women and girls.

Three village women were attempting to sell vegetables at the side of the road from large rattan baskets. Two market inspectors closed in on them, forcing them to move with violent shoves and loud imprecations. Thoroughly shocked, Carol raised her eyebrows. Though no words could pass between the Burmese and the British woman, an imperceptible shrug and a hint of sympathy in her eyes showed Carol that the *thanaka* seller loathed the autocratic regime.

* * *

Carol was re-packing the striped plastic bag in a hotel room near Rangoon's airport when there was a loud knock on the door. She thought it was James, who had left the room to settle their bill.

Two men in uniform were standing in the doorway. Green uniforms, army uniforms. As she opened the door they pushed it violently against the wall. Carol staggered back. 'You come with us. Now. Bring your passport. Now.' The English was thick. It was peremptory. She understood every word.

'But I . . . My husband — '

'Is in our custody. You must come with us.'

The second man, who had not yet spoken, emptied her bag on to the bed, picking the contents over. 'Where are your papers?'

She wanted to conceal them, to leave them where they were, but her eyes had gone instinctively to the black folder where James kept all their documents.

The second man smiled and picked up the folder. 'Now you come with us.'

So the nightmare had begun.

★ ★ ★

The overhead light, which was also protected by bars in that small, barred room, came on without warning. Carol realized that it was evening in Rangoon, that it had become dark outside. She had been — wherever she was — for many hours. She wondered if she would ever see home again. See James? Suddenly exhaustion swept over her. She could not remember ever in her life feeling quite so tired, quite so helpless.

'It is all nonsense,' she said weakly to her interrogator, for the umpteenth time. 'I am not interested in your politics. James and I came to Burma because it is a beautiful country. We wanted to see the pagodas and the temples. There was no other reason. We fly back to Bangkok tonight, then we are flying home. We should have been taking a flight this evening. I want to see the British Consul.' She put her arms on the table and sank her head on to them and burst into tears, not caring any more that tears would be construed as admitting defeat. She cried inconsolably for several minutes.

Eventually she felt something being thrust into her hands. It was a box of tissues. Slowly she sat up, took a handful and began to blow her nose and wipe her face.

'We believe you, Mrs Morgan.'

'You believe me?' she said incredulously.

'Also, we do not wage war on children. Brian and Kimberley Pickering have been arrested. Their children merely do what the parents tell them. They must leave Myanmar immediately. You will take them with you.'

'To Bangkok? What am I supposed to do with them there?'

'That is not our problem, Mrs Morgan. You will come with us.'

(It was only some time afterwards that Carol appreciated the use of her formal title to signify her change in circumstances.)

'Where is my husband?'

'We have not yet finished with your husband.'

Carol could do nothing other than accompany her two guards to a lift and out of the former colonial building into the night, though she was sick at heart over the non-appearance of James. They took her back to the hotel where this had all started, and they took her to the room which had been given to them on their arrival. They opened the door — but did not give her the key — standing aside to allow her to enter.

'You will be put on a plane tomorrow morning, Mrs Morgan. Please be ready. You may use room service but you may not leave the room until we fetch you.'

She went into the room and the door closed behind her. Inside stood Jessica and Dan Pickering, facing her. They were white-faced, plainly terrified. The three stood looking at each other without saying anything for a long time. Eventually Carol realized that Dan Pickering was crying silently. She hesitated, wanting to put her arms round both of them but she was too uncertain how they would react. She was furious; with Brian

Pickering and his wife, with the Burmese authorities, even with James (who could be dead, for all she knew) for suggesting that Burma was an interesting country to visit. She was furious with herself for being incapable of being anything other than useless in the face of what she could not understand. But her heart smote her for the even greater helplessness of the children. The Burmese authorities did not torture children? She recalled stories she had heard of atrocities wreaked on women and children of the Karen, the Karenni and the Shan minority tribal groups and she shuddered inwardly. Jessica and Dan might not have been touched physically, their evident terror was torture enough.

'When did you last eat?' she asked, struggling for normality.

'We're not hungry,' said Jessica.

'I am.' Surprisingly that was true. It had been many hours since she had eaten. 'We need to eat or we shall fall apart.' Carol went to the dressing table and picked up the hotel folder. 'I should think a few sandwiches would be a good idea. And something to drink.' There was a mini-bar in the room but all it contained was two bottles of water. She thought she could murder a gin and tonic. It was the first time she had really wanted anything more alcoholic than the local beer since they had left home. Then she felt bad because plainly James was not in a position to chose for himself whether he ate or not. Don't think about that, she told herself severely. She went to the door and turned the handle. It was locked. She made a face at the children and went instead to the bedside table and picked up the phone.

'Would a selection of cheese and ham sandwiches be all right?'

'I'm a vegetarian,' said Jessica.

Carol ordered cheese and tomato and some ham sandwiches and asked for biscuits. She ordered a large gin and tonic for herself and Coke for the children.

'Dad doesn't like us to have Coke,' said Dan primly.

'You can have water, if you prefer. Do you like Coke?'

'Yes.'

'I don't suppose he'll mind, for once.'

She motioned them to sit on one of the twin beds, as there was only one chair in the room. Then they sat in further silence until the door was opened and a stony-faced man, whom she supposed was one of their new guards, entered with a tray of food, followed by another with a tray of drinks. To Carol's relief the children fell on the food as though they were starving. She sat and nursed her gin and tonic and let them get on with it. Jessica looked guilty when she realized they had demolished all the sandwiches.

'Don't worry. We'll get some more.' She got up and went to the phone and placed a second order.

'We don't have any money to pay for food,' said Dan, when Carol put the receiver down.

'We don't have anything,' said Jessica bitterly.

'Do you think, perhaps, you would be able to tell me what happened today?'

'Yesterday,' observed Dan. It was long past midnight.

'You should be asleep,' she said. 'We should all be in bed. I guess, though, that none of us is ready to sleep, yet. Will you tell me what happened?'

It was as she had feared. In the morning, the Pickerings had left their small hotel and had made their way to the street where Aung San Suu Kyi, the elected leader of the National League for Democracy, was living under house arrest. Carol observed to the children that she thought the police guarded the entrance to this street to prevent anyone undesirable in the eyes of the authorities from getting to the house. Dan replied scornfully that of course they hadn't gone into the street itself, for there wouldn't have been any point.

'We stood on the street corner with our stickers and leaflets which we handed out to anyone passing by who would take one from us. At least I tried to hand them out,' Dan said. 'Some people refused to take them. A lot of people wouldn't even look at me. I suppose it was because my Burmese isn't very good,' he ended, with an ingenuous grin.

'Some people smiled at me, took my stickers and hurried off,' said Jessica. 'I don't think it made any difference that we don't speak more than a few words of Burmese.'

It was what Carol had feared, a planned political protest. The family had stood near the street corner for maybe half-an-hour, handing out the leaflets. Both Brian and Kimberley Pickering had also shouted slogans in Burmese.

'They were shouting: *Release all political prisoners*, and *Open the universities*. At least, that was what they were supposed to be saying. I don't think Dad's Burmese is very good, either,' said Dan miserably.

'The stickers had the same slogans,' said Jessica helpfully. 'Half of them were in Burmese, half in English. Like the slogans the *Tatmadaw* have put up in the streets,' she added, referring to the large, red posters in both languages erected by the army. These were four statements of what was called the People's Desire, one of which urged the people to *Crush all internal and external destructive elements as the common enemy.*

Inevitably several cars had driven up at speed, screeching to a halt beside them. Men in uniform had jumped out and forced the Pickerings into the backs of the cars.

'They separated us,' said Dan. 'It wasn't very nice.'

'Did they hurt you?' asked Carol, appalled.

'One of them slapped my face,' said Dan. His eyes were large and he shivered at the memory. Then he added proudly, 'They slapped me because I screamed at them that I wouldn't tell them anything. They were mean.'

'He didn't have anything to tell,' pointed out Jessica.

'Get real. Nor did you.' He shoved her and she hit him on the shoulder in retaliation.

'I don't suppose either of you could tell them much, Jessica,' said Carol diplomatically. Then she asked the girl, 'Did they touch you? I mean, did they hurt you in any way?'

Jessica shook her head. That was a relief, thought Carol. If they had actually got the girl into a prison there was no telling what would have happened to her.

'Have you seen your parents since you were all detained?'

The children shook their heads silently.

'Are we going to get our things back, Carol?'

'Do you really have nothing?'

'We left everything we have with us in the hotel room yesterday morning. We've not been allowed to fetch it. We had our passports with us, but they were taken by Military Intelligence.'

'And no money,' added Jessica. 'Dad always said that as we had to carry dollars he would look after those.' Dollars were generally used by tourists for larger purchases. English pounds were not recognized at all.

'Mum had a few kyats in her bag. They were useful for buying water and things like that.'

'What's going to happen to us?'

'I don't know, Jessica,' said Carol honestly. 'I was told that you were to come to Bangkok with me tomorrow morning.'

'What would we do there?'

'I don't think we should be worrying about that now,' said Carol, who found it difficult to think of anything else. 'I think we should all try to get some sleep. We'll just have to wait and see what happens in the morning.'

Brother and sister took off their shoes and

curled up on one of the twin beds together without a murmur of protest. Carol decided she would have a shower, getting under the water and letting it soak away the sweat and the fear that made her feel so disgusting. The dirt was easy to get rid of, the fear remained. They had not yet brought back James and there was no telling when, or if, he would be freed to join them.

The insistent ring of the telephone woke them before dawn. 'We need food,' Carol told the man on the other end of the line. Police? A hotel worker?

'You will be fetched at seven o'clock,' she was told.

She woke the children and urged them to have a shower. 'I have found a clean shirt belonging to James that you can use,' she told Dan, 'and some clean underwear, though that might be a little large. Jessica, here are a few things for you. Just in case yours isn't brought to you, you understand?'

While Jessica was in the shower, the door was unlocked and a man Carol had not seen before entered with a tray of food. To their general delight, this was croissants, jam, orange juice and a pot of coffee.

'Would you prefer tea?' Carol asked Dan, who looked amazed that she was even suggesting they should have something different.

'I guess Jess and I'll stick to the juice.'

Later they were shown to a large black people carrier, the intelligence officers plainly disgruntled at being asked to stow the Morgans' two bags and two backpacks. But there was no way Carol was going to leave any of their belongings behind in the hotel. She was certain that if she did, that would be the last James saw of any of his possessions, whatever was the outcome of his current predicament.

The airport formalities were the briefest she had ever known. The three of them were taken through the airport by a side door and then immediately driven by another car across the tarmac to a waiting plane. There they were escorted up the steps and into the plane where they were put into their seats. No one even mentioned boarding cards or passports — though Carol was handed all of these as they sat down.

There were brief nods and the men left. At no time had they seen anyone from the consulate. Carol surmised that no one had even been alerted as to their arrest. Probably no one, except the authorities and those few at the hotel who had witnessed her first, hurried departure, knew anything at all about the incident.

After a pause the plane started filling up. The Pickering children were sitting together. Behind them was Carol, in the window seat. The seat beside her was empty. It remained empty until the very last moment when their plane began to move. As it did so, a man dropped wordlessly into it.

Carol took one look at him, tired, unkempt, a day's growth of stubble on his face, scruffy shirt, crumpled trousers. Tears welled into her eyes. 'James.'

'Hey,' he said. 'It's all right. I'm here and we're about to take off.'

'Fasten seat belt, sir,' a stewardess touched his shoulder.

'Oh, James. James, you smell,' said Carol indignantly, and the tears fell. She sniffed and fumbled for a handkerchief.

James actually chuckled. 'Just so long as the Thais let us into Bangkok. I'll have a long soak in the hotel. Are the children here?'

'In front of us. Thank God you're here. Where are Brian and Kimberley?'

He shrugged. 'Insein?' He named the notorious prison in Rangoon. 'Who knows. They've only themselves to blame, wherever they are.'

'Ssh.'

'I can't help that. All I know is, they've been arrested.'

'Are Mum and Dad in prison?' Dan's head appeared over the top of the seat. 'Are they all right? When are we going to see them again?'

'I don't know, Dan,' James answered wearily. 'I only know they have been arrested for . . . well, you know what for.' His voice said, *Damn idiots*. Dan flushed and Carol winced. 'Look, I'm desperate for some sleep. Let's talk about it once we get to Bangkok, huh?'

★ ★ ★

'Somewhere down there is a snake farm,' Carol said aloud.

She pulled aside the thick net curtain that hung across the window of their room on the fifteenth floor of the Hotel Montien in Bangkok and gazed at the scene below, a jumble of low concrete roofs, decrepit wooden shacks, corrugated iron and haphazard rubbish. The sun had not yet risen to gild the red and green roof of the nearby temple but despite the early hour the road that bounded the hotel was busy.

'What do they farm snakes for?' James sat up in the huge bed behind her. His hair was tousled and his face sleep-softened.

'Venom? For their skins, food? I don't know.' She moved an upholstered chair to

66

face the window and sat in it, hugging her arms to her chest as if she were cold.

'Do you want to see it?'

'I should think not. You know I can't abide snakes.'

James grunted, fell back against the pillow and gave every appearance of going back to sleep.

Carol watched the sun rise, a small red disk which hung in a murky sky. Two weeks ago, before they had gone to Burma, it had rained unexpectedly and the sunrise had been reflected in the roads, greasy from the water. This morning it was quite dry and promised to be hot.

There was a rustle behind her as James turned over, flinging an arm towards her side of the bed. How had it come to this? They had been married for twenty-seven years and in a few hours he was planning to leave her.

'It doesn't have to be like this, Carol,' the voice behind her murmured softly, persuasively. 'Come with me?'

'You — we never intended going to Australia.' She stiffened in the chair as she answered him indignantly. 'The plan was that we'd go home after Burma. You said you would need to find work for a few months. We talked about me finding a job, too, to help pay for the next trip.' It was an argument that had raged since the previous evening. It made no difference that she already knew what his reply would be.

'Finding a job isn't that urgent. It seems stupid to go home when we've already come halfway.'

'It can hardly be halfway when we never intended going on,' she pointed out heatedly. 'And that's not the reason, is it? Why you are doing this? Why, James?'

4

It was all very different when they reached Thailand.

Immigration at Bangkok Airport had obviously been notified by the airline before the plane landed that there was a problem with the children, for they and the Morgans were taken from the plane and escorted to a small room. Carol noted thankfully that this time the windows were unbarred and the chairs, though unpadded plastic, were a cheerful blue. The room was also air conditioned.

After a short wait, two people entered the room. One was a young woman, who introduced herself as Susan Walker, from the British Consulate. She was accompanied by a Thai immigration official whose name they never discovered.

'I regret these formalities,' the official said politely. 'You understand that we have to check on all our visitors to Thailand, especially where there are irregularities.' He spoke perfect English. Yet again, Carol was dismayed that so many officials could do so.

James had bristled noticeably at the

official's use of the word 'irregularities'.

Susan Walker noticed this. 'Suppose you first tell us what has happened,' she said to James, her voice conciliatory. 'We only know that, apart from you, the children are unaccompanied and appear to have been deported from Myanmar.'

'It is on account of the children that we wish to question you. They are not your children? I am correct?'

'That is so,' Carol agreed. 'But . . . '

'Have we been deported?' interrupted Jessica. 'What about Mum and Dad?'

The adults looked at each other without replying.

'Anyway, we don't need accompanying,' said Dan indignantly. 'We are perfectly capable of looking after ourselves.'

'Except that we have no money,' said his sister quietly.

'So tell us what happened,' encouraged Susan Walker.

The four told their stories: separate interrogation, kept apart until Carol and the children were taken to the Morgans' hotel room. James told them that he had been shouted at and not once had he been given food and only one, small bottle of water, but that otherwise he had not been physically abused.

'It was Military Intelligence who questioned me. Somehow they were convinced I had helped Brian and Kimberley from the start. They actually accused me of bringing illegal literature into the country for them.'

'That's not true,' said Jessica. 'I told them that.'

'Where did the stickers and the leaflets come from?' asked Susan Walker.

Jessica said, 'Mum had the stickers hidden in a box of tampons. I needed one and she refused to let me open her box. I told her she was mean but she insisted we would have to buy something for me in Bangkok.'

'Your mother might have thought it wouldn't be easy to get tampons in Burma,' said Carol tactfully, though having had no reason herself to inspect the shelves of Burmese pharmacies.

'Mum took the stickers out of the box when we were getting ready to demonstrate.'

'And the leaflets? Could your father have picked them up in Mandalay?'

'At the pagoda in Rangoon I overheard Brian talking to a Burmese man about something he had to be given,' said Carol reluctantly.

'That was money collected in London to help the people who run the Friendship House,' said Dan. 'It's where Burmese on the run make for when they have crossed the border into Thailand.'

Carol and James exchanged glances. 'The Friendship House. So he didn't just mean a house for friends,' observed James.

'I carried the leaflets from home,' continued Dan. 'Dad said it would be too dangerous for anyone in Burma to print them there.'

'You did?' James sounded appalled. 'Your father actually gave you illegal leaflets to take into Burma? He must have been mad.'

'He only gave them to me because I found them when we were packing. I said they'd be safer with me. I put them in my science work-folder.'

This entailed an explanation about the children's schooling and the books they carried.

'We have a laptop at home,' said Jessica. 'But Dad didn't think we'd be able to use it in Burma so we had enough worksheets printed out to last us while we were away.'

'Were your possessions at any time searched by the authorities?' the Thai official asked them.

The children said that no one had seemed interested. 'Dad was pretty sure no one had gone through our things at any of the hotels, either,' said Dan. 'They hadn't touched mine, anyway.'

'How do you know that?' asked Susan.

'I put a hair under the band which fastened my folder,' Dan said. 'It wasn't moved.'

James grinned. 'Good stuff,' he commented.

'But what about Mum and Dad?' asked Jessica, distressed. 'When are they joining us?'

'That is what I have come to tell you,' answered Susan, uncomfortably. 'It appears that your parents were tried and sentenced yesterday afternoon. We believe they have been taken to Insein prison.'

'But they can't do that!' exclaimed Carol. 'It can't be right to have a trial and a verdict so soon after anyone is arrested. And aren't they entitled to legal representation?'

'It is certainly against international law not to be given impartial representation,' agreed Susan. 'However, the Myanmar regime is a law unto itself. I'm afraid that both Brian and Kimberley have been imprisoned as a result of their demonstration.'

'How long for?' whispered Carol, aghast.

Susan Walker sighed. 'Mrs Pickering has been sentenced to three years imprisonment, Mr Pickering was given five years,' she said reluctantly.

Jessica burst into tears. Carol got up clumsily and put her arms round the girl. 'Hush, love,' she said, rubbing Jessica's back soothingly. 'We can't know that's right, just yet. I mean, it's too soon.'

'I'm afraid it's all been confirmed by the British Consul in Rangoon,' said Susan. 'A Burmese dissenter was able to observe the demonstration at a distance and once the Pickerings were arrested, which, of course, was inevitable, he got the news to the British Consulate.'

'And what about us? Why have we been involved when we had nothing to do with the demonstration? And why weren't we visited once we had been taken into custody?' demanded James furiously. 'I asked and asked for a consular visit. And a lawyer.'

'So did I,' said Carol. 'Though I forgot to mention a lawyer.'

'The British Consul did ask to see you. She was refused permission.'

'Even this morning?'

'Yes, Mrs Morgan. You said you were taken directly to the plane, by-passing the authorities?'

'That's correct.'

'Which would explain it. It is not the first time. Myanmar is a difficult country, you understand.'

'Mr and Mrs Morgan,' interrupted the immigration officer quietly. 'An unfortunate episode, I am sure. You understand, however, that we now have a problem ourselves that is equally pressing. I am speaking of the children. We understand they have nothing with them except one small bag.'

'We have our passports but no bags at all,' said Jessica.

'Ah. Please excuse me.' He left the room and returned almost immediately with a small backpack. 'Does this not belong to one of you?'

'It's mine,' said Dan. 'It has my name on it.'

'That is what we thought. Would you mind opening it?'

The bag had been packed hurriedly, and haphazardly. It contained a few items of underwear, two wash bags, a dog-eared bear which a red-faced Dan hurriedly pushed underneath a white T-shirt which had seen better days, and a flowered *longyi*.

'They might have, like, included my diary,' complained Jessica bitterly, 'and our Burmese travel guide. I mean, I made all sorts of notes in the margins.'

'I guess all your books were taken away to be examined,' said James.

'You mean for incriminating evidence?' asked Dan. 'Awesome.'

'Well, I don't suppose you wrote anything down that was particularly bad.'

'I definitely did. I had a notebook because Mum said we had to do a project on Burma when we got home,' admitted Dan. 'Do you think that . . . ?'

'No, of course not,' said Susan Walker hurriedly. 'I am sure nothing that you wrote anywhere had any bearing at all on your parents' trial.'

'So-called trial,' said Carol.

'Precisely.'

'What's this?' Jessica had wiped her eyes on tissues handed to her by Susan and she was now brandishing a sealed envelope addressed *To Whom It May Concern*. It had been at the bottom of the bag.

'That's Mum's writing!' exclaimed Dan.

'Can we open it?' asked Jessica.

'I think you should,' replied Susan.

The letter was just a scrawled note. It read:

I authorize James and Carol Morgan to care for and protect my children, Jessica and Daniel Pickering, until such time as my husband, Brian, and I are at liberty to return home.

It was signed *Kimberley Pickering*. It bore the previous day's date.

'I don't understand,' said Jessica. 'Why should Mum have written a letter like that?'

'I believe it means that your mother made a

bargain with the Burmese authorities for your release. You see, we understand that while your father insisted that he had broken no law because he was demonstrating against an illegal regime, your mother pleaded guilty to all the charges. This seems to be reflected in their different sentences.'

'It's not fair,' burst out Dan. 'We all did the same thing. Why should Dad be in prison for longer?'

'Five years is the sort of sentence that is handed down for anti-government demostra- tions.' Susan Walker shrugged helplessly. 'Unfortunately your parents are not the first dissenters to be treated like this.'

'I bet they are the first to involve their children,' muttered James.

'We just have to hope that after a few months they are freed.'

'I must emphasize that we cannot permit the children to remain alone in Thailand until such time as that happens,' the immigration official broke in. There was a pause while the phrase, *If they are lucky enough to have their sentences reduced*, registered in the minds of the other adults. 'It would be quite out of the question. I believe the British authorities would support us?' He nodded towards Susan Walker.

'That is indeed so. We are able to authorize

airline tickets home — since these have not been included in your bag. The money for the tickets will, naturally, have to be refunded in the UK. That is not an immediate problem,' she said to Jessica, who was about to expostulate. 'But the real problem is that no airline will fly unaccompanied children under fifteen nowadays because of the insurance involved.'

'We understand that you, Mr and Mrs Morgan, are flying back to the UK imminently?'

'Yes. We are planning to get a flight as soon as possible,' Carol told the immigration official.

'Then we would ask you to escort the children home.'

'That would be the best solution,' said Susan Walker. 'Though I do understand that it is one thing for Mrs Pickering to have appointed you as guardians of the children, you would have to agree to act *in loco parentis* until a member of their family meets them at Heathrow.'

'We don't have any family to meet us anywhere,' said Jessica.

'We do have Uncle Peter,' said Dan.

The two exchanged enigmatic glances which were not lost on either of the Morgans.

James sighed heavily. 'I'm really not sure about any of this.'

'Of course we will escort them home,' insisted Carol.

'Then,' said the Thai official, 'if Miss Walker will take over the arrangements, we will pass the children over to your custody and permit them to stay in Thailand for forty-eight hours. That should be sufficient.'

'As if we were nothing but parcels,' muttered Jessica resentfully.

★ ★ ★

Parcels the children were not. They had needs. They needed a change of lightweight outer clothing. Fortunately, like the Morgans, the Pickerings had left a suitcase containing warmer clothes in the small Bangkok hotel they had used on their arrival in Thailand. This, with the help of Susan Walker, they were able to reclaim. It had a combination lock, the numbers of which Dan remembered, and they opened it back in the Montien. To the children's surprise (and to Carol's relief) in the pocket of Kimberley's fleece jacket there was an envelope containing £1,000 in large denomination notes.

'As if she knew exactly what was going to happen,' said Carol, who still found it quite extraordinary that parents were prepared to go to such lengths to safeguard the interests of their children, while not appearing to worry that they themselves were responsible for putting these children in danger in the first place.

Carol had always hoped that she would have more children after Matthew. Tests available two decades earlier had suggested that there was no reason for her not to conceive again. It had just not happened, which had been upsetting at the time. James would not consider adoption and so reluctantly and, after some years, Carol accepted that Matthew was to be an only child. Matthew had always said that he had preferred it that way and as he surrounded himself with chosen friends, Carol did not believe he had suffered too much.

After a minute's reflection Carol observed, 'I think we'll not admit to having found this money. 'I mean, your Uncle Peter can sort out the matter of the tickets once you're home. It was obviously meant for you two and you may need it over the coming weeks.'

James merely grunted.

★ ★ ★

It was late. They had fed the children in the restaurant and settled them for the night in the room next door. Alone, and with the mini bar broached for the second time, James, who had been uncharacteristically quiet during the meal, said his piece.

'I am not having anything to do with this nonsense over those kids.' He sat down in one of the chairs by the window.

'What do you mean by nonsense?' Carol was methodically folding soiled underwear into a large polythene bag. She stopped what she was doing to regard her husband with consternation.

'How dare that woman charge us with the guardianship of her children! The gall of it. How many times did we see them? How many conversations did we have, two? Three? We could be child molesters, for all she knew.'

'If, by 'that woman' you mean Kimberley Pickering, she obviously did what she thought was right. And as for it being nonsense, we really don't have a choice, do we, James? We have to look after them until they are handed over to one of their relatives. James?'

'I am not going home with those kids.'

'But we are going home,' she said reasonably, returning to her packing. 'We might just as well see them to Heathrow on our flight and hand them over to their uncle ourselves. I mean, they have suffered such a dreadful shock. We can't abandon them now.'

'Their parents have.'

'Not through their choice.'

'Come on, Carol. Do you mean to tell me that Brian Pickering wasn't aware that they'd be arrested the moment they began waving anti-government leaflets in the street? His wife obviously was, otherwise she wouldn't have left money in that suitcase. £1,000. Can you believe that? At least it is real money, not just a credit note.'

'So all we have to do is escort them to Heathrow and pass them, bag and all, over to their uncle. Finish.'

'If there is an uncle. Which I doubt.'

'How can you say that? You sound so cynical.'

'Did you see Jessica's face when young Dan mentioned Uncle Peter? Not a lot of joy there, I imagine.'

'You imagine too much. Are you really going to have a third whisky?'

'After the day we've had, I most certainly am.' James was already opening the door of the mini bar. 'Then I'm going to bed. And tomorrow I'm going to change my ticket to Heathrow for one for Sydney.'

'You can't do that!'

'I most certainly can.' He threw away the miniature Glenfiddich bottle and settled himself again in one of the chairs by the window.

'But what about me?' Carol, who had been standing by the case gazing unseeingly at the pile of clothes while her husband opened the mini bar, sat down in front of him on the end of the bed. There was an unaccustomed throb in her temple and her mouth was quite dry. 'I mean, if you are going to Australia, what am I supposed to do?'

'Carol, I'm not about to leave you, you know. Come on,' James said jocularly, taking a generous swallow of his whisky. 'What do you take me for?'

'I don't know,' she answered quietly. 'What am I supposed to do, James, if you fly to Australia? Look, I just can't understand why you are doing this. It's not as though what we have been asked to do is life changing.'

He ignored that. 'Carol, we've always been good together. Why must you spoil it now. Come with me.' His voice was cajoling, his words were persuasive.

He was right, Carol conceded, they had been good together. It was a relationship that had never floundered as had that of some of their friends. In all those years Carol had never been unfaithful to her husband. She wasn't one hundred per cent sure — could you ever be? — but she was almost certain that he had been faithful to her. And it was not for the lack of opportunity, she was as sure of that, for both of them. There was still passion. They always had been and they still were, kind to each other.

It was true that James was didactic, overbearing — witness his sudden decision to retire. He regularly forgot their anniversary and sometimes he forgot her birthday, but in the main they were content with each other. Nothing in these idyllic recent weeks had so much as hinted that he could contemplate leaving her.

Yet he had declared that he was going to buy a plane ticket to Sydney instead of going home.

'Come with me,' he repeated softly. 'We'll have a look at Sydney, perhaps for a couple of weeks. Then we'll go home either through the Centre and up to Darwin, or maybe after spending a few days in Perth. But I've always wanted to see Alice Springs. We could take the Ghan instead of flying.'

Carol was continuing to regard her husband as though he had taken leave of his senses. Perhaps he had taken leave of his senses, she was thinking.

'And what about Dan and Jessica? You know I can't just leave them,' she replied now, as she had repeated over and over again.

'I know you have developed a totally unjustified compulsion to act in an uncharacteristic way. You call it a moral necessity. I

84

don't see it that way and I know it doesn't have to be like that. Come with me.'

'James, I can't.'

'Then promise me you'll follow me. In a couple of weeks. That ought to be time enough.'

'I can't see why you have to abandon us. Why can't you come home as we planned. We can always forget India next winter and go to Australia instead, if that's what you'd prefer. We could maybe find temporary jobs there,' she said wildly, not knowing even if this were feasible.

He sighed. 'Carol, I'm not abandoning you. I've told you my solution to a problem that *isn't ours*. In the end, you must do what you think best.'

'Very well. I guess I must,' she said coldly.

'You don't want me to buy a second ticket? You know, Susan Walker can take care of the kids,' James declared. 'If it's anyone's problem, it's hers. After all, that's what she gets paid for. Looking after Brits in trouble. I bet there'll be any number of Brits who won't mind looking after them on a flight back home. They are not our problem,' he ended emphatically.

'I cannot believe you are saying that. It was us Kimberley said were to look after Dan and Jessica. Not any number of strangers.'

'Which is exactly what we are. Strangers, Carol. Strangers.'

'But less unknown than most. I don't see we have a choice,' she said stubbornly.

'Well, you may do what you want to do. I've told you my decision.' James put down his empty glass with a small thump. Then he got up out of the chair and picked up the shorts and T-shirt he wore in bed and went into the bathroom, closing the door behind him.

Carol got undressed, hanging her cotton skirt in the wardrobe and putting soiled underwear in another plastic bag which she would put in her case in the morning. When James emerged from the bathroom she went into it herself. How could he have turned this trip upside down? She wondered about that as she brushed her teeth too vigorously, then examined her gums anxiously. Australia had never been on their agenda. It was time they returned home. She had actually been looking forward to going home. What was so dreadfully difficult about being asked to escort two teenagers — well, Dan was only twelve, but a mature twelve, she thought — on a plane journey to meet their uncle? It was the whisky that was talking, she decided. In the morning James would have seen sense and they would be on their way home, as they had always planned. They would hand over Jessica and Dan to their Uncle Peter and everything would return to normal.

James was lying on his side of the bed, facing the window, when Carol returned to the bedroom. His bedside light was off and the covers were tucked firmly round his neck. Carol adjusted the air conditioning and turned off all the other lights except her own. She got into bed and picked up her book. But Margaret Atwood totally failed to take her mind off the blow James had dealt her, and after she had read a paragraph three times without understanding what it was about, she put the book down and turned off her own light. James stirred, but Carol turned away from him, lying on the edge of her side of the bed.

Really, she had no choice. She had to undertake what Kimberley Pickering had charged her to do. It wasn't in the least what she desired, but she had no choice.

A restless night followed on Carol's part — though she was fairly sure that James slept dreamlessly. It was unnerving to discover that the man she thought she knew so well had a facet to his personality that made of him as much of a stranger to her as Brian Pickering. There was nothing she could recall that suggested anything like this would ever happen to them; no warning that he could be so ruthless. It seemed he was casting her aside without a qualm.

And in the morning Carol discovered that it had certainly not been the whisky talking. James's very silence about anything more mundane than making sure the children were ready to have breakfast with them indicated that he had not changed his mind.

For James, in that obstinate way he had, refused to admit he was wrong and did exactly what he wanted to do. He came back from the hotel's business centre with his ticket to London changed for one to Sydney. They would all fly out in the evening.

Within twenty-four hours they would be at opposite ends of the world.

★ ★ ★

'I'm sorry it has turned out the way it has,' said Susan Walker, who had met them at the hotel with the children's tickets and was escorting the three of them through the formalities at the airport. 'I mean I . . . '

'Never expected to be involved in a marital crisis?'

'Mrs Morgan, you could have refused to do what the Pickerings wanted. No one could have forced you to do something for which

88

you were never prepared. We should have understood.'

Carol looked round hastily to make sure that neither Jessica nor Dan was in earshot. The two of them were examining the machine which encased fragile luggage in bubble wrap.

'That was what my husband said. In the end, though, I don't think I would have been comfortable if we had just left them. Poor things. Whatever their parents did, or did not expect to happen to them in Burma, the children didn't have a choice.'

'I suppose you could always join your husband in Australia?'

'There is always that possibility,' agreed Carol, without much conviction.

'Then all I have to do is wish you a good flight.' The children had returned to the adults. Susan handed Jessica some Thai currency. 'When you have gone through the security controls buy yourselves something to read on the plane.'

Dan said, 'Thanks, but I expect there'll be entertainment on the plane. Games and things.'

'Thanks, Miss Walker,' Jessica said hurriedly. Overnight she had lost her tan, and her skin had an unhealthy pallor.

'If the films aren't to your liking, perhaps

you'll be able to sleep.'

'You're sure their Uncle Peter is meeting us?' Carol said, as the two women shook hands. It was more for something to say, to elicit reassurance that what she was doing had some relevance. How could a consular official in Bangkok really know the circumstances of the two children now in her sole charge? Or if Uncle Peter actually existed?

The prospect of discovering that Peter Pickering did not exist she put resolutely to the back of her mind.

5

The flight from Bangkok to London passed uneventfully. While they were waiting for it to be called, Dan had wondered aloud if they would be given an upgrade. 'After all, we have suffered a trauma,' he said importantly. 'Maybe Susan will have arranged it.'

'I don't think it works quite like that,' said Carol. She was right, though since there were three of them, they shared a row of seats in economy.

'Cattle class,' observed Jessica scornfully.

Carol could not suppress a raised eyebrow at the comment. With Jessica's parents' egalitarian beliefs this was an unexpected reaction. 'I expect we'll be comfortable enough,' she said.

It was a long flight. The food was just passable. Carol was offered, and accepted, two bottles of airline wine. (It seemed that the steward had been told who they were and was being particularly solicitous.) There was a minor fuss since Jessica had not been able to pre-order her vegetarian meal, but eventually something was found that was acceptable to her. The films were either violent or banal.

Carol gave those a miss and was totally uninterested in any of the other offerings except the map of their flight path. She had packed the Margaret Atwood and had found a Joanna Trollope in the airport bookshop. It was something she had read before but at least that meant she did not have to concentrate too hard. She hardly slept at all. Both Dan and Jessica, however, appeared to be dead to the world for several hours, once Jessica had watched a film and Dan had exhausted the games.

Only during dinner did they have any conversation about what would happen when they arrived at Heathrow.

'Where does your Uncle Peter live?' Carol asked.

'In Hay-on-Wye,' said Jessica.

That meant he had quite a journey to meet them, though actually Hay was only an hour's drive from Otterhaven. 'I can't keep calling him Uncle Peter,' she said. 'What is his surname? I mean, I assumed he is your father's brother.'

'That's right. He's a Pickering, too. Dad's elder brother.'

Probably not too elderly, though. That was a relief. Do you have any cousins?'

'Uncle Peter's a bachelor,' said Jessica. 'I gave Miss Walker his address. I couldn't remember it properly, but I do know he lives in Hay.'

'We don't see much of him,' said Dan helpfully. 'I don't think he approves of us.'

Susan Walker had advised her to take the children to the meeting point at Heathrow. There they would be met and arrangements would be made for their onward journey. 'There will be a car to take you to South Wales,' she had said to Carol. 'Under the circumstances, that's the least we would expect the Pickerings to arrange.'

The luggage — what there was of it was reclaimed without a problem. Their passports were hardly examined. There was no Uncle Peter at the meeting point.

'Now what?' exclaimed Jessica pettishly. 'I knew this was going to happen.'

She had felt the same, Carol decided. There was no Uncle Peter, but there was a woman bearing a placard with the name, 'Morgan', on it, exciting no interest whatsoever. They were led to the inevitable small room.

'What happens now?' Carol asked despairingly.

The woman had flashed an identity card at Carol who was too exhausted to have taken in the name at the time. She replied, 'I'm afraid Mr Pickering is not able to meet the children.'

Jessica shrugged. 'So what do we do? Do we just go to Hay on our own?'

'I'm afraid there is a small difficulty,' the woman said.

'As in Uncle Peter doesn't want to have anything to do with us?' suggested Dan.

He sounded a lot more cheerful than she felt, thought Carol, a presentiment of doom flooding over her.

'It would seem as if, for the time being, that is indeed the case,' said the woman carefully.

'No sweat,' said Dan. 'I never liked Uncle Peter much.'

'What happens now?' asked Carol again.

'I wonder if you and I might have a word in private?' said the woman. 'We won't be long,' she told the children.

They left the room and went down a corridor to another room, identical to the last one. As they entered this one, it registered that the man sitting on a chair outside the first door — who had not been there when they originally arrived — was airport security.

'Look, who are you?' Carol asked, when the door closed behind them. 'Excuse me, I didn't take in your name.'

'I'm Jenny Wilson. Sorry, I expect you're exhausted. I'm from the Department of Health, Social Services and Public Safety and

I'm here because of the children.'

'I don't understand.'

'It's a bit tricky. I didn't want to say too much in front of Jessica and Daniel but their uncle absolutely refuses to have anything to do with them. We can't force him to take them in, you see. So — '

'So?' Carol interrupted. 'What is going to happen to them?'

'That rather depends on you.'

'On me?'

'I understand that you have a letter, signed by the children's mother, giving you their guardianship. Would it be possible for me to see it?'

'Yes, I have.' Carol opened the small backpack in which she kept her personal belongings. The letter was in the same pocket as her passport. She handed it to Jenny Wilson who read it carefully. 'The letter wasn't witnessed,' Carol pointed out. During the flight something James had said as they parted had come into her mind. If Kimberley Pickering's letter hadn't been witnessed, it wasn't legal.

'I'm not sure that is a problem, exactly,' said Jenny Wilson, after a pause. 'At least, not at this moment in time. Anyway, as we see it, there are two solutions. The happiest would be if you continue to act as the children's guardian, as their mother plainly wished.'

'For how long?'

'Well, I can't exactly say. I mean, three years was her sentence, wasn't it?'

'Three years!'

'But I understand that often these sentences are reduced,' the woman said hastily. 'We would ask the Foreign Office to make representations to this end. After all, she did plead guilty, and we can claim extenuating circumstances.'

She did not elaborate on what these might be and Carol was too shattered to notice the omission, then.

'And what is the other alternative?'

'We would have to take the children into care.'

'Could you explain that to me a little more fully?'

Jenny Wilson opened her mouth as if she were about to comment that most people understood what was meant by putting a child into care. Then, realizing that the woman in front of her had been through a lot in the past few days, she thought better of it. 'It will be up to me to find them somewhere to live,' she said, a little less brusquely. 'Since Mr Pickering won't have anything to do with the children I don't think there would be any point in trying to place them in, or near,

Hay-on-Wye. Unfortunately places near Heathrow are usually heaving — um, because of the asylum seekers problem, you understand? The most suitable solution might be to place them near their school in Woking. At least then they would have less of a disruption to their lives. I mean, they could keep their friends.'

'They don't go to school,' said Carol wearily. 'Woking, you say? I didn't even know where they live. As for friends . . . ' She left that point hanging in the air. 'Why don't you ask them?'

'Do you mean to tell me they are home educated? Oh, my God! That's the last thing I needed. A school and a care home.'

'Wouldn't they be fostered?'

'Not initially. Foster parents aren't too thick on the ground anywhere. Besides, the children would have to be assessed first.'

The two women regarded each other, compassion compounded with dismay in their expressions, though Jenny Wilson's silence had something of expectancy in it.

'It's a nightmare,' sighed Carol. 'I suppose . . . I mean, I suppose I could take them home with me. Just until you find something permanent for them, I mean.'

Jenny Wilson shook her head emphatically. 'That's a generous and impulsive gesture, but I'm not sure it's a good idea.'

'You mean it would be better for Jessica and Dan to go to some care home in the hope that you might be able to find them a foster parent eventually?'

'Foster parents. We can never guarantee that siblings stay together. Especially at their age.'

'That's outrageous!'

'I agree with you. Nevertheless, that's how it is. That's why you have to be very sure about making your offer.'

'Hang on, it was you who said that doing what Kimberley Pickering wanted would be the best solution.'

'And it most certainly would be. But if you are only prepared to be in this for the short haul, then it might be just as well if the children go straight into council care.'

Carol opened her mouth, and shut it. She shook her head. 'If I agree to take them home, it could only be for as long as I thought I was doing the right thing by them. If we rowed; if they hated me, I couldn't possibly keep them.'

'If your husband sent you a ticket to join him in Australia?'

'You seem to know an awful lot about me,' Carol said bitterly. Then she thought that of course Jenny Wilson and her bosses did. They would have checked up on her before ever she was permitted to get on the plane with the children in Bangkok. Did that mean being police vetted, or whatever they called it nowadays? Probably, and by the fast track, too.

'I spoke to Susan Walker in Bangkok,' Jenny Wilson said, proving Carol right.

'Then you will know that my husband is most unlikely to send for me.'

'He might return home.'

'He might. Unfortunately I find that I know my husband a lot less well than I thought I did. Just what he will do over the next six weeks or six months, let alone the next three years, I couldn't possibly predict. So, do we go and tell the children that they are coming home with me to South Wales?'

★ ★ ★

'Why can't we go back to Woking where we live?' asked Dan.

'Is that where you would like to live?' Jenny Wilson made a note on the file she was carrying.

'It's where we used to live,' Jessica corrected her brother. 'We gave up our rented house just before we went to Burma.'

'You did? Everything?' exclaimed Carol.

'Dad rented a large lock-up from a

neighbour. We kept a few things. Like our beds, a table and a few chairs.'

'Our laptop and a few reference books,' added Dan. 'Can we take them with us to South Wales?'

Carol thought of the small house into which she had crammed as much as possible of her favourite things from Windrush. 'I think we might have to find out exactly what you need before I promise anything rash,' she said. But she did smile.

'Cool,' said Dan.

'It's term-time, isn't it?' Jessica looked troubled. 'Who is going to teach us?'

'I think you should understand that Mrs Morgan will need to send you both to school,' said Jenny.

'I couldn't possibly teach you myself,' added Carol. 'I'm not in the least qualified to teach you anything.'

'But Dad says that schools today are crap.'

'I doubt if he used that word,' said Carol drily, proving to Jenny's satisfaction that it was unlikely she would be a complete walk-over as far as disciplining the children was concerned.

'So I'm certainly not going to any crap school,' declared Jessica, her challenge one of complete malice.

'I think any decisions other than that you

100

will be living with me, that is unless we all hate it, can safely be left for a day or so,' said Carol. 'Did Susan Walker say something about transport?'

'We'll go and find it.'

★ ★ ★

The Pickering children regarded 14, The Lane in Otterhaven in impassive silence while the taxi driver unloaded the large Vauxhall which had brought them from the airport to South Wales. Carol, unsure if they were jet-lagged or were being deliberately unhelpful, ignored them, chattering with the man inconsequentially. Then she signed his chit, thanked him profusely and waved him off as though he were a dear friend before finally she steeled herself to deal with the more pressing matter of the children, and took her keys out of her bag.

The house in the centre of the village which she and James had bought, was still relatively unfamiliar to her, even its appearance alien, the idea of living anywhere other than Windrush remained almost painful. An end of terrace house, Number Fourteen occupied a corner site. 'Inside it is larger than you think,' she said defensively. The first key did not fit the lock. 'I think this must be the key to the garden gate.'

'There is a garden, then?' said Jessica. The front door opened off the pavement, the flags of which were in need of repair. Though there were windows on either side of the front door, they were narrow. 'Net curtains. Naff.'

'When I was young I vowed I would never live in a house with net curtains,' said Carol apologetically. (Afterwards she was furious with herself for minding the criticism.) 'I changed my mind when we came to live here. I mean, how many of us resist the temptation of looking into other people's houses through uncurtained windows?'

'How sad can you get?' Jessica made a face.

'Obviously very sad,' muttered Carol. The second key had unlocked the door but it was only opening with difficulty. 'Could you help me, Dan? I think there must be mail obstructing it.'

Together they got the door open and between them they carried the luggage into the small hall. Leading from it, to one side, was a sitting-room which was now the depth of the house and opened into the garden. Daniel took in the old beams, the open fireplace which was laid with a log fire, French windows and the paved terrace beyond.

'Cool,' he said. 'Will we have our own bedrooms?'

This had been worrying Carol. There were three bedrooms. The largest was hers and James's, with a view over the garden. It had a small, ensuite bathroom which the previous owners had carved out of the generously sized family bathroom. Carol intended keeping that room for herself. After all, there was no saying when James would return ... Of the other two bedrooms, one was Matthew's and he had claimed a front bedroom. Yet he was unlikely to visit frequently. It made no sense to keep his room sacrosanct.

'I suggest Jessica has the spare room in the back and Dan uses Matthew's room.'

'What happens when Matthew comes home?'

'Shall we worry about that when it happens?'

To the left of the front door was a tiny room which James had taken over as his study. This left space for a kitchen which was big enough for a table and chairs. To Carol's relief, the house was clean and reasonably warm. At Windrush they had employed a housekeeper who did for them on three mornings a week. Vera Preece was coming up to retirement age but declined to be passed on to the new owners of Windrush.

'A terraced house in The Lane will do me

fine,' she announced. 'I can even walk to work.'

This also suited the Morgans admirably, especially when Vera agreed to go in twice a week while they were away, to sort the mail, twitch the curtains and generally look after the property. Carol had telephoned Vera from Bangkok and asked her to switch on the boiler, make up the beds and put some milk in the fridge in preparation for their unexpected arrival with guests.

'I'm going to light the fire. Then I must make a shopping list Do you think you would like a curry for lunch? An Indian restaurant opened in the village last summer. It's really very good.'

'No,' said Jessica ominously. 'It'll be tough lamb or chicken, with prawns as a vegetarian option.'

Carol sagged inwardly. 'Actually they do a very good vegetarian curry with lots of spinach and lentils. But I think you and I are going to have to talk about your diet.'

'I'm not going to eat meat,' declared the girl.

'Of course not. I didn't mean that. What I meant was, I suppose you can cook vegetarian food? You see, I'm not very experienced in menus for vegetarians as James and I have always eaten meat and fish.'

'Mum did all the cooking.'

'Then it would be fun for us to experiment together. Wouldn't it?'

'Whatever,' Jessica shrugged. 'But that restaurant. I bet they'll use the same oil for veggies as the one they cook the meat in.'

'I never thought of that. Do you think . . . '

'Jess didn't worry about that in Burma,' said Dan brightly, earning himself a glare. 'Well, you didn't, so,' he added indignantly. 'Dad said that if you made too much of a fuss we would all be con-conpers something or other.'

'Conspicuous?'

'That's it. Butt out, Dan.'

'So Jess stuck to vegetable curries and rice and no one asked if the meat had been cooked in the same oil.'

They glared at each other as if mutual antipathy were their natural bond.

'I think maybe we need to look up some cookery books and make up menus,' said Carol, profoundly grateful for any support. 'We'll do a shop once you've seen your rooms. I guess you can manage in the clothes you have until tomorrow? Then we'd better go into Monmouth and stock up on a few things like jeans and so on.'

She was so out of touch with what the young wore nowadays. Should she give them a budget and let them get on with it? Already the £1,000 was rapidly being spent, in theory at any rate. There would be school unifoms too, though perhaps these were not quite a priority. Before they left Heathrow, Jenny Wilson had mentioned benefits in a vague way, but Carol had no real knowledge of the support she might expect. Peter Pickering, however much he disapproved of his brother and his brother's way of life, must be her first point of contact. At least she had managed to persuade Jenny to give her his telephone number. She'd get in touch that very evening.

Unfortunately all Carol got was Peter Pickering's answer phone.

'Uncle Peter gets involved with things in Hay,' Dan said vaguely, when Carol told them that she had left a message for their uncle to contact her. 'We hardly ever speak to him.'

'I can be very persistent,' said Carol. 'I'll try again tomorrow.'

★ ★ ★

The following morning they went into Monmouth.

'I thought you said there was a choice of shops here,' said Jessica scathingly. 'I mean, like you can't expect us to wear stuff we've bought in Monmouth. And if we come here at all, there's almost as little to do as there is in Otterhaven.'

'I know it's not like Woking,' said Carol, 'or Cardiff or Bristol. But later on, once you've got used to the place, you'll find there's quite a bit on offer. Monmouth has even got its own cinema.'

Jessica and Daniel exchanged glances.

'I know, your father disapproves of the cinema.'

'Actually it's our mum who disapproves of the cinema. She says you get germs from places like that. She sometimes got us DVDs as a treat.'

At least Kimberley appeared not to be totally opposed to television, thought Carol with considerable relief. 'I'll think about that, Jess,' she said. 'In the meantime you'll need underwear and socks, a few warm things, slippers and wellie boots.'

'Slippers!' exclaimed Dan. 'Only old men, like Uncle Peter, wear slippers.'

'You may have noticed my carpets are new, and pale. You will be wearing slippers indoors. House rule,' said Carol firmly. 'And by the way, fashion statements will have to wait until we see how far the money stretches.'

The morning passed amicably enough. Never before had the children been given the opportunity of buying as many clothes at the same time and once certain ground rules had been laid down, (concerning price and suitability), they were very co-operative. Carol could see that they were actually enjoying the experience. Then they ate at a small café and afterwards they did a large supermarket shop.

'I like to use Otterhaven shops wherever possible,' said Carol. 'But occasionally it pays to come here and buy in bulk.' Though she knew they had bought sensibly, as she had feared, there was already a hole in the £1,000. Peter Pickering had better be home that evening, she thought grimly. She was not used to watching the housekeeping money and the prospect of feeding two extra mouths on what was in her own bank account was not one she relished. She supposed it was salutary to discover just what it was like to have to live on a very limited budget.

★　★　★

They went back to Otterhaven and unloaded the car. Daniel was unimpressed by Carol's eight-year old Nissan. He was even less impressed by the lack of a garage. Like the whole terrace, Number Fourteen did not have one, but fortunately the Morgans had

108

been able to rent a garage for the time they were expected to be away. The house, being at the end of the terrace, did have a parking space inside the garden gate and because the lane curved at that point it was not obvious from the road that the two plots were part of the same property.

'James sold his BMW before we started to travel. We haven't decided whether to apply for planning permission for a garage or not,' said Carol. 'I suppose it depends on what happens when James comes home.' She suppressed the depressing thought that it could be a long time before she saw her husband again.

'We had a Peugeot 206. It was second-hand when we got it. Dad doesn't approve of gas guzzlers,' Dan said righteously.

Carol was in the kitchen putting away the groceries when there was a knock on the back door. It was opened almost immediately and Marion Henderson walked in.

'You are home. I thought you must be,' she said. 'I was passing and saw the lights were on and I wondered how your journey back was. Then I realized the garden gate was unlocked, so here I am. Hey, that's a lot of stuff you're putting away. I didn't know you ate porridge oats for breakfast.'

'Marion. It's great to see you, too!'

The two women, who had been friends for many years, were not in the habit of embracing. They stood and smiled at each other, Marion — who had not changed in the least in the intervening months — clearly assessing Carol. A door slammed upstairs and Jess's voice could be heard upbraiding her brother.

'How's James? What's going on?' Marion asked curiously.

'Do you have time for a cup of tea?'

'Why do you think I came over now?' Marion grinned and sat down. 'Start at the beginning, Carol. I've all the time in the world.'

Carol made the tea and sat down opposite her friend. She hardly mentioned the trip — they could pore over photographs at some other time. She glossed over her interrogation at the hands of the Burmese Military Intelligence. But she told her about the children and how it had been impossible for her to abandon them in Bangkok, even though James had been so vehemently against the whole business of bringing them back to the UK.

'I don't know what to feel, now he's been proved right,' Carol grimaced. 'Oh, damn it. It's such a mess!'

Marion had let her talk, only interjecting a

110

few sympathetic murmurs, which Carol found immensely reassuring.

Now Marion said robustly, 'For what it's worth, I think you had no choice. Of course you had to help them. Just think how you'd have felt, if it had been Matthew.'

'Precisely. But James wouldn't have that. He said we'd never have allowed ourselves to get into that situation in the first place.'

'I guess he's right about that,' agreed Marion. 'Still . . . '

They were interrupted by the doorbell. 'Sorry. I'd better get that.' Outside it was already dark and a strange man was on the doorstep. 'Are you Mrs Morgan?' he asked politely.

'I'm Carol Morgan,' Carol answered cautiously. She had opened the door wide, though she had not stood aside for the man to enter.

'I'm John Price.' He named a South Wales newspaper, flashing an identity card. 'You've just got back from Burma with the Pickering children, haven't you? Their parents are in prison in Burma, aren't they. A political thing, I understand. How difficult for Jessica and Daniel. Do you think I could come in and talk to them?'

The press. How? When? Oh God, thought Carol. Not the press! Why hadn't it occurred to her that this would happen?

'I don't think that's really a very good idea,' she said, and went cold as the man nodded sympathetically. She had just confirmed what he thought he knew.

A light bulb flashed in her face.

'Thanks, Mrs Morgan. That'll be a scoop for our next edition. I'll be in touch in the morning,' he said. 'Perhaps you could all give me an exclusive interview then?'

Carol closed the door firmly in his face, then she stood with her back against it. In front of her, their own faces white and shocked, Jessica and Dan were poised on the stairs. She did not doubt that the powerful camera had caught them, too.

Marion was poised in the open kitchen door, looking equally startled.

'Oh, Lord! Whatever am I going to do now?' Carol said helplessly.

6

There was a moment's appalled silence. 'I can't think why I wasn't prepared for something like this to happen!' Carol cried, stunned by this latest complication.

'Dad says any publicity for the cause is a good thing,' said Dan virtuously.

'I don't think he meant that Carol should be involved with reporters, though,' said Jessica unexpectedly.

Recovering herself, Carol said, 'I'm sure your mother would prefer you to be kept out of it, too.'

'I think what you need is a solicitor,' suggested Marion practically. 'I'm sure you can invoke privacy laws, or something.'

Also Peter Pickering, thought Carol grimly. They needed him, whether he liked it, or not. 'But before that, let me introduce you to my friend, Marion Henderson,' she said to the children. And when that was done, she added, 'Marion is quite right. We need a solicitor. But first I'm going to try to speak to your uncle.'

Marion took her leave, promising to be in touch in the morning.

This time Peter Pickering answered the phone himself. After the shock of being accosted by the press on her doorstep, Carol was seething with rage that the man had not yet bothered to answer her previous calls. She told him so.

'I saw no point in telephoning you,' he answered coldly. 'I told the woman who contacted me from London that the children are nothing to do with me.'

'I don't care whether you disapprove of your brother and his beliefs or not,' she said. 'I'm not going to cope with this unaided. I intend to call my solicitor. You will pick up the bill. No doubt I shall have to give the press some sort of an interview. If you are not there to support me, I shall tell them just what I think of a father and mother who sacrifice their children for a whim, not to mention an uncle who abandons his kith and kin to a stranger.'

Carol slammed down the phone. She turned to find brother and sister regarding her with almost as much astonishment as they had the reporter. In her anger with Peter Pickering, she had forgotten they would inevitably overhear her conversation.

'Have Mum and Dad sacrificed us?'

'Daniel. I shouldn't have said that. It was a stupid thing to say and not true.'

'Well, it is true, in a way,' said Jessica. 'I mean, Mum and Dad did know they would be arrested by the police in Burma.'

'Mum said it would be just for a few hours. She said I wasn't to worry. That we'd all go home after the protest.'

'I don't think it works like that, Dan. Not in a totalitarian regime like the one in Burma,' said Carol uneasily.

'But Uncle Peter isn't helping much.'

'I'm not surprised. He's a pig,' declared Dan.

'You're only saying that because he had a row with Mum and Dad that time when he came to see us at Christmas. He did give us book tokens. Generous ones.'

'Did he? That was nice,' Carol said circumspectly.

'I've still got mine. If the lock-up hasn't been broken into.' Jessica sounded as though this was a distinct possibility.

'I expect everything is safe enough. We'll arrange to go over there and for you to bring some of your belongings back. Once things are a bit more settled. Um . . . Do you mind telling me what the row with your uncle was about?'

'Burma, of course. He said we should be staying in Woking.'

'There was no question of your staying with him?'

115

'Uncle Peter doesn't do children.'

'That's a funny way of putting it. Though I think I know what you mean. What does your uncle do?'

'He has a second-hand bookshop.'

In Hay-on-Wye. How very suitable, thought Carol. She wondered what a thirty-something man bought and sold. Science fiction? Thrillers? She might even have visited his shop herself. A thought occurred to her. 'What about godparents? Does either of you have a godmother or godfather who you could stay with? I should have thought about that before.'

Jessica sighed. 'Uncle Peter is my godfather. I did have one godmother but she died in a car crash with her whole family when I was still a baby. Mum and Dad didn't ask anyone else.'

'What about you, Dan?' asked Carol hopefully.

'By the time he was born, Mum and Dad had decided they didn't do religion,' Jessica answered for her brother.

'No life guardians, or anyone else? I mean, most parents appoint someone to be a guardian in case anything happens to them.' Carol was thinking about Matthew, who had the regulation two godfathers and one godmother. All three had remained family friends and all of them had been generous and supportive.

116

'There was Uncle Michael and Aunt Cindy. They were sort of life guardians,' said Dan gloomily. 'But they emigrated to Canada when I was nine. They send me a money order every Christmas, but I don't s'ppose they'd want me to go to Canada to live with them. And what about Jess? I couldn't leave her.'

'Of course not.' Another avenue closed. 'Well, I must do something about contacting that solicitor. I'm not sure if it should wait until the morning.' Carol brought her mind back to the immediate problem.

James and Carol had been friendly for years with a solicitor and his wife who lived in Otterhaven. Alison Firmer remained a stalwart of the WI and now that her husband, Luke, had retired, he spent most of his time in the garden, growing the produce that Alison sold in Monmouth's market. James approved of Alison but he tended to despise Luke, who he said should have been called to the bar, an opportunity open to him when he was young. Now Carol rang Luke, apologizing for intruding on his evening.

'I was only watching rubbish,' Luke said. 'I didn't know you were back. Tell me what's happened.'

The tale was told succinctly. 'I'm sure we need legal advice. I don't know where to start.'

'Why don't I phone Polly?' Polly was Luke and Alison's daughter, who had joined Luke's old firm a few years before. Polly had married a local farmer but practised under her maiden name. 'She's better at things now than I am.'

'Do you think she would mind?'

'Of course she won't.'

* * *

Whether she minded that her evening was disturbed, or not, Polly Firmer was efficient. By the following morning, the privacy of the children had been guaranteed. It was too late, though, to prevent the South Wales paper from getting its scoop and the picture of Carol and the two children behind her was splashed across the front page with a reasonably accurate report of what had happened to Brian and Kimberley Pickering in Rangoon. By breakfast time eight assorted reporters and cameramen were camped outside Number Fourteen.

Polly Firmer had been adamant. 'Absolutely no individual interviews,' she said to Carol. 'Through me you can issue a statement to keep them happy and maybe later do an interview. It depends on how much of a nightmare develops.'

'I suppose we do have to remember Brian and Kimberley in all this,' observed Carol. 'After all, however the children are affected, they are the ones in prison. They are the ones who wanted the publicity in the first place,' she ended wryly. 'Good, or bad.'

Vera Preece turned up at breakfast time, her hair immaculate, a determined look on her face.

'I thought you might like somebody to mind the door,' she said.

'Vera. How very thoughtful of you. If you could also fend off the phone calls? We've taken to only answering every other one. But I don't really think that is a good idea in case we miss something important.'

About five calls later, Vera said, 'There's someone called Peter Pickering who says he's parked round the corner. Will you see him?'

'Tell him, of course. Oh, Vera,' Carol said, as the housekeeper turned to go back into the study, 'suggest Mr Pickering comes in through the back. With a bit of luck the reporters won't have realized that the back gate is part of our garden, particularly as it never even occurred to me to cut back the old honeysuckle before we left on our travels.'

Peter Pickering was not what Carol had expected. She registered a man who loomed over her in her low-ceiling sitting-room; who was inches taller than his brother, Brian, and had grey hair which curled over the collar of an elderly sports jacket. Peter Pickering must be in his late fifties, older than she had surmised, feeling for the first time some sympathy for him. He was no less a victim of Brian and Kimberley than she was.

'As you see, I came.'

His voice was low, cultured. His handshake was firm. Though his face was lined, his eyes were a dark, intense blue under bushy eyebrows and his gaze was intelligent, not unkind, as he took in the strain of Carol's expression.

'I gather you are having a time of it. Hello, Jessica, Daniel.' He approached his niece and kissed her cheek. Then he held out his hand to his nephew. But the boy stood stubbornly with both his hands behind his back. Peter smiled ruefully and let the ill manners go. 'What would you like me to do first?' he asked Carol.

It was not the response Carol had expected. 'Perhaps we should talk? Coffee. I expect you would like coffee? Jessica, would you ask Vera to make a pot, please? Do sit down, Mr Pickering.'

'Peter,' he said easily. 'May I call you Carol?'

It was worse than she had imagined, she

thought as she nodded assent. What had she imagined? A man like Brian Pickering for a start. Brian was brusque, sometimes almost rude. Brian was not a particularly attractive man, though maybe if his glasses were not the rimless sort they might have helped to give his face more structure. Brian was also badly dressed. Maybe not so much badly as carelessly dressed, as though clothes were the last thing on his mind. They probably were. Now Peter was not smartly dressed but the cloth of his jacket was good, the worn patches on his elbows were leather, as were his shoes, and his trousers had been well-cut and were clean and pressed. What had she expected, imagined she would be meeting, a man she could dislike enough to blame him for all that was happening to her? How childish!

'I am sorry you have been embroiled in all this,' Peter Pickering said. 'It is unforgivable of my brother.'

'Dad couldn't help it, Uncle Peter,' said Dan loyally.

'Of course he could, Daniel,' answered Brian's brother resignedly. 'If you recall, I predicted something like this would happen. I warned him he was not to rely on me for help when he got himself into a mess. Carol, I didn't really think that Brian would involve Kimberley, let alone the children.'

121

'Mum wouldn't have left Dad alone in Burma,' objected Jess.

'No, my dear. She was prepared to leave you, though, wasn't she?'

It was an unkind comment, though true. Carol felt that her original, bad opinion of Peter Pickering was being reinforced.

'I'm not your dear,' said Jess, through her teeth.

'Jessica!' protested Carol, who also felt that adult solidarity should be seen to be maintained. 'Your uncle is here to help, now.'

'Only because you shouted at him down the phone.'

'That's true enough,' said Peter, with a smile. 'Look, we all know this is a real predicament. Do you think we might call a truce, stop sniping at each other and decide what we have to do now?'

'Polly Firmer, the solicitor I called, is coming to see us at noon,' Carol told him.

'A house call's going to be expensive,' he retorted.

'I expect it might be. There was no way I was going to take the children in to Monmouth to see her and run the gauntlet of what's happening outside. Were there reporters at the back gate?'

Peter shook his head. 'Mrs Preece opened the gate just as far as I needed to get through,' he said. 'The reporters are all clustered at the front.'

'I don't think we can suggest the same mode of entry for Polly. She's never gone in for skulking.'

'Solicitors are likely to be better able to cope than the rest of us.'

'So what are we going to do?' asked Jessica brusquely.

'Carol, you do understand why I said that I cannot look after Jess and Dan?'

'Not really. You are their uncle, after all.'

'I live in a small flat over the bookshop. I have one bedroom and a study-cum-sitting room. There just isn't the space.'

Carol opened her mouth to protest, then closed it. Bedroom space — of which she obviously had more — was just one of the problems she was facing.

'Jess, Dan, why don't you leave Peter and me to talk things over?'

'If you're going to talk about money, we are staying,' said Jess.

'Uh-uh,' murmured Dan emphatically.

Carol shrugged her shoulders. 'I hate to sound mercenary, but, yes, there is the question of finance.' She went on to explain about the money they had found in the bag in Bangkok. 'It sounds substantial but I can assure you it isn't going to go far.'

Peter Pickering raised his eyebrows. 'It seems adequate to me. At least, for some considerable time.'

Carol got up abruptly. 'That shows you have absolutely no idea what things cost nowadays.' She left the room and went into the study where she picked up a folder from the desk. She returned to the sitting-room where the three Pickerings had remained in silence. She placed the folder on the small table beside her seat and took out a sheet of paper which she passed to Peter.

'I have kept an account of every penny I have spent since we left Heathrow,' she said coldly. 'Here also are the receipts. On my accounts' sheet you will see that I have divided the food bills into three. Naturally I expect to pay my own expenses. But the children needed clothes. You will see that nothing has been spent that has not been necessary. There is also the matter of their plane tickets.'

'Insurance money . . . ' muttered Peter, visibly taken aback by her belligerence.

'You would hardly expect me to have the first idea whether your brother had insurance, or if, in fact, any insurance company would pay out under these circumstances,' she snapped, uncontrite.

'Carol,' began Dan. His face was white and

124

his eyes were large and shiny.

'Oh, Daniel,' said Carol, her voice full of regrets. 'I'm sorry. This is why I didn't want you and Jess to be here while I talked to your uncle. It's not that I . . . '

'Yes, it is,' said Jessica fiercely. 'You never wanted to take care of us in the first place.'

'That's not . . . Well,' she admitted helplessly. 'I never envisioned this situation in my wildest dreams. Of course I didn't. I was expecting to come home with my husband, not two children whose parents are in prison in Burma. I was expecting us to . . . and now James is in Australia . . . Excuse me . . . ' Once again she got up abruptly, this time more clumsily. This time when she left the room she fled upstairs to her bedroom and took refuge in her bathroom, subsiding on to the lavatory seat where she sat and trembled for several moments.

There was a tentative knock on the door.

This was outrageous!

'Go away,' she cried fiercely.

'Mrs Morgan. Mrs Morgan?' It was Vera. 'Do you think you'd like a nice cup of tea?'

Carol smiled through her anguish at Vera's panacea for any trouble. 'I've only just had a cup of coffee. No, thanks, Vera.' There was a pause. Somehow Carol knew that Vera had not gone away. 'Thanks, Vera. I'm all right. I'll be down in a minute.'

She took several deep breaths to calm herself. Then she got up and went over to the basin. She looked at herself in the mirror. 'Stupid woman,' she said aloud. 'Losing it, like that. You are an old fool!' She reached for her flannel and ran it under the cold tap then she pressed it gently against her flushed face. 'So humiliating,' she murmured. 'I bet they're laughing their socks off.'

The Pickerings were not laughing. When she went back downstairs they were sitting where she had left them though she had a feeling that a great deal of substance had been said in her absence. The children looked subdued. Peter Pickering appeared even more shaken than before. He got up when she entered the room.

She said immediately, 'I'm sorry about that . . . '

'I'm so sorry. I hadn't . . . '

'I don't usually react in that sort of way,' said Carol, her voice apologetic. 'I think it must be those reporters outside. I just hadn't thought through the implications of the publicity angle. So stupid of me. Of course the press wants to know about what happened in Burma. And of course both Brian and Kimberley have the right for as many people as possible to know what's happened to them.'

'Not to mention what's happening to the Burmese who oppose the government in Burma,' said Jessica firmly.

'That, too. I suppose,' agreed Carol. She lifted her hands. 'Of course. But not at your expense.' She sat down, feeling exhausted and helpless.

'Carol, I do apologise,' said Peter, actually sounding as though he meant it. 'I hadn't realized your husband — '

'Let's leave James out of it,' she interrupted tautly.

'As you wish. What I meant to say was that I hadn't appreciated the children were just dumped on you.'

'Thanks, Uncle Peter,' said Daniel, earning himself a frigid glare.

'I think I assumed that you were a part of all this. I mean, you were together in Burma.'

'We were not together in Burma,' Carol glowered at him.

'Carol is right, Uncle Peter,' said Jessica reluctantly. 'They just happened to be in the same places we were. Dad said it was a God-sent opportunity to-to . . . '

'Use us? I knew it.' Carol continued. 'It wasn't just coincidence, was it? All those times when we had to share our transport with you?'

'It wasn't a put-on the first time. We really had a breakdown then. After that, well . . . '

'Brian said we were sitting ducks.'

'Dad never said that, exactly.'

'Dad would never use a shooting metaphor,' said Jess. 'He doesn't approve of blood sports.'

'I can believe that. I expect he said something quite different. All the same, he meant that we were ripe for exploitation.'

'It wasn't a kind thing to do,' said Peter unexpectedly. 'Both Brian and Kimberley must have known that things could go disastrously wrong and that the children might be left with no protector. If you ask me, I think they were very lucky to have found you.'

Peter Pickering was looking at her in a way in which no man had regarded her for many a year. It made her feel inexplicably fortified, as though nothing in the future would, or could, be too difficult to cope with. Dangerous, she thought.

'Maybe so,' Carol conceded aloud, warily. 'Though that doesn't help much with what happens now.'

The doorbell rang and Vera, blatantly hovering in the hallway, from which vantage point she could hear the conversation in the sitting-room, even if she could not see the people concerned, went to answer it.

'It's Miss Firmer, Mrs Morgan. Shall I make some more coffee?'

'Please, Vera. For anyone else?' Carol introduced the young woman to the Pickerings: 'Do sit down, Polly.'

'I'd prefer a cup of tea, please, if that's available,' said Polly. 'Now, I expect you want to hear what I've achieved so far?'

She went on to tell them that an injunction had been set up to preserve the anonymity of the children. That meant that while their circumstances might be public knowledge, there could be no more newspaper pictures of them.

'What do you mean their circumstances are public knowledge?' asked Carol.

'I mean that while what happened in Burma is already in the public domain, nothing can be written about Jessica or Daniel that might identify where they are staying or what might happen to them in the future. You won't have to worry about being followed in Otterhaven, Mrs Morgan.'

Polly Firmer then said that it would be politic to issue a statement — most usefully in the name of Brian Pickering's brother.

'Half-brother,' said Peter firmly.

So that explained quite a bit, thought Carol.

'In the name of Brian Pickering's half-brother,' Polly corrected herself. She said that she would be most happy to continue to represent Mrs Morgan and to represent the family's interest, if that was agreeable to everyone concerned.

It also appeared that there were many people in the country who would be working on behalf of Brian and Kimberley, ensuring on-going publicity for their imprisonment in Burma and trying to obtain their release. At the same time they would be reiterating all the injustices from which the Burmese, particularly the minority tribal groups, were suffering. Friends of the Pickerings recognized that, while it might have helped to focus on their children as victims, they would avoid this in case they infringed the law.

'I've started to draft a statement to which you might agree,' said Polly. 'Perhaps you could have a look at it? I think we should issue the statement as soon as possible so that the reporters won't have any reason to stay here.'

It was a simple statement verifying the fact of Brian and Kimberley Pickering's imprisonment; dwelling on the length of their sentences; mentioning that the present regime was notorious for such injustices, and stressing the fact that this regime was illegal.

It thanked well-wishers, gave assurances that the Pickerings' children were being cared for and requested that their privacy in these dreadful circumstances be respected.

It seemed to cover everything, Carol and Peter agreed.

There was also the matter of the invoice Polly Firmer's company would be submitting.

'To whom should it be sent?' she asked carefully. 'We would be happy to submit separate accounts.'

Peter Pickering answered promptly, 'Anything that pertains to the children while they are in Carol's care, should be sent to me.'

'Thank you,' said Carol simply. Once again Peter looked at her for a long, brooding, moment. She shivered as though a ghost had walked over her grave.

A further point of importance was the custody of the children and where they would live until their parents were released. 'You might be glad of legal advice,' Polly said. 'I'm not an expert in family matters so you might like to consult one of my colleagues. I am most happy to recommend one of them, if you need advice.'

Peter made a non-committal reply and shortly afterwards Polly, flanked by Carol and Peter, stood outside the front door while she read their prepared statement.

Both reporters and cameramen departed promptly, followed a little later by Polly and Vera Preece, who had left them a huge plateful of sandwiches and said that she had some shopping to do and would see them in the morning. This left the three Pickerings alone with Carol Morgan.

★ ★ ★

'I hope we can manage without expensive legal advice from now on,' said Peter, tucking into the sandwiches.

Carol, who had also cut into the large fruit cake provided by Vera, allowed her lip to curl. Her opinion of him nose-dived once more.

'I should hope so, too,' she replied. 'However, as I mentioned an hour or so ago, we do have to agree on some financial settlement, and also what is to happen about the children's schooling. I've already said that I can't possibly teach them myself.'

'Of course you can't. Ah, I suppose another apology is called for. Carol, I had no intention of insulting you. What I meant to say was that naturally you couldn't be expected to teach the children yourself when there is a perfectly good school in the area.'

'You are talking about the comprehensive, I assume? You may or may not know that we

132

have two good independent ones also in the area.'

'Quite out of the question, unless there's a scholarship involved,' said Peter firmly.

'But, Uncle Peter, Dad says . . . '

'Not now, Daniel,' said Carol gently. 'I'm sure you'll do very well at the comprehensive.'

'I don't expect Matthew went there.'

'No, Jessica. But that is rather different, isn't it?'

'Absolutely different,' her uncle said fiercely. 'And take that mutinous expression off your face, girl! If you were living with me in Hay there wouldn't be any question of where you went to school.'

'Peter . . . '

'Yes, I know. Make allowances for all the trauma etc. Pure psychobabble, all of it, and my sister-in-law is one of the worst exponents of it.'

'Mum isn't . . . '

'I'm not staying to argue. Thank you for the sandwiches, Carol, and I'll be in touch. I do mean that,' he said, actually taking her hand and squeezing it. 'I think you've been handed a tough deal, with my nephew and niece, and I hope they don't run you ragged. I'll phone you in a day or so to tell you what I've sorted out and you must bring them over to Hay soon. Don't come out. I guess I can leave by the front door now.' He looked at the children. 'Behave. Promise me? Your mum and dad would expect no less.'

He hesitated, then he gave Jess another quick peck on the cheek and Dan a pat on the shoulder. Then he picked up his ancient overcoat and was out of the door.

Jessica and Daniel looked at each other. Then they looked at Carol who was standing in the middle of the sitting-room appearing for all the world as though she had passed through a hurricane.

'What did we tell you about Uncle Peter?'

She was spared an answer — wouldn't have known in the least what to say — for once more the phone rang.

The wretched instrument had been ringing on and off all morning and they had got used to it being answered by Vera. Now, as if he knew this one was important, Daniel was up and out of his chair and into the study soon after the second ring. But unexpectedly he came back into the sitting-room without answering it.

Carol went to pick up the phone herself, thinking it was probably Marion. Afterwards, she wondered if Dan had thought it might be his parents.

'Hi, what took you?' The easy, familiar voice of James came down the line to her.

7

Carol felt a surge of resentment at James's greeting. She could think of nothing she wanted less than to speak to her absent husband. How dared he just call and speak so casually to her after all this time! What could he possibly say to make any of this awful situation better?

Of course she wanted to speak to him!

'James? Where are you? What are you doing? Why are you calling me?'

'Hi, Carol,' he said again, as easily as if he had only seen her the previous day. 'How are you doing?'

Her mind reeled. They had parted in Bangkok on Tuesday evening. She and the children had landed at Heathrow early on Wednesday morning — according to international time. It was now Thursday. She had been with James only two days before. (She had been locked in an interrogation room only hours before that.) If anyone had suggested — less than a week ago — that she and James could have parted in the way they had, she would have thought it a sick joke. How could a trip through South East Asia have disintegrated so very suddenly in the way it had?

'Where are you?' she repeated weakly. Did she really expect him to reply that he was already at Heathrow and that he was on his way home?

'I'm in Perth. It's a great city. You'd love it. You really would. I'm calling from an internet café. I had thought about e-mailing, but I wanted to hear your voice.'

Carol smiled wryly. It was the sort of emotional answer that, coming from her, James would have ridiculed in days gone by.

'Then I wondered how many times you've checked your e-mail since you got back.'

'You know me,' she said, vaguely wondering if her computer was still half-concealed under the desk. Why had it not occurred to her that James would try e-mailing? She thought that this lapse could definitely be classed as a 'senior moment'. She peered down. Of course the computer was still there. 'I haven't even had time to switch the thing on yet.'

'That's what I wondered. Anyway, I'm about to go back to the hotel as it's just after eleven o'clock and I'm a bit exhausted from the sightseeing. We're nine hours ahead, since you haven't asked, though it'll be different in Sydney.'

'Sydney.' Carefully Carol pulled the flex for the landline as far as it would reach and pushed the study door closed. The thought that this was yet another conversation it was preferable the children did not overhear had just crossed her mind.

'I've got a berth on the train across the Nullarbor Desert to Sydney. Looking forward to that immensely.'

'It's a desert. There's nothing to see.'

'Precisely. It'll be great.'

'James. When are you coming home?' As she asked, Carol already knew what his decision was. There was a slow intake of breath down the line, then came his reply:

'I don't know. Soon,' he added encouragingly.

There was a longer pause. She would not beg, Carol thought, gritting her teeth, concentrating hard on neither losing her temper nor bursting into tears and pleading with him. She was not sure which was the more difficult. Yet, if James did not know how very much she needed him; if he did not care that she needed him, there was no point in begging.

'I'm sorry you're not with me. You really would like Perth.' The disembodied voice interrupted her thoughts. 'It's hot, but the sky is so blue.'

'Not so very different from Asia, then.'

'The streets are a lot cleaner, though.'

'James, you are supposed to be in Sydney already.' She gripped the telephone receiver, thinking how nonsensical this conversation sounded.

'I couldn't get a seat on a direct flight unless I flew business class, which seemed a bit extravagant. Then the airline offered me Perth as an alternative, so I took that. Which was when I thought of the Nullarbor. I've always wanted to do that train journey. Carol, there was another reason why I phoned. I was hoping you were going to tell me you've had time to buy your plane ticket and will be meeting me in Sydney. Have you?'

'Have I what?' She was thinking that it hadn't mattered to him where he went, so long as he got away. From her? The idea was sickening.

'Have you bought your ticket?'

Money wasn't the real problem. Although she would have needed to transfer money for a long-haul flight and the subsequent funds that she would require. 'You haven't asked about the children,' she temporised.

'Matthew? How is Matthew?'

'Matthew is not a child,' she said tightly. Actually, now she came to consider that, she hadn't even spoken to her son since her return. She supposed she ought to, now that the papers were involved with her affairs. She thought it might be better not to mention the press to James just yet.

'You mean Jessica and Daniel? Actually, I was sure you'd have passed them over to their uncle by now. I supposed that little adventure must be over for you at last. And a good thing, too. So, when are you joining me, Carol?'

'I'm not.'

There was another pause. His thought processes clear to a wife of many years. James said uneasily, 'This call is beginning to cost. Are you trying to tell me you are still looking after the children?'

'Yes, James. Jess and Dan are here with me, in Otterhaven.'

'Why?'

'Why do you think? Because their uncle can't take them.'

'Can't, or won't?' he demanded sharply.

'It's a long story.'

'Like this call. Look, e-mail me, Carol. There might be e-mail facility on the train, but I'll wait and check my messages as soon as I arrive in Sydney. Probably telephone you once I've found a hotel and made a few plans. Let's hope you've got rid of the kids by then.'

'I'll take it you don't mean that literally?'

Again he laughed. This time it was much more of a guffaw. 'I'll trust you don't have to resort to that, love.'

It was the first term of endearment he'd used. Though in a context that was far from loving.

'James, I . . . '

'Got to go. Speak to you soon. Byee.'

Before she could answer, the line was dead. Of all the conversations she had had with her husband during their marriage, that was one of the most unsatisfactory.

★ ★ ★

The children were in the kitchen. They were just finishing the washing up.

'Thanks,' said Carol. 'I think the rest of the cake had better go in this tin,' she said, producing from the pantry a National Trust container, the lid of which was decorated with flowers. 'By the way, you could have put the plates in the dish-washer.'

'Dad says dish-washers use too much water,' Dan pontificated.

'Mum says you use more water if you wash the dishes by hand.'

'Well,' said Carol. 'That's interesting.'

'Not really,' said Jessica. 'What did James want?'

Carol ignored the rudeness. She thought she might as well tell the truth. They deserved to know exactly what was going on. After all, this whole situation could hardly be more traumatic for them. 'James thought that you would be with your uncle by now. He wanted to know when I would be joining him.'

'What did you tell him?'

'Jess,' said Dan awkwardly, 'I don't think you should ask Carol that.'

'Get real,' the girl countered. 'After all, it's us they were talking about behind the closed door.' Her pent-up feelings overwhelming her, she wrung the dishcloth out hard and flung it down on the draining board.

'Why don't we go into the sitting-room and I'll tell you about my call and perhaps we can decide what we are all going to do next?' Carol ignored the tantrum and turned and left the kitchen. She had no intention of getting into an argument with the children over the propriety of closed doors and telephone calls. Particularly calls with James. If — or when there was another.

'There is something you could do to help me,' she said, when eventually the two trailed reluctantly into the sitting-room after her. 'It's my computer. I haven't even turned it on since we came back and James says he's sent e-mails. He probably isn't the only one.'

141

'So you do have a computer.'

'Of course. It's in the knee-hole of the desk, covered by a rug. We left it connected, but not switched on.'

'Is it any good?' asked Dan eagerly.

'I'm not sure how you define good in terms of a computer,' smiled Carol. 'James seems to think it's state of the art. We go in for Apple-Macs, if you're interested.'

'Cool,' said Dan, a little doubtfully. 'Got any games?'

'Only what's part of the hard drive, or whatever,' confessed Carol. 'That is, we don't go in for special games at our age. James bought this computer a few months ago when he retired because the laptop he was using belonged to the firm and so had to be returned and our old computer was a bit past it.'

'Have you got broadband?'

'Oh, yes, because of its speed.'

'Cool. Have you got an iPod?'

So many questions. Still, at least now she knew what interested Dan. 'Not here, Dan. James bought one for us to take away. I know he down-loaded a lot of our music before we went and he still has it with him.'

'So it's not here now?'

'I'm afraid not. Anyway, if you know about computers, perhaps you could get it going again for me so that I can send James an e-mail? He wants to know all about what we've been doing.'

'I bet,' murmured Jessica.

Once again Carol ignored her, saying brightly, 'Which one of you is the computer whiz?'

'I am,' said Dan. 'Jess just uses it for Google searches for homework.'

'That's pretty clever,' said Carol.

'Sometimes we needed information for the homework Mum set us,' Jessica shrugged. 'It was no big deal.'

'James says that the research you do on the Net is only as good as the person who's typed it in. Did you never use reference books?'

'It was good enough for us, and of course we had reference books,' Jessica glared.

Carol's patience snapped, but she took a deep breath before she reacted. Then she got up from her chair and went over to the girl. She put her arm round Jessica's shoulders and managed to keep it there, though Jessica made an attempt to shake her off.

'I think we need to establish a few ground rules, don't you?'

'Like the house rule about slippers?' Jessica sneered.

'Yes, Jessica. Like house rules. They are the same thing really. You use slippers in the house to keep my new carpets clean. You are polite to me — we are polite to each other — because in that way we preserve the peace between us. This is important because you are guests in my house.'

'You'll be getting money for looking after us.'

'Then you're paying guests,' said Carol brightly. 'Since when did paying guests, of any age, have the right to be insolent?'

'Dad says . . . '

'But your father is not here, and I would so much rather you were not insolent to me. Or perhaps I should say that unless you can manage to be reasonably polite while you are staying with me, I might feel that flying to Australia to be with my husband was a better option. You know the saying about worms turning?'

Jessica's face turned a dull red. 'Sorry,' she muttered.

'Sorry,' said Dan brightly. 'Can I go and sort out the computer now?'

'Won't you have to make sure it's properly warmed up, or anything, before you do something complicated?'

Daniel looked at Carol witheringly. Then he remembered his manners and smiled winningly. 'Trust me,' he said.

'Can I go to my room?'

'If you want to, Jess,' said Carol. 'I think

while Dan is sorting out the computer I might make a telephone call to the school and arrange for us to go and see the head. It would probably be as well if you started school as soon as possible, don't you think?'

'Whatever.'

★ ★ ★

Jessica climbed the narrow stairs slowly, hauling herself up by the banisters as if she were an old woman (maybe even older than Carol). Inside her new bedroom she stood in the middle of the room for some time, her eyes unfocused, her mind a blank. Finally she went over to the window, sitting on the padded window seat to gaze through the glass. The scene outside was wintry; a thin rain was blowing across the garden, driven by a wind that had come up suddenly from the east. The garden itself was small and walled, and filled with overgrown shrubs that hung over the path which led to the back gate. Unkempt was the word that came into her mind. Unkempt. She let the word roll round her brain. Edging the path and drifting across the patch of grass near the house were masses of snowdrops, most of them past their best, but a few late varieties stood erect, their white heads nodding bravely as their green leaves rustled. In other parts of the garden there were clumps of bluebells, some already in bud. Jess had never seen bluebells in a garden before. She thought they were wild flowers. Bare branches, bedraggled grass, sparse colour; it was so different from Burma.

Tears came into her eyes and Jessica allowed them to fall unheeded for several minutes until her cheeks felt uncomfortably wet and cold. Then she wiped her face with a tissue from a box on the dressing table and went and lay on the bed. Mum would never have put tissues on the dressing table. She would have insisted on a proper handkerchief, Jessica thought.

But Jessica had no choice. It had not occurred to her to ask Carol to buy handkerchiefs. She buried her face in the pillow and wept silently.

After a while the tears seemed to stop of their own accord. She sat up. She supposed she had been a bit bitchy to Carol, she thought grudgingly. After all, Dan was right. It wasn't really Carol's fault that she and Dan had been foisted on her.

As a godfather, Uncle Peter was rubbish.

Then Jessica remembered the bookshop in Hay and Uncle Peter's flat above the shop. Every surface was covered with books, she recalled. There was no way two beds, even two camp beds would fit into his sitting-room.

What was the alternative? Jessica shuddered. She imagined the children's home. There would be a dozen or so other children, of all ages, noisy, rough. Girls who would call her names and be jealous of . . . Though what was there to be jealous about? Neither she nor Dan had anything much. Not now. In a children's home there would be boys, too. Bigger than Dan, probably. Jessica supposed they wouldn't be too much bother. I mean, they wouldn't be allowed to interfere with you, would they? The thought crossed her mind fleetingly, and was discarded as quickly. No boys messed with her. Jenny Wilson had discounted the idea of foster parents. Social services were picky. (Jenny Wilson'd sort of implied that foster parents were also picky.)

You were put into care for how many years? Didn't they look after you until you were eighteen nowadays? There was a time when you had to leave child care when you were sixteen. She tried to imagine herself on her own when she was sixteen. Fending for herself. That would be less than two years away. And what about university? Dad and Mum had insisted that both she and Dan would go to university. Did social services pay for further education? What would she do, could she do, instead of having a university education?

School . . . Jessica went cold at that thought. They'd tried school, for a term. She'd been nine at the time, Dan was seven. She'd hated every minute of every day. Got bored out of her skull with the lessons. Lessons! Huh! She'd told them she'd read all the Readers (Readers!) in the first week and that at home she was reading 'The Secret Garden' and was thinking of reading 'Jane Eyre' next. Her teacher didn't believe her, of course. Jess could see that by her raised eyebrows which said plainly, 'As if.' Of course after that she had read 'Jane Eyre', which was a bit long, but it had made her weep buckets, so she'd read it again at home when she was eleven and she'd really, really loved it then. Mum had borrowed a DVD of *The Sound of Music*, and Jess, imagining herself part Jane Eyre, part Maria, had superimposed Christopher Plummer's face on that of her illusory Mr Rochester. It was all so romantic, so idealistic. Instead of allowing her to read another proper book, that stupid school had insisted that she did page after page of silly sums. Which she couldn't be bothered with.

It was weird that Dan was disappointed when Mum and Dad decided school wasn't such a good idea after all.

148

The local comprehensive was bound to be dire. They'd be expected to wear uniform, too. Indubitably.

The door burst open. 'Don't you ever knock!' Jessica sat up abruptly, yelling at her brother.

'Come and have a look at the news about us on the Net,' Dan said excitedly. 'There's several pieces about Mum and Dad, too.' He went over to the bed and patted her leg. 'Don't cry, Jess,' he said softly. 'Things aren't really all that bad, you know. Carol's great, when you get to know her, and I guess Uncle Peter'll help us a bit after he's had a moan.'

'I don't want to go to stupid, beastly school.'

'Well, I do. I think it'll be awesome. Dad always said he'd get us to do sport, but he never did, except the swimming once a week. I thought that was boring. I expect we'll do footie. D'you think Carol supports Liverpool?'

'Idiot. How should I know? She probably doesn't even watch sport. If she's any sense, anyway.'

'Well, I wouldn't really mind if she prefers Arsenal. Come on, come and see these articles. Carol's getting supper. Macaroni cheese. She said we could print out any articles we liked. She said she'd buy us a scrapbook to paste them in. That'll be cool.

We can show them to Mum and Dad when-when . . . ' he gulped.

Jessica knew that Dan would be so embarrassed if he actually cried in front of her. It wouldn't be his fault, of course. Twelve wasn't really very old to have to cope with having no mum or dad, having to live with a stranger and wondering if you might be shoved into a children's home at any minute.

'OK. Let's do it,' she said determinedly, swinging her long legs off the bed. 'Hey, a scrapbook sounds a great idea.'

When they'd cleared up after the macaroni cheese (using the dish-washer), Carol settled the children in front of a DVD. She had a copy of *The Railway Children* which neither of the two had seen. Then she went into the study to telephone Marion.

Marion was aghast at James's behaviour, which naturally had the effect of making Carol feel defensive about him.

'I wouldn't have minded seeing Perth,' she confessed to her friend, 'though a four-day train journey across a desert isn't exactly my idea of fun. I expect James'll be home very soon after that.'

'You mean he needs time to get used to the idea of keeping the children? You plainly seem to have accepted it as a fact.'

'What gives you that idea? I mean, all

sorts of things could happen, Marion.' She thought of the things that weren't going to happen — like Peter Pickering having a change of heart, or the life guardians in Canada absolutely insisting that both children should live with them for the duration of Brian and Kimberley's sentences.

'But you are going to put them into school. That sounds pretty significant to me.'

'Well, yes. That seems the best way of occupying them until-until . . . '

'Their mother is released? Sorry. I didn't mean to be yet another one to harass you, Carol. You just phone and weep on my shoulder whenever you need to.'

★ ★ ★

They were interviewed by the head teacher on the Monday morning. Mrs Meredith was in her mid-forties, a tall woman, with sleekly bobbed, black hair. She was immaculately dressed in a navy blue suit with a white and navy spotted blouse. Her manner was gracious, assured. Carol's initial impression of a well-ordered school — the absence of litter in the playground, clean, neat corridors and an overall air of purposeful occupation — was strengthened.

With no fuss but with no waste of time, either, Mrs Meredith despatched Jessica and Daniel with one of the senior girls to be interviewed individually by their prospective year head. There was absolutely no question but that they would do as they were told.

'I suggest you come back to fetch them at noon, Mrs Morgan.' Carol was on her own with Mrs Meredith. 'I thought it best for my staff to assess their capabilities before we assign Jessica and Daniel to a class. Under the rather unusual circumstances, you understand?'

'I was going to ask if you were aware of what has happened to their parents.'

'County Hall rang me on Friday. The Department for Education and Skills had alerted them that you would probably be getting in touch. We are a bit short of spaces, you understand.' Mrs Meredith smiled complacently. Her school's excellent reputation ensured that parents were anxious to be included in her catchment area. 'But considering what has happened to Jessica and Daniel, I have been urged to accept both of the children. Actually, though, I was referring to their home schooling. I imagine that the other children will hear about Burma sooner or later. We shall try to minimise the effects, naturally.' She opened the door and stood to one side. 'Until noon, Mrs Morgan.'

★ ★ ★

Carol did some shopping and returned home. Vera was upstairs cleaning the bathroom. Carol went to talk to her about her availability to do an extra morning in the house.

Vera seemed pleased to be asked. 'Of course, you would expect the children to keep their rooms tidy, but there'll be a lot more dirt, you mark my words.'

Carol put a second load of washing into the machine and hung up the first lot to dry. Then she went into the study to check her e-mails. She re-read the two which James had sent from Perth before he phoned her.

There was no note of apology that he had left her to cope on her own with the children. There was little understanding of her position, of her absolute certainty that she was doing the right thing in escorting them back to London. With, or without him. Instead there was a great deal of enthusiasm for his new experiences. Carol read into that an eagerness to make the most of all the new events that were happening to him. For which you couldn't blame him, even if he were doing it without her.

Once Dan had got the computer going again, Carol had sent James an e-mail. She had thought long and hard before she wrote

153

it. In the e-mail, she had tried to be rational. She had tried to make James see that her choice — to comfort and support two children, strangers though they were — was essentially far less of a radical change in their plans, hers and his, than his sudden decision to fly to Australia.

There was a reply. It was very short.

'*I cannot understand how you could choose them over me. I thought you loved me. When did you stop loving me?*'

She printed it out, thinking, hoping illogically that the words might have altered in the interim, that at the very least their meaning might be less uncompromising. What had loving James got to do with helping a child?

She could not believe how irresponsible and immature he sounded. Was this the man whose life she had shared for twenty-seven years? She had always looked up to James. She had always believed his judgement to be impeccable; she had taken his advice, deferred to him. Was it only now that she saw him for what he was; an essentially selfish man whose personal comfort came before the welfare of others?

It was unbelievable that a man of his age could be jealous of his wife's attention to two vulnerable children.

No, Carol thought. She must have got it

wrong. Lost in translation: at the very least, he had not read what he had written before he pressed 'Send'. There was every possibility that he regretted each word of that e-mail the moment it had gone. No doubt he was composing something this very minute (allowing for the time difference) to show her how wrong he knew he was.

She typed in: *'James, I have never stopped loving you. Jessica and Daniel have nothing to do with us, as a couple. But just now they need me more than you do. Actually, they could do with a man about the house. As could I.*

'I wonder, did the desert put us into perspective?'

Vera came in with a cup of tea. Carol accepted it with a smile of thanks. After she had drunk it she went into the kitchen to have a word with the housekeeper about the sort of food to give the children, allowing for the fact that Jessica was a vegetarian.

'I'd get that one to cook her own suppers.'

If not cook her own, Jessica must at least help to plan the menus, thought Carol, sitting down once more at the desk. She read through what she had written to James. It seemed to her, after what, admittedly, was only a short interval for reflection, to say exactly what she meant.

She pressed '*Send*'.

8

Jessica and Daniel were sitting on chairs in the secretary's office when Carol returned promptly at noon to see Mrs Meredith. The head teacher ushered her into her room, indicating that the children should wait.

'So interesting, the belief that home schooling is much more satisfactory for a child than a state secondary school. By no means accurate,' Mrs Meredith began after they had both sat down. 'Then, naturally you would expect me to say that,' she added, with a deprecatory smile.

'Though I can imagine a situation where a child does better with intensely individual attention than he, or she, would in a large school,' said Carol cautiously.

'We aim to educate the whole child.'

'Of course. Are you suggesting that there are problems with Jessica and Daniel?'

'Not problems, exactly. Shall we say that the results of the tests they did this morning were definitely out of the ordinary. Jessica, for example, has an extraordinarily mature grasp of both English literature and the English language though I suspect she is capable of relapsing into playgroundspeak along with her peers. She also knows far more than our children of her age are required to learn about what you and I called history and geography. She is familiar with the basic principles of Buddhism and Hinduism. She says their parents don't think highly of organized religion. She says she understands Spanish and a little Burmese. You will appreciate we were unable to test that. Her maths are adequate. Just. She has some knowledge of biology, almost none of physics or chemistry.'

'Will that matter?'

'Most certainly it will, when it comes to university entry. Jessica insists that her parents want her to go to university. However, she is bright enough to catch up with what is lacking in her knowledge of general science. It is a pity she has neither French nor Welsh.'

'You would hardly expect Welsh from a child brought up in Woking,' said Carol sharply.

'Quite so. Jessica herself said that Mandarin would be a far more useful language to learn. Many business men would agree with her. Unfortunately not all our educationalists are that forward thinking.'

'And how did Dan get on?'

'Another bright child. Quite different in his skills from his sister. Daniel's maths are first-rate. His computer skills are advanced — and he seems to be interested in physics and chemistry. His English . . . abysmal written work. Appalling spelling and, as with so many of his peers, he reads very little fiction. Still, like Jessica, I am sure that with some judicious coaching he will more than catch up by the time he comes to do his GCSEs.'

'That's four years away.'

'Ah. You must be referring to the length of the mother's sentence. Is there any suggestion that the children might need to move school in the near future?' Her tone softened. 'I appreciate how hard all this is for you but moving the children while they are in the middle of coursework is not wise, especially now, in Jessica's case.'

'You must think me extremely foolish,' said Carol weakly. 'It must be so obvious I haven't thought this through properly.'

'Not at all, Mrs Morgan,' said the head warmly. 'You may be a little unprepared, but the way in which you have coped with the children since their parents were arrested, is nothing short of saintly, in my opinion.'

'I only did what anyone would do,' protested Carol. Then thought scornfully,

158

what utter nonsense, remembering James's reaction to the way in which she had presented their part in Dan and Jess' future as a moral dilemma. Even to herself, her motives remained hidden. 'I confess that I am more than a little unprepared. For the long term, you understand. But what alternative is there?'

'Is there really no relative who would take them on?'

Carol shook her head. 'It would not appear to be feasible for their uncle.' She explained about Peter Pickering's situation. 'I have also asked about legal guardians. There don't appear to be any others in this country. Of course, there is always the possibility that Kimberley and Brian could be freed. At any time.'

Mrs Meredith looked anything but convinced. 'I think it might be advisable for you to have a long talk with the children's uncle. In the meantime you may trust us to do our very best for them.'

The children were called in. Mrs Meredith gave them a potted version of what she had told Carol. 'I am sure you will find that we have some really interesting subjects for you to tackle,' she said. 'There are also clubs that might divert you. Sports, music. You can discuss those with your pastoral care tutor.'

She suggested that they might like the afternoon off to acquire items of school uniform — the secretary would give them a list.

'Please come straight to the office tomorrow morning. You will be told then which classes to join. Goodbye, Mrs Morgan. No doubt I shall see you again soon.'

If Carol had expected mutinous outbursts following the visit to the school, she was mistaken. Both Jessica and Daniel were very subdued on the way back to Otterhaven. Even the acquisition of school uniform in Monmouth had not provoked more than a, 'That's just so totally gross,' as Jessica held out the navy blue skirt on its hanger.

'In uniform you blend in with the crowd,' said Carol, in an attempt to console.

'Yeah, right,' murmured the girl.

It was pouring with rain by the time they got back to Otterhaven. Carol dropped the children off at the front door with their parcels, then she drove the car to the garage to leave it there. On her return, some ten minutes later, she was surprised to find the children still outside, their parcels in a tumbled heap by the door.

'What's going on? I thought I'd given you the key.'

'Oh, Carol. It's Splodge. He's found us!

160

It's-it's fantastic.' A red-faced Dan (with tear-stained cheeks) and an ecstatic expression was standing there, a small bundle of what appeared to be filthy fur held tightly in his arms.

'Dan, Jess?' Carol turned to the girl, who shrugged noncommittally. 'Who's Splodge?'

'Splodge is my cat. I thought I'd never see him again. Oh, Carol. D'you think he's all right? He's very thin.' Scarcely releasing his hold on the animal, Dan approached Carol.

Not knowing in the least how to react — was it truly possible that a cat had found its way from Working to Otterhaven? — Carol's first thought was that Dan had picked up a stray. And then, oh, Heavens . . . *fleas* . . . was what occurred to her. She wanted to say, Put it down, but the words stuck in her throat.

'Ah,' Carol exclaimed. As a reaction it was pathetic. 'Wow,' she continued. 'You mean your cat has actually found you? Well. Well, why don't we all go inside. It's far too cold to be standing out here. Jess, you take the parcels inside. Dan, you take the cat into the kitchen and let's have a look at him.'

In the kitchen Carol carefully shut the door. Then she found an old towel and placed it on the kitchen table. 'Let's have a look at you, Splodge.'

A very young kitten was placed, with some reluctance, on the towel. It resembled nothing more than a drowned rodent, even its tail was rattish. 'Are you sure this is your cat?'

'Must be. Look, the markings are exactly the same.'

'What happened to your Splodge?' Carol thought this animal was probably a tabby with three paws that looked as though they might once have been white. As Dan had pointed out, though, it was extremely thin. It also had no collar.

Jess, who had been standing at the other end of the table, said, 'When we went to Burma we gave Splodge to some friends. He was a bit old . . . ' Her voice tailed away.

'Did Splodge wear a collar?'

'No,' said Dan. 'Mum said it was an unnecessary expense. Don't you think Splodge looks very hungry.'

'I think he looks starving,' declared Carol. It was quite plain to her that it was out of the question — whatever its provenance — to push this animal out into the night, both for its own sake, let alone Dan's. 'Dan, why don't you run down to the shop and buy some cat food. Kitten food,' she corrected herself. 'The shop should still be open, if you hurry.'

'Splodge only eats fishy cat food,' objected

Dan, taking the money Carol was holding out to him.

'Kitten food,' she repeated. 'He's starving. We don't want to overload his digestion, do we? Kitten food would go down best,' she ended softly. 'Jess and I will dry him off while you get the food.'

The door slammed almost immediately. There was a pause while Jess and Carol regarded each other wordlessly for a long moment.

'Oh, dear. This is a kitten, Jessica,' Carol said eventually.

'I guess. D'you like cats?' Jessica asked unexpectedly.

'Yes. Matthew had a cat. Of course, I was the one who fed it. And cleaned up after it.'

The kitten mewed plaintively.

'Pass me the rag bag, will you?' Carol came to another decision. She found several pieces of old towel, one of which she soaked in a bowl of warm water. 'Let's see if we can get Splodge a little cleaner.'

'Why are you using a wet towel?'

'Cat fleas. Though I suppose it's probably too late for Daniel. I'd like to give it a bath, but I don't think it would care very much for that.'

'I thought cat fleas didn't attack humans.'

'Take my word for it. They do,' said Carol

darkly. 'There was something about my blood that attracted Blaze's fleas. When she had them.'

'Blaze?'

'She had a white streak down her back. It was very distinctive.'

'What happened to her?'

They were rubbing the kitten gently with the towel that was as wet as itself. Filth (and fleas?) were coming off in dark streaks. 'That's enough, I think. Let's see if we can dry him off. Actually, I'm not even sure if this is a he, you know. Blaze died of old age. We never had another. I missed her for years.'

'Mum didn't tell Dan. I think Splodge died.'

Carol was spared an answer. The door was flung open and a breathless Dan reappeared. 'What are you doing? Have you fed him yet? Is Splodge better?'

Carol said, 'I thought you'd like to feed him yourself. We've been cleaning him up. See?'

The kitten had been transformed from a bedraggled rat into a bundle of almost fluffy fur. It was a tabby, with the white feet Dan said he knew. The boy put out a gentle hand and the kitten's tiny pink tongue licked it tentatively.

'Pour a little milk into a saucer, Jess, and

warm it slightly in the microwave.'

'Why?' asked Dan.

'I think Splodge would prefer something warm in his tummy, don't you?'

The saucer was placed near the kitten who lapped up the milk eagerly. They gave it a small spoonful of kitten food. While the children were watching it feed, Carol found a cardboard box which she lined with newspaper, then, after a moment, placed a piece of dry rag on top of it.

'I've bought cat litter,' said Dan, leaning over the kitten with a yearning look that brought a lump to Carol's throat.

'That was thoughtful,' she said faintly. 'I think I've an old roasting tin we could use for that. Splodge used a tray, I gather?'

'Only in the few weeks before we went away. We had a cat door.'

'Well, I think we should leave Splodge to have a little sleep now while we have something to eat ourselves. You can give him a little more milk before you go to bed.'

Carol heated oven chips for them that evening to go with the chops she and Dan were eating and Jessica's lentil bake. She expected complaints that their parents didn't allow chips, but instead there were appreciative comments. She thought comfort food had to be a good idea, occasionally. It had already been decided the two would take sandwiches for lunch with a yoghurt and a piece of fruit. 'As long as we have wholemeal bread,' insisted Jessica. They would all eat together in the evening.

'I'll phone your uncle later,' Carol told them. 'I expect he will be interested to hear how you have got on today. You can talk to him yourselves, if you like. Tell him about Splodge.' She ignored the look of scepticism that passed between the two.

Splodge was dead to the world, curled up into a tight ball, his nose covered by his one dark paw.

★   ★   ★

However, it was Matthew she spoke to first. Her son had come off the oil rig that morning and had picked up a letter from James which had been sent to his flat. James had put down a hefty deposit on a flat when Matthew left university, knowing how important it would be for his son to have a base when he had leave. He shared this flat with a friend, a local solicitor. Carol knew that when he was at home, Matthew's girlfriend, Rosa, stayed with him most of the time. She, herself, was not very keen on Rosa, who she thought remarkably dense on the one occasion when

166

they'd met. Although Rosa was very attractive, if in a somewhat obvious way.

So James had actually sent Matthew a letter! Matthew sounded as amazed as Carol was — though possibly more gratified. It appeared that James had been quite frank in it about his disapproval of Carol's decision. Matthew himself said he couldn't understand why two otherwise sensible adults were acting the way they were. His other comments were along the lines of: what the Pickerings did in a foreign country were none of the Morgans' business and he'd thought his parents had more sense at their ages. Though whether he sympathized more with his father, all alone in Australia, or his mother, coping with two strange children, was a little uncertain.

When Carol asked if he would be coming home to visit soon, Matthew's answer was: 'It doesn't seem as though there's any room for me.'

Another alpha male bristling with the effects of offended pride, was Carol's first reaction. Obviously, if they'd still been at Windrush, there would have been no problem at all, with bedrooms for everyone. That was another thing Matthew had pointed out.

'I'd love to see you,' she told her son, wistfully. 'It seems such an age since you were down here. I know I have had to put Daniel in your room, but we can always put him in the study for a night or two.'

'Thanks, Ma, but I've things to do, people to catch up with. I'll give it a miss this time. Maybe when you and Dad are back together again, huh?'

He made it sound as though James and Carol had separated.

Then, as if in an attempt to refute the very suggestion, Carol checked her e-mails. But there was no response, yet, from James. E-mails were supposed to make it easier for people to keep in touch, weren't they?

Peter Pickering was a far more sympathetic ear. 'Head teachers are so fearsome, even the ones who've retired.'

'Mrs Meredith seems extremely capable. It was just her comments about home schooling that threw me.' She explained that Jessica was going to have to work very hard at all her science subjects and her French.

'I don't see why taking Spanish instead of French should pose too much of a problem for the school. What are they going to do about the science?'

'Possibly a remedial class. That wasn't explained thoroughly.'

'We may have to monitor that. Don't want to jeopardize her university prospects for a lack of forethought. Poor you. It sounds as though you've had a really rough day.'

'It wasn't so very bad,' said Carol, feeling buoyed up already. If Peter was going to be this supportive she thought she could manage well enough. 'The children are both being very good.' As the children had not asked to speak to their uncle she had decided not to mention the kitten.

'So I should hope. Bring them over to Hay on Sunday. I only open the shop on a Sunday during the literary festival and in the summer months for the tourists, so I'll cook lunch for all of us.'

'That would be kind. Um — Jessica is a vegetarian.'

'Why am I not surprised?' he commented drily. 'Never mind, so long as she eats eggs she can have plenty of Yorkshire pudding to go with the vegetables. By the way, did you know there is growing support for Brian and Kimberley, and not only in this country? There is talk of them being adopted as prisoners of conscience. That should help. Tell Dan he can read about it on the Net. Usual site.'

The children were in bed. Carol went round the house, picked up the inevitable book which had been left lying around; and plumped up the cushions. The last thing she did was to check up on Splodge. The kitten was nowhere to be seen. Carol smiled to herself. No need to panic, she thought. As she expected, there was a dark lump at the bottom of Daniel's bed, lying cosily between his feet.

As she stood looking down uncertainly at the kitten, Splodge opened one green eye. Steadily he looked at her, as if defying her to pick him up and remove him. At least Dan had put Splodge's towel on his bed for the kitten to lie on. She shook her head.

Splodge shut his eye. Then he stretched, flexing his four legs and all his claws, bracing his back against Dan's ankle. After a moment he relaxed and curled up once more. His eyes tightly closed, he began to purr like a little engine.

★ ★ ★

Carol packed the children off to school the next morning complete with new uniforms, the requisite stationery paraphernalia and healthy lunch boxes. They went with less reluctance than she had anticipated. Indeed, Dan was positively eager to set off.

'You do know where to go?'

'Yes, yes.'

'You'll come straight home?'

'Yes, yes. Don't worry!'

'I'm not worried. I know you can't wait to get back to Splodge. Don't forget the vet's appointment I've made.'

She had scarcely said goodbye to the children before there was a knock on the door. Thinking one of them had left something behind — she had not yet had time to have front door keys cut — Carol hastened to open it.

On the doorstep was Sandy Williams, the manager of the local Citizens' Advice Bureau. 'I've come to throw myself on your mercy,' Sandy said cheerfully, not looking in the least like a supplicant. 'May I come in, or is it dreadfully inconvenient?' She was inside the door before Carol could formulate a reason why she was extremely busy.

Sandy was a woman of indeterminate age, a formidable organizer whose talents many thought were wasted on a small-town project. Sandy, however, was married to a man with MS and said, honestly and quite without a demand for sympathy, that since they could manage on her salary and Desmond's pension, she preferred not to undertake any work that might involve travelling to Bristol or Cardiff.

'I heard from Marion that you were at home. Would you believe it? Alison fell downstairs last week. She's only gone and broken both her wrists.'

'Good heavens. The poor woman!' Carol interjected. They exchanged views on how the luckless Alison was going to cope over the next few weeks and how other people they had known with multiple fractures had managed — and had made full recoveries.

'The thing is,' began Sandy.

'You are short-staffed.'

'How did you guess? But of course. So you see that even if you could only offer just one session a week it would make a tremendous difference,' Sandy ended winningly.

'I'll think about it.'

Carol did think about it. She thought about the work she had done for Citizens Advice over many years, and she came to a rapid decision. She picked up the phone and talked over her situation with Sandy, finally agreeing to go in regularly on a Tuesday afternoon. She was quite frank about her current problems. 'I think it'll make a change from worrying about two children I seem to be fostering, an errant husband and a kitten who might, or might not, be a reincarnation of a lost family pet. I'll try not to let anyone down, but you must understand though, that I'm not at all sure what my commitments are going to be over the next months,' she explained.

Overjoyed at getting back one of her most

competent members of staff, Sandy said she could see no problems there, suggesting only that Carol took on nothing that was likely to want on-going contact with a client.

While the children were at school, Carol went to the charity shop in the village. There she was fortunate enough to pick up very cheaply a cat basket (which she took home and washed in disinfectant before putting it out in the garden to dry). She also picked up a bowl suitable for water for a cat.

Daniel had been unwilling to take Splodge to the vet but Carol insisted. 'You never know,' she pointed out, 'the vet may recognize Splodge. He may be micro chipped.' That needed some explaining.

'Our Splodge wasn't micro chipped.'

Did this mean that Dan was acknowledging that the kitten could not be his first cat? 'Then if this one isn't micro chipped and we can't find the owner, I think we should get him done.'

Her done, it transpired. The vet also advised spaying, in due course, and insisted on various injections. 'You don't want Splodge to catch cat flu, do you?'

Oh, Lord, thought Carol ... All the obligations of pet ownership, too. She did so hope that Kimberley proved sensitive to her son's newfound love, when she came home.

'What do you get paid?' asked Dan, when Carol told them that evening that she proposed to go back to work for a few hours for Citizens Advice.

Carol smiled and shook her head at Jess who had nudged her brother sharply. 'It's a fair question. Actually, I'll be paid nothing. It's voluntary work, you see.'

'Dad says everyone should be paid for what they do. He says doing voluntary work sucks.'

'Getting a wage for what you do is a splendid idea, in theory, Dan,' Carol said gently. 'Unfortunately, if everyone were always paid there would be a lot less care available for the vulnerable in this country, like the elderly and those with disadvantages.'

'The state should take care of them.'

'Of course, Jessica. But that would mean James and I, and your parents, would have to pay a lot more taxes. You must have discussed that sometimes.'

'We talked about it at home, and that's what Dad said. Volunteering is for mugs,' Jessica commented scornfully.

'Oh, dear,' said Carol. 'Well, I happen to think he is wrong. You'd be amazed at the problems we help to solve, the CAB, I mean. All sorts of financial matters, consumer advice, housing. That's to say, we don't always have the answers. Mostly what we do is to advise people where they have to go, the people they must see, and what they can expect to happen. We signpost, if you like. For some, we make phone calls. You'd be surprised how many people either don't have a phone or who can't afford to spend their money hanging on while a government department takes its time to answer. It's a very satisfying thing, helping to solve problems for other people.'

'Is that what you did, before?' asked Jess.

'I was a volunteer for the CAB in the beginning. Then, after about two years, and because I enjoyed the work, I did some more training to become an advice sessions supervisor. That's a sort of assistant manager. The CAB has to have someone on the spot to advise the volunteers. I worked three mornings a week and I was paid for that. This time, though, I shall just be one of the volunteers.'

'Will you go back to becoming the supervisor?'

'I don't know, Jess. It depends on how I feel about it, not to mention whether or not there is a vacancy.'

★ ★ ★

There was a message from James at last in Carol's in-box on Friday evening. It was a lengthy one, detailing the pleasures of a long-distance train journey across the Nullarbor, on its dead-straight track. There was nothing to see from the train except for a few rabbits and kangaroos in the early evening he had written, but the food had been excellent and the bar well-stocked. His compartment — which he had agreed to share with a young lawyer who was on his way to Adelaide — was comfortable and had its own shower etc. James had also met some other interesting people, including a couple who had recommended an excellent small hotel overlooking the harbour in Sydney's Watson's Bay. They had invited him to dinner and he was looking forward to that very much, especially as they intended to introduce him to someone they thought would interest him.

'Russ and Betty were very sympathetic when they heard that you had felt it necessary to return home instead of coming to Australia with me,' the e-mail said.

I bet, thought Carol grimly. She read on, looking in vain for some reaction to her own previous message. James did, though, give her the address of the hotel, where he intended to stay for a week. Then he was going to do a couple of coach tours, going first to the

176

Hunter Valley where the vineyards were, then south to Melbourne and Adelaide. Apparently he had been advised that Uluru — Ayers Rock in the Red Centre — was too hot at that time of the year, and that the weather was too wet in the Northern Territory. Such a shame.

At the very end of his message James said that he did hope the children were not proving too much. 'Any news of the mother and father?' Not even Brian and Kimberley; she noted the unfeeling nomenclature with dismay. James had been unable to find out anything about them from the local papers.

There was always the BBC World Service, thought Carol. Or CNN. While they were getting ready to go out to dinner on their travels, she and James had developed the habit of picking up one or other of the news channels on those evenings when they were staying in a hotel with a TV. She found it difficult to believe that James could not find out anything at all in Australia about the welfare of the Pickerings, languishing in their Burmese prison.

9

The small town of Hay-on-Wye on the borders of Wales and England calls itself the world's largest second-hand bookshop. Premises bought by Richard Booth in the early sixties are now independently owned and one of these, Peter Pickering's bookshop, close to the castle, was small, its interior old-fashioned, with tall wooden bookshelves and narrow aisles between them. Peter specialized in classical English literature with a small section of biographies. He also had a stack devoted to local history.

'The literature is for me,' he told Carol, when she took the children over for Sunday lunch. 'Mostly my favourites and in good quality bindings though I don't go in for first editions which need to be kept under lock and key.' She expressed shock. 'You'd be surprised what walks,' he said darkly. He told them that the biographies sold well, as did the books on local history. 'You can have a good browse after lunch, if you like. But I must go upstairs now and see to the vegetables.'

Upstairs, Peter's flat seemed to be an extension of the bookshop. It was just as

Daniel remembered it — as he had told them on the way over that morning — with piles of books on the floor and heaps covering most of the surfaces.

'Can't bear television,' Peter said disarmingly, as he swept aside a pile of John Galsworthy so that Carol could sit down, 'so I put on some music and do my cataloguing in the evening. Then, when I've space downstairs these will go on the shelves.'

'What happens when you run out of space?' asked Carol.

'Oh, I'll have a sale of stuff that hasn't moved. Do it once or twice a year, actually. People are very happy to have a two-for-one offer, you know. You have a good second-hand bookshop in Otterhaven, haven't you? Philip Gerard is quite knowledgeable in his own field.'

'I believe so, though I don't buy from him very often,' she remarked.

'You should introduce the children to him. I'd happily pay for a book a month for each of them.'

'Would you, Uncle Peter?'

'Yes, Jessica. Owning a shelf-full of books is the best thing in the world, especially the ones you read again and again. You must already have a few of those.'

Jessica made a face. 'Mum made us get rid

of all our kids' books as she said we'd never read them again. Anyway, she was more into music. I remember she used to play the piano when we were small. Things like the 'Moonlight Sonata'. Sometimes I'd sit on the stairs to listen to her.'

'She must have been good,' said Carol, impressed.

'Not really. I suppose I just didn't know much about music then. And the piano's base keys stuck so none of us minded when that had to go. Mum did accompany my flute, though.'

'I didn't know you played an instrument, Jessica,' said Peter.

The girl shrugged. 'A bit.'

'You should foster a talent like that. It's not something I've ever been good at.'

'Nor me,' said Carol.

'Don't you ever get bored of books, Uncle Peter?' Dan interrupted.

'Bored with books, dear boy. Why ever should reading bore anyone? Of course I don't.'

'Hay is a very small town, though, isn't it?' commented Jess.

'Thank Heavens for small towns, I say. Though Hay does have its backbiters and critics.'

'Doesn't everywhere?' commented Carol.

'Quite so. Sherry, Carol? Excellent. Though I've only got a Tio Pepe. I never thought . . .'

Carol assured him that she never drank anything but dry sherry but when he produced a schooner, said that she would prefer to have a small one since she was driving.

'Now, Daniel, you set the table while Carol relaxes. Jessica, you come with me and give me your opinion of my trifle.'

The meal was delicious: roast beef and the promised Yorkshire pudding with four different vegetables, including cauliflower cheese especially for Jessica. The trifle was filled with cream and decorated with hundreds and thousands — which Carol said she hadn't seen for years. At the end of the meal Peter sent the children down to the shop to look around while he and Carol had coffee.

'You may go for a walk round the town, then come back and choose one book each,' he told them. 'Give us an hour's peace and quiet.'

'What about the washing-up?' asked Carol, who wasn't sure what they would talk about for a whole hour if they were not occupied at the kitchen sink.

'Goodness me, no. Your first visit is as my guest and guests do not wield tea towels.'

What had she expected? Afterwards Carol

181

could not remember, nor why she had ever thought Peter Pickering was dour or uncommunicative. Their conversation ranged from the theatre, about which he seemed to know a great deal, to current events and, naturally, the latest authors to watch. He never once mentioned Brian and Kimberley and the trouble they had brought upon their children, though he encouraged Carol to talk about James.

She found herself telling Peter how very difficult it was to maintain any real communication with James. 'We use e-mail,' she said. 'I never imagined I would be writing e-mails to my husband. Also, I thought they would be so much more instant. You know, you ask a question and you get an answer almost immediately. It doesn't work out like that. Or at least it doesn't with James and me.'

'More coffee?' Peter waved the coffee pot towards her. It was of elegant and well-polished silver, and looked as though it was of an age to be valuable.

Carol shook her head. She thought she should change the subject. Caution told her that she might be unwise to confide too much in Peter, though she wasn't sure why she felt this way.

'Surely it doesn't make any difference

whether it's letter-writing or e-mailing,' Peter was objecting before she could think what other subject to introduce. 'All that matters are the intentions of the correspondent. If there is a reluctance to reply, there are always reasons for procrastination.'

'Well, I know that,' said Carol. 'At least, I know that logically.' She paused, but found herself continuing, 'It's the emotional factor behind it that is confusing me.'

'You were travelling for some weeks before you found yourselves involved with the children, weren't you?'

'We left Otterhaven immediately after Christmas. We did have a fantastic trip.'

'And you were living out of a small suitcase in a hotel room?'

'Are you trying to suggest we were getting on each other's nerves and that that was why James decided to go to Australia?' She bristled at the very idea. There had been the odd disagreements — what couple never had differences of opinions? But she couldn't remember that they had disagreed over anything of significance, certainly nothing that could have been called a row.

'It's a possibility.' Peter was picking at a loose thread on the sleeve of his jacket and wasn't looking at her.

'You shouldn't pull that. It'll go into a

hole,' she warned him. 'Sorry,' she said penitently, 'but it's easy enough to work a loose thread through the cloth.'

'Is it?'

'I'll do it for you, if you have a needle.' Without a word, Peter produced a small workbasket from a cupboard under one of the overfilled bookcases by the fireplace. She was impressed, though she supposed that a bachelor needed the wherewithal to sew back the odd button. It occurred to her that that particular skill was not one that James had ever needed to learn. Or if he had in his youth, he had deliberately forgotten it. Just then, it seemed the most normal thing in the world, to be taking this man's jacket, threading the loose end on to a needle and carefully working it into the rough cloth. As she worked, the subject of James's attitude on their trip came back into her mind.

'You know, James and I were seeing so much that was strange, new, exciting. I'd never imagined I could become so involved. Usually on holiday it's a matter of seeing sights and forgetting most of them quite quickly.' She stopped. She replaced the needle in to its case and handed the jacket back to Peter. Then she confessed. 'By the evening, James and I were both pretty exhausted. Part of it was the heat, I suppose.

But there was so much to absorb, so much I didn't want to forget. Anyway, we usually got up early, so what with one thing and another, we went to bed very early.' There had been physical contact, though that wasn't quite the thing to mention to someone who was essentially a stranger. Lovemaking between them had been as good, if not better than for a long time.

'I'm sure you were exhausted,' Peter said with feeling. 'It can't be easy to maintain highs like that for too long a time. I wouldn't be surprised if your husband didn't look out at the emptiness of the Nullarbor and rejoice in that very thing, the lack of needing to respond to what he was seeing.'

'It's certainly an interesting theory,' she conceded.

'But not one to which you would subscribe?'

'I've not thought about it in that way.'

Peter leant forward, patting her knee — their chairs were placed by a window where they could look out across the town. 'When you got to Heathrow, what was the first thing you and the children did?'

She was taken aback, both by the question and, possibly, the touch of his hand. 'I don't know. You mean, after we had collected our cases? Oh, that was when we were inter-viewed by the authorities.'

'And then?'

'We had to wait for the car which they had arranged would take us home. The children were hungry. They'd not liked the breakfast the airline served. I took them for something to eat'

'What did you have?'

She smiled, seeing immediately where this was leading. 'You're absolutely right. We all had a full English breakfast. I had coffee. The children had orange juice.'

'And what was the first thing you cooked for them once you had reached Otterhaven?'

'Well, it wasn't baked beans. But only because I had just the one tin in the house. We had a takeaway.'

'You see, what I'm getting at is that your mind craved the familiar on the plate as much as your taste buds rejected the unusual.'

'Yes, I see that. I can also accept that maybe James decided to go to Australia rather than India, or anywhere else in the East, because he was going to somewhere basically familiar.'

'I understand that Australia can hardly be said to be familiar to your average whingeing Pom,' Peter commented ironically.

'That aside, it still doesn't explain why he

186

seems to . . . oh, I don't know. If James wanted a rest, even if he wanted a rest from me,' she reiterated fiercely, 'there was no reason why he couldn't have come home as we planned. The new house may be small, you can still have some privacy.'

'Even with the children?'

'Are you trying to warn me that James won't come home until they have left?' she cried, aghast. No matter that Carol had considered that possibility in more than one wakeful moment in the night, hearing it spoken gave it a dreadful reality. Tears that she never knew were anywhere near the surface sprang to her eyes. She sniffed.

'Hey, Carol!' Peter got to his feet swiftly and knelt by the side of her chair. He fumbled in his pocket and produced a clean, white hanky. 'Here, use this. Heavens, I'm so sorry. I never know when to keep my big mouth shut. It's living on my own, I suppose. Idiot that I am. I never intended to upset you.'

Carol blew her nose. 'No, forgive me,' she said. 'I was being totally stupid. I just seem to have got myself into such a peculiar situation and because James is unexpectedly part of it, yet no longer a part of it — if you see what I mean — I don't know how I am expected to react.'

'You react just the way you feel,' he urged her, as he touched her shoulder briefly and got to his feet again. 'If you ask me, pussyfooting around the subject isn't going to get you anywhere. But I am so sorry if you think I have been intruding on what must be painful. It never occurred to me . . . I mean, if I had thought for one moment that you and James . . . If Brian and Kimberley . . . Oh, darn it, I am sorry.'

Carol shut her eyes briefly, wondering if she should say . . . No, Peter was only trying to help. She missed the look of dismayed helplessness that crossed the man's face.

'I guess we just have to wait and see what happens next.'

What happened next was that Daniel burst into the room, followed by Jessica. The interruption was welcome. The atmosphere, which, Carol noted, had become charged in a way that was totally unexpected, lightened.

'I see you are both carrying books,' said Peter, deliberately standing so as to obscure their view of Carol. 'That's good. What have you chosen?'

'Actually, I hope you don't mind,' said Jessica, diffidently. 'We went out to look round the town . . . '

'Cool castle,' Dan broke in. 'But there are books everywhere.'

'There would be, considering that Hay makes most of its living selling books,' commented his uncle drily.

'Anyway, one bookshop had cookery books outside, and there was this one with vegetarian recipes. They look yummy and quite easy to do. Do you mind, Uncle Peter? I thought that was a good idea.'

'Absolutely,' he said, producing a handful of change. 'So long as you do the cooking involved in the recipes. As a matter of fact,' he went on, this time bringing out a well-worn wallet, 'it occurred to me that when you have a moment, you might like to buy something casual to wear. Carol has been extremely careful with your money, just getting you the necessities and school uniform, so I know you've very little choice for after school. Could you spend this? I've no idea what clothes cost — at least, I've no idea about fashion clothes. Would this do?' He held out a couple of notes.

'Wow,' said a gratified Jessica. 'That's really kind.'

'Thanks, Uncle Peter,' said Dan.

'My pleasure. And what book did you buy, Daniel?'

'I found *The Heart Must Break* down-stairs. It's by James Mawdesley. It's about what happened to him when he was thrown

189

into prison by the Burmese.'

Carol Morgan and Peter Pickering exchanged a brief glance across his cluttered sitting-room, a glance which expressed alarm at Daniel's choice of reading matter which could hardly be said to have been written for a twelve-year old.

'That's an interesting book,' said Peter, his voice neutral. He held out his hand for it. 'I knew I had a copy of that on my shelves but I thought you might have preferred an adventure story.'

'I don't read fiction. Besides, I think going to prison is an adventure,' said Dan scornfully.

'Doesn't that depend on your point of view? I mean, on whether it is you who is in prison,' objected Carol. 'Not to mention where,' she said pensively.

'You've read all the Harry Potter books,' said Jess. 'You pinched the last one from me before I'd even started it.'

'Well, that's different,' mumbled her brother. 'George was going on about it so. I thought I'd better know what he was talking about. Anyway, I finished it before he did.'

'I've noticed that a lot of boys prefer something factual to fiction.'

'I said. This is factual, about Burma.'

'I've not read the book, but I remember the

circumstances,' said Carol carefully.

'I remember Dad telling us about it when we were younger,' said Jess. 'James Mawdsley wasn't all that much older than me when he first went out to Burma and shouted slogans in the street. He was arrested and put in prison. But in the end they did let him go before his sentence was up.'

She sounded reflective. Carol wondered if Jess thought this was incontrovertible proof that her parents would be freed soon. If so, it was a rash belief. Deliberately she did not look at Peter, who she was sure would agree with her.

'So I chose the book because I want to know exactly what's happening to Mum and Dad,' said Dan doggedly.

The boy looked wretched, thought Carol compassionately. She wanted to hug him and reassure him that everything was going to be all right. She could do neither. She could not hug him because she was afraid he would be mortally offended by her touch. A mother could hug her son, at any age, and not be rejected. A stranger could never do so; that is, not hug a twelve-year old. (Especially not nowadays.) Nor could she assure Dan that his parents were going to come out of prison unscathed. Apart from the fact that prison scarred everyone who was sent there, the conditions in a Burmese prison were likely to be unspeakable. She remembered the loo to which she had been taken at the interrogation centre in Rangoon, and shuddered inwardly. She did so hope that Kimberley was more robust than she appeared. She looked at Peter. It was plain that he was as helpless as she was. Men didn't hug men — not his type of man. Nor would this man lie to his nephew.

'I think you might find parts of the book heavy-going,' Peter said circumspectly, as he handed the volume back to Dan. 'All the same, he's very good on the state of the hill tribes.'

'And what happened to him in prison?'

'He's telling his own story.'

'Which doesn't mean that what happened to one young man is happening to your mum and dad,' said Carol, trying to sound reassuring.

'But you don't know that,' said Jessica obdurately.

Peter Pickering gave a deep sigh. He sat down. Carol went back to her chair. The children stayed where they were in the centre of the room.

'What do you want us to say?' he asked at last.

'The truth,' said Jessica fiercely.

'Oh, my dear,' said her uncle, 'if only I could. The truth is that I know no more than you do. Probably less, because I have never been to Burma. I have no idea what happens to political prisoners — except, it has to be remembered, that officially your parents are not political prisoners. The Junta doesn't have political prisoners. Your parents are deemed guilty of a civil offence. That is, they have broken the law. Imprisonment is their punishment.'

'It sucks,' said Jessica.

Far from reprimanding her, Peter smiled. 'Yes, Jess, it does. However, there is nothing that either you or I can do about it. Dan, read the book, if you like, but please don't let it upset you too much. Heavens, it will upset you, I'm sure. But I won't tell you not to read it. Hey, and next time, choose something more cheerful? By then, who knows, we may have good news about your parents.'

His attempt at optimism failed dismally. Carol judged that the time had come for them to leave.

'Won't you stay for a cup of tea?' Peter seemed loathe to be left so abruptly.

'I think not,' said Carol firmly. 'The children still have homework to do.' She could see Jess about to contradict her and sent the girl a silent plea to keep quiet. 'Thank you so much for lunch, Peter. You gave us a splendid meal and it has been great to see your bookshop.'

'You've hardly looked at it.'

'Well, next time I really will. Though I'm sure we'd all like to return your hospitality first and offer you Sunday lunch in Otterhaven. How about it, folks?'

The children agreed, with a fair degree of enthusiasm, Carol noted thankfully. They collected their belongings and very soon they were walking towards the car park.

'I don't have any homework,' said Dan, as he got into Carol's car.

'It seemed to be a good way of saying goodbye,' observed Carol, wondering if she was going to have to explain about the nuances of social behaviour? She thought a judicious bit of side-tracking was called for. 'Would you like some music?'

'Only if we get to choose it,' said Jess, who had won the tussle over the front seat and was already switching on the car radio.

Resigned to something raucous, Carol agreed, thinking philosophically that, for the moment, there need be no post mortems about choices of reading material. Besides, this was the first time they had left Splodge on her own. She knew that Dan would be distracted by the health and hunger of his kitten as soon as they returned.

★ ★ ★

Jessica sat on her bed with a science book open. She was not reading it. She had no intention of reading it. Well, some of it looked quite interesting. She thought the physics were dire, but the chemistry might be all right. Over lunch the day before, Uncle Peter had suggested that if she found the classes difficult he might be able to see about some coaching to get her up to speed. She'd had one science class. Difficult didn't describe it. If you were able to shut out of your head the noise made by the rest of the class, the work was easy. But she wondered how anybody could concentrate. That was one of Mum's firmest rules. You weren't allowed any background noise while you were studying. She leant across and switched on the little radio on the bedside table. (You had to say this for Carol, she did have most of the necessary modern technology.) She found the channel they'd been listening to in the car on the way back from Hay and turned up the sound. Loud.

She waited. After five minutes there was a knock on the door. She smiled, pretending not to hear it.

'Jessica! Would you turn down the volume, please?'

195

She ignored the request. After a moment the door opened. Carol put her head round it.

'Excuse me!' exclaimed the girl righteously.

'Actually, no,' said Carol. 'Please turn the sound down. In fact, if you are studying, turn it off altogether. I'm quite sure that was one of your mother's rules.' Without waiting for a response, she went out and shut the door firmly.

'Old cow,' muttered Jessica. She put the book down. What was the point of trying to study. She couldn't understand any of it. She plumped up the pillow to make it more comfortable. Then she lay down. After a moment she sat up and readjusted the sound, turning it down.

What was she going to do without her mum?

Jessica thought she'd have a cry. But this time, try as she might, the tears would not come.

What was she going to do to help her parents? What could a fourteen-year old do? She remembered the articles Dan had found. At least he had been able to do something practical. Something practical. Now there was a wicked thought . . .

* * *

Two weeks later, while they were eating their evening meal, Jessica asked, 'Carol, do you think it would be possible to go to Working and get our stuff out of the lock-up?'

'What stuff were you thinking about?' asked Carol cautiously.

'Nothing big,' answered Jess, interpreting correctly Carol's caution. 'Just, you know, our reference books. The projects we were doing with Mum for lessons. One of my teachers said she'd like to see some of my work.'

'So did my maths teacher,' said Dan.

'Right. Well, I suppose they would like to have some idea of what you've covered already.'

'I left my flute there, too, remember?' said Jess. 'I can only join the orchestra if I have an instrument.'

'In that case we'd better go as soon as possible.'

'How about a week on Sunday?'

Carol shook her head. 'That Saturday would be more convenient, I think. Besides, I expect your uncle will come to lunch again on the Sunday. By the way, how do you get into this lock-up?'

'We have to ring the friends who own it. They have several lock-ups and they're all quite private. I can't remember their telephone number but we can get it from the Net.'

'Can you?'

'Of course I can,' said Dan.

'Then we'll arrange it after supper.'

Getting hold of the key would present no problem. That call having been accomplished, Jessica asked Carol if it might be possible for her and Dan to spend an hour or so with friends after they had collected the possessions they needed. Both Jessica's friend, Rachel, and Dan's friend, George, lived in the same road not far away, so please would Carol drop them off?

Carol thought the idea was not unreasonable. It was such a long time since the children had been with their friends and the opportunities to meet would be few and far between in the future.

'We shouldn't leave it too late to return home,' she said. 'Hey, but why not? So long as it's not inconvenient for your friends' parents. Suppose we came home around five o'clock? That would give you several hours with your friends. We could eat at a motorway service station on the way back and still not be too late. See what you can arrange?'

'What will you do, Carol?' asked Daniel.

'I'll think of something.'

★ ★ ★

Marion Henderson, who always maintained that she had absolutely no head for facts and figures and couldn't possibly imagine herself giving sensible advice to anyone distraught enough to ask her for it, called round a day or so later to ask how Carol was getting on at the CAB. As usual, Carol took Marion's protestations with the proverbial pinch of salt for, in her time, Marion had been a county representative at the annual WI meeting in the Albert Hall. Without being specific, Carol said that it was good getting back to the old routine. She also knew it was salutary to realize that other people had worse problems than she did.

'It was trading standards stuff this morning,' Carol said. 'You know, one of those sad cases of faulty goods which should have been recalled, in this case a pushchair. The parents didn't know what they could do about it and they certainly couldn't afford a new one. We got it sorted for them. I'm glad I was persuaded to go back. It's just what I need to take my mind off everything else.' She went on to tell Marion about Jess's suggestion that she and Dan should spend the afternoon with their friends. 'It seemed mean not to say yes, though what I shall do with myself, goodness only knows.'

'If the weather's bad, you could always find a cinema. Or there are the shops. I daresay you could while away an hour or so buying something decadent.'

'Multiples,' Carol said, though really she had no idea what Woking had to offer. Still, retail therapy did sound seductive. Also, it wouldn't do at all to wrangle an invitation to stay for the afternoon from one of the parents. Nor could she just sit in the car. It was probably all going to be utterly boring, but it was the least she could do for Jess and Dan to help maintain their friendships. She thought that there probably weren't too many of those in the children's lives.

10

The trip to Woking went smoothly. They were away by half-past eight and at the lock-up by eleven o'clock. This was one of a row of purpose-built, double garages situated where the slate-roofed coach house had been in years gone by. They were in what had been the grounds of a substantial house, built in the early years of the previous century on the St John's side of Woking. Though the woodwork was in need of a lick of paint, the lock-ups were all secured by modern padlocks and, inside, the Pickerings' was quite dry. Everything, the children assured Carol, was perfectly secure. They spent an hour moving boxes and rooting around for what they wanted to take back to Otterhaven — the most elusive item being the music for Jessica's flute, as it and the music had not been packed together. When they had finished, the boot of the car was full and there was a suitcase and a box on the back seat.

'Oh, dear,' said Carol dubiously. 'I had intended taking the car into town and finding a multi-storey car park. I don't think I should leave all this in clear view.'

The children looked at each other. 'George's house has a big drive,' said Dan eventually. 'I guess you could park the car there and take the bus in. There's a stop in the village.'

'What a good idea,' said Carol. 'Provided George's parents don't mind the car being there.'

George's mother, Ellen Kennedy, made no objection, even insisting that Carol put her car into their garage as her husband was playing in a golf match and wasn't expected back until the evening.

'Are you sure you won't stay?'

'Thanks, but no.' Carol turned to go. She noticed that Dan seemed a little tense, but thought nothing of it other than surmising that there must be a certain uneasiness in the resumption of the relationship between the two boys. Not unforeseen, she thought. They must both have moved on, found new friends, but hearing about Dan's experiences would bridge the gap between them.

★ ★ ★

Carol found a small café for an early lunch and afterwards she wandered round the shopping centre. It was something she rarely did and she enjoyed the experience, even deciding that she would buy herself a new pair of smart linen trousers for the summer; a pair of flat suede shoes and various items of underwear to replace what she had taken abroad and which was all looking sad and saggy. All most uplifting, she said to herself righteously, and at her age definitely an investment. For what, exactly, she did not examine further.

Laden with carrier bags, she took a taxi back to St John's. When she went into the garden Ellen was there, mulching her roses.

'Heavens, is that the time? I'll get cleaned up.'

'You must have a splendid display in the summer.'

'These are 'Iceberg'. I love the way they glow in the dusk on a summer's night.' They talked roses for a bit and then Carol admired a large ornamental pool which contained a number of goldfish.

'I don't feed the fish,' said Ellen. 'They seem to manage on what is in the pond and they maintain more or less the same population from year to year.'

'Do you get any herons?'

'Not round here, thankfully.' She tipped the last of the compost on to the rose bed and put her tools into the wheelbarrow. 'Let's go and find the boys. Is Jess coming to us, or are you calling for her?'

'She is walking here. I guess that means she hasn't arrived yet?'

'I haven't seen her. She probably won't be long.'

They went into the house and Ellen sat Carol down in the family kitchen while she washed her hands at the kitchen sink. 'How about a cup of tea?'

'That would be good. If it isn't any bother.'

'I could certainly do with one myself.' Ellen went to the bottom of the stairs and called: 'George! Dan! Carol is here. We're going to have a cup of tea. Come down in five minutes, will you?' She put the kettle on and when it had boiled and the tea had been made, she sat down at the table, opposite Carol, and poured tea into mugs decorated with wild flowers. There was a biscuit tin beside them. Ellen opened it and offered the tin to Carol who declined to take one. Ellen helped herself to a chocolate biscuit.

There was no sign of the boys. Carol glanced at the large kitchen clock on the wall. It was already nearly 5.30. When she had finished her tea, she said, 'Jess is very late. I'm sorry about this. We must be delaying you.'

'Not a problem.' But Ellen frowned. 'I'd better go upstairs and fetch those boys. Maybe they didn't hear me.'

She was back almost immediately. 'They aren't upstairs. Drat George. He knew you didn't want to be too late leaving.'

'Do you think they're in the garden?'

'Unlikely. I'd have seen them when I put the wheelbarrow away. They've probably gone to see Jake who lives just down the road. I'd better give his mother a ring and ask her to send them back.'

'Jess still isn't here. Personally, I'm not too bothered about the time and after all, they won't have the opportunity of seeing each other for some while.'

'As long as you're sure you don't mind. Shall we wait until six then start doing the heavy stuff?'

They began talking about the travelling Carol and James had done, Carol managing to avoid having to explain why it was that James had not come home with her. She could see, though, that Ellen was becoming increasingly uneasy.

'I'm so sorry about all this. It is thoughtless of both Dan and Jess not to be back by now. Especially Jess. She should know better at her age. It's almost six. Why don't I ring Rachel's mother?'

'Do you have the number?'

'Fortunately I had the foresight to get that last night.'

Jess was not at Rachel's. It transpired that Rachel's mother was just about to phone George's mother to ask her to send her daughter home at once, as the family planned to go out and Rachel had promised to be back in time.

'Promised to be back?' Carol repeated.

'They went out just after two o'clock,' Rachel's mother told her. 'They said they were going to do some window shopping.'

The kitchen door opened and George walked in.

'George! Where have you been, wretched boy? We were beginning to get worried. You should have told me where you were going.'

'Where's Daniel?' asked Carol.

'Um . . . ' George began.

'You haven't quarrelled?'

''Course not, Mum,' he said indignantly. 'Um . . . '

'Where is Daniel?'

'He's gone to . . . ' the sentence ended in a mumble as George turned his head away, his hand going to the biscuit tin.

'Leave the biscuits alone!'

'Where did you say Dan had gone?'

George heaved a sigh and turned to face the adults. 'He's gone to London. With Jess.'

There was a stunned silence.

After a moment Ellen opened her mouth to

206

protest vociferously. Carol interrupted quickly, 'Suppose you sit down and tell us all about it, George?' She said to Ellen, 'Lord, I suppose Jessica and Daniel have done something extremely stupid and left George and Rachel to do the explaining.'

The phone rang. Ellen, shaking her head in bewilderment, went to answer it. Carol and George, avoiding each other's eyes, could hear her expostulating to Rachel's mother. It seemed that Rachel had just arrived home and told her own mother where Jess was.

'Right, George,' Ellen said ominously, when she came back. 'What have you done?'

It had been planned meticulously. George told them that Jess had it all worked out before she phoned Rachel to suggest they spent the afternoon together.

'What plan?' asked Carol.

'To join the demo in London.'

'Demo? Do you mean a demonstration?'

'Yes, Mum.'

While he was surfing the Net for information about his parents in Burma, Dan had discovered that there was to be a demonstration by pro-democracy activists in front of the Burmese Embassy in Charles Street in London. Jess had decided that she would join it and Dan had refused to be left behind.

'When is this demonstration?' asked Carol.

'Tomorrow. Sunday.'

'But you said they have gone to London today, this afternoon.'

'They caught the 16:26, Mum. They wanted to be in London long before anyone knew they were going.' His hand went back to the biscuit tin and hovered over it. His mother, grim-faced, nodded reluctantly. George helped himself to three biscuits. 'I'm starving.'

'You had soup and bread and cheese for lunch,' resumed Ellen. 'You said you had things to do this afternoon. Oh.' She glanced at Carol. 'I was gardening. I didn't hear them go out. Don't we have a strict rule,' she said tightly to her son, 'don't you always tell me when you are going out?'

'Sorry, Mum.'

Carol said quickly, 'So what did you actually do?'

'Me and Dan got a bus into town. We met Jess and Rach at the station. They caught an earlier bus. Jess had to buy a mobile phone . . .'

'Buy a mobile phone!' exclaimed Carol. 'What with?'

'Er . . . money?'

'Don't be impertinent.'

'I'm not, Mum. She bought a pay-as-you-go phone,' he told Carol. 'She said she'd ring you about now to set your mind at rest.'

Carol was about to repeat his comment — 'parrot his statement', she amended, recalling James's objection all those months ago — when the phone rang again. This time it was Jess.

Carol took a deep breath and forced herself to remain calm. Hysterics — which she thought entirely justified, given the circumstances — would be counter-productive. She demanded, instead, her voice commendably firm and quiet, to know where they were, were they safe — what was Daniel doing — and when were they coming back?

In London, Jess said, 'We're perfectly safe. Don't worry, Carol. We're going to stay the night with some friends . . . '

'Friends? What friends have you got in London?' Carol interrupted harshly, before it could occur to her that it was not impossible for the Pickerings to have any number of entirely suitable friends in that city.

Jessica partly confirmed Carol's initial misgivings. 'They're not exactly friends. Well, Mum and Dad have met some of them because of Burma. You know. But they know all about us and they're quite all right about us staying. We're going to join the demo tomorrow, then we'll go back to South Wales. Could you pick us up at Newport?'

'Money, Jess. What are you doing about money?'

'We're using the money Uncle Peter gave us, along with what we took out of our piggy banks. You know, from the lock-up? It's quite all right, Carol. Don't worry about us,' she said again. 'Look, would you like to have my mobile number? You can have it as long as you don't ring every hour, or something humiliating like that. If you do, I'll just turn it off.'

Her head spinning, Carol wrote the number down. Peter, she thought. Peter gave them money (though not to finance an escapade such as this, her mind reasoned). It was up to Peter Pickering to sort out this mess. She couldn't cope.

Carol produced her own mobile, an ancient instrument that caused George (silent) mirth. She only ever had it with her when she was away from home, for an emergency. Fortunately Peter was in and he picked up his phone straight away. Succinctly she told him what had happened.

'I don't know what to do, Peter. Should I phone the police? Jess did say they were with family friends whom they knew because of the Burma-thing, but they could be any-where, with anyone. In grave danger.'

In Hay, Peter said, 'Don't worry.'

Carol could have screamed.

'They are both responsible children. They know what they want to do. I doubt if they are in any danger. Give me Jess's number and I'll try to get a little more information out of her. I'll ring you back in a bit when I've got some sense out of her.'

'Oh, Heavens,' said Carol hopelessly, sitting down again heavily. 'Responsible children, he says! I just don't know what to do.'

'What did their uncle say?' asked Ellen.

Carol told them. 'But you don't know what kind of strangers they are mixed up with. Friends? They don't have friends of their own in London. At least, they've never said anything to me about having friends in London. And to think they are going to sleep there.'

'With friends,' responded Ellen tentatively. It was all absolutely fascinating but she was extremely thankful that George's father wasn't home. He had a short fuse and would have thought of the police, and acted on that thought immediately. 'I should do as their uncle said,' she continued, 'and wait until he has managed to contact Jess,' Ellen cautioned. Feeling like one herself, she suggested a drink?

Carol declined. 'I'm driving, to London.'

'Oh, I do hope not.'

'I'd so much rather be driving home.'

Peter Pickering phoned back. He had not sounded concerned, Carol told Ellen. He had even spoken to the friend in whose house the children were to sleep. It all seemed quite genuine. He had suggested to her that the two of them should meet in a travel lodge that night. They would go up to London in the morning and see the demonstration . . .

'Take part in it?' interrupted Ellen.

'I very much doubt that. But we can look out for the children. After all, it probably won't be that big a demonstration. Then we can bring them back ourselves. At the moment they are making banners.'

'Making banners! Way cool!' said George.

'Forget it,' said his mother. 'You are going nowhere.'

Then Ellen fussed gently over Carol, making sure she had a clean towel for the bathroom and re-filling her water bottle with fresh water. Did she know exactly where she was meeting Peter Pickering?

Carol allowed it all to waft over her. It was even comforting to have someone worry about whether she was all right. As for Peter, he had the long drive ahead of him and they would not meet up until late. She would buy a toothbrush, check into the travel lodge and go and have something to eat. 'Thank goodness I had the sense to bring a book.'

'You could have a meal with us here.'

'That's very kind, but you must have had enough of us to last a lifetime.'

Ellen did not protest, so Carol knew she was right in her assumption and left soon afterwards.

Peter had told her where they were to spend the night so Carol expected to find that he had booked rooms for them. But when she arrived at the travel lodge she discovered that there was only one double room available for that night. Once more she floundered, not knowing what was best. Two beds, but only one room. On the other hand, it would take time to find anywhere else, and Peter was going to be tired when he arrived. She took the room. Then she went to have something to eat.

★   ★   ★

Peter Pickering knocked at the door of their room in the travel lodge soon after eleven o'clock. Carol opened the door to find him standing there, brandishing his own key.

'I didn't want to scare you by entering unannounced,' he told her.

'That was kind. You must be very tired,' she said immediately, relieved that he was here, at last. She had watched the late news to keep herself awake but her eyelids had begun to droop and now a yawn escaped her. 'Excuse me, it's been a long day for both of us.' She went back to the chair she had been occupying while he put down a small, overnight bag.

'I'm more hungry than tired. I guess that's really a manifestation of exhaustion. I could murder a steak and a drink.'

'I've already eaten,' Carol said apologetically, 'but I'll join you in that drink.' She got up again. 'Um . . . you must have been told we just have the one room.'

'Sorry about this,' he said easily. 'It never occurred to me that we needed to book.'

'I thought it best to go ahead and take it,' she said nervously. 'I mean, I don't know this area or how long it would take us to get somewhere else.'

'I'm sure we could pick up something around Heathrow, if you'd prefer to do that.'

'Don't let's bother,' she said. 'It's only for the one night and I'm far too tired to drive any further. Besides, I've already had one drink and I don't drink and drive.'

'Sensible woman. Let's go and find the restaurant.'

In the end, Peter settled for soup and a roll. 'I suppose I can do without indigestion in the middle of the night.' They both ordered red wine. 'Tell me about this demonstration,' he said, when the waitress had finished setting their table.

'I only know what George told me,' Carol replied. She explained how Daniel had apparently discovered from his researches on the Net that a demonstration was to take place and that it was Jessica who had decided immediately that she would take part in it.

'We probably can't blame Daniel for refusing to be left out. These friends,' he asked. 'What do you know about them?'

'Absolutely nothing. Peter, I'm sorry to have dragged you all this way, but the responsibility is too great for me. You do understand? I mean, I know nothing about these people. They could be . . . '

'Child molesters? I very much doubt that.'

Carol sighed and lifted her glass. 'I expect you are right. I daresay they were as much taken aback as we are now. This contact number which Jess used, I mean, what else could they do when the children announced who they are and that they wanted to take part in the demonstration? They could hardly go to the police.'

'Of course they could. Though the demonstration isn't illegal, they could still have insisted that the children were under age and therefore needed police protection until a guardian arrived to pick them up.'

'Well . . . Anyway, it is right that Kimberley and Brian should have all the publicity they can get. I know that we have tried to keep Jess and Dan from the press but I can see that having the Pickering children take part in a demonstration has to be about as big as it gets from the point of view of the Burmese.'

'I hope you are not going to be all sweet reasonableness tomorrow when we've found the children. They deserve the book throwing at them,' Peter said.

'Of course they do, but getting them home safely is what concerns me most.' She yawned.

Peter smiled. 'It's very late. Let's go to bed.'

It could have been awkward, two strangers in a hotel room. Perhaps it was because they were still essentially strangers to each other that they managed the accommodations without embarrassment. 'I guess this bed is mine,' Peter said, indicating the one which bore no indication of having been touched. He threw his bag on to it and unzipped it. 'Do you want the bathroom first?'

Carol nodded. Before leaving Woking she had bought a toothbrush and toothpaste. Her shopping spree had fortuitously left her with clean underwear for the morning and a new pair of summer pyjamas. She always carried moisturizer in her bag and the travel lodge provided soap and a towel. She washed her face and smoothed on moisturizer. There were lines on her face that she had not seen before — not that nowadays she scrutinized her face so very minutely, she conceded. There was tension behind her eyes. It was hardly surprising, she thought, given the stress she was under. She added another dollop of moisturizer. She would have a shower in the morning. Things could be worse, she philosophized, though not itemizing them.

While Peter was in the bathroom, she finished undressing and got into bed, turning out her light before he emerged. But when he did, she could not help exclaiming almost resentfully: 'Slippers and pyjamas! I suppose you packed for a night away. And I bet you've got a clean shirt and socks for tomorrow.'

'Don't sound so disapproving.' There was amusement in his voice. 'Of course I'm prepared. Ah. That must mean you have nothing with you.'

'Thankfully I'd gone shopping in the afternoon.'

'That's all right, then,' he said. 'Now, go to

sleep. Good night.'

Predictably, sleep would not come. Carol thought that she would drift into oblivion immediately but it was all too strange, the circumstances, the room, the bed, the virtually unknown man asleep just feet from her. She knew that Peter was asleep because his breathing was so regular. Lucky man, she thought, with yet another surge of unreasonable resentment. Just like James. It hadn't mattered where they slept while they were travelling. Each night he fell asleep as soon as his head hit the pillow. She invariably tossed and turned for at least an hour, occasionally woke in the night and lay sleepless for ages — or sometimes she went into the bathroom where she could read. (To give him his due, wherever possible James insisted that they paid for private facilities. He said that at his age he couldn't be doing with lurking in corridors waiting for some unknown to finish with the loo.) But in the morning, after a disturbed night like that, Carol was sometimes jaded, finding it difficult to get going until she had consumed a large, strong coffee. She did so hope she would get to sleep soon, otherwise coping with the children was going to be a real effort.

The children. Carol tensed, wondering what they were doing at that moment. Logic said that they were asleep, like Peter. Banners finished, the adults they were with would have wanted a good night's rest before the exigencies of the following day. The adults. The men. Jessica was a very attractive girl, but she was still fourteen. There was bound to be one unscrupulous man among the adults they were with. One who would want to take advantage of a girl like Jessica. And Jessica? She was no fool, but Carol was sure that despite the girl's travelling, she was essentially innocent, and though she might put on that appearance of being streetwise — like all her peers — this was a carapace. Admittedly she had her brother with her, but Daniel was only twelve. You could hardly expect a boy of that age to assume the responsibility of looking after his older sister.

Carol took in a sudden and deep breath which, mindful of the sleeping man, she expelled slowly. Deep breathing was meant to calm you, though she found that it rarely worked for her. Then, maybe she was the sort of impatient person who needed to work at relaxation. On her back, she practised deep breathing. It didn't work. Carol turned over irritably. How could they do this to her?

If Peter hadn't given the children that money, they would all be asleep in their beds in Otterhaven. If Brian and Kimberley hadn't

219

demonstrated in Rangoon, she would be in Australia with James.

No she wouldn't, Carol realized. But they would both be in Otterhaven together. James. She stifled a sob. Whether the sob was one of sorrow, or sheer rage at her present situation, Carol never worked out. The side of her bed sagged as Peter sat down on it beside her.

'Hey,' he said. 'Can't you sleep?'

'I . . . ' she turned on to her back again. Peter was nothing more than a vague shape. 'Oh, Heavens, did I wake you?'

'It was probably intuition that woke me,' he said. He did not sound all that dismayed. 'What is it?'

'I don't know. Well, the children. I was thinking about Jess. She's so young.'

'You are wondering if she's been raped yet?'

'How can you joke about it?' she asked reproachfully.

'Look at it this way. She's young, yes, and she's very pretty. But she's their main asset for tomorrow — today. If any harm comes to her, or to either of them for that matter, what sort of publicity is that going to give the Burmese? Their entire credibility would be demolished at a stroke. Pro-activists for democracy who couldn't keep two children safe? My guess is that Jess and Dan had a

220

marvellous evening making banners and eating Burmese food, and that they're dead to the world at this very moment, dreaming pleasantly fantastical dreams of causing the Junta to have a change of heart and order the immediate release of their parents, for which Brian and Kimberley will always be immensely grateful. Pure poppycock, of course.'

He was right, Carol conceded. 'I guess so,' she said grudgingly.

'Of course I'm right,' he said bracingly. 'Go to sleep.'

It would have worked. Carol would most likely have turned over and gone to sleep, but Peter bent forward. He told her later that, truly, he only meant to kiss her on the forehead, as an expression of gratitude for her care of his niece and nephew, but in the dark he kissed her lips. In the dark, their lips clung.

To Carol it was like a dam bursting. All the bitterness she was feeling about James, what she saw of as nothing short of betrayal, flooded through her. All the loneliness, the abandonment, overwhelmed her. She missed a male presence in her life (in her bed?), the everyday support of living with another adult — especially in her dealings with the children. All these emotions were compounded by fright over these children and what might be happening to them. To all this was added the enormous sense of relief that here was someone else with whom she might share the liability she had taken on so carelessly (it seemed to her).

What followed was cataclysmic as they came together.

Afterwards she was languorous with release. She was asleep before Peter kissed her on the forehead, stroked her shoulder gently, hesitated for a long moment, then returned to his own bed.

11

In the morning, things did look a lot better, at first. Carol woke and stretched. She felt extremely relaxed. What had happened was extremely therapeutic, she convinced herself. Peter was still asleep. She got up quietly and went into the bathroom where she had a long, warm shower. Dressed and made up and with her hair done, she felt infinitely better. Was she just cloaking emotions?

Peter was fully awake when she entered the room. He gave her a beaming good morning smile.

'Hi,' she said cheerfully. It seemed to her very important that what had happened in the night should be accepted as one of those things. It might be a cliché, but there were times when clichés expressed exactitude. Peter should need to feel neither guilt at having taken advantage of her nor committed to an ongoing relationship. (Heaven forbid!) She had no idea what relationships he had had in the past, though it had been evident in the night that he was certainly not a clumsy fool. Carol hardly flinched as she recalled

James; she was sure she was vastly more experienced in the moods of a man than he was in those of a woman.

'Bathroom's free.'

'I'll shower and shave.'

When he emerged, also fully dressed, Carol was sitting by the window reading. She closed her book and got up. 'Breakfast,' she said. 'Let's go and eat.'

She was hungry enough to order a full English breakfast. 'Then, we don't know when we'll be able to eat again.'

Coffee arrived. 'Are we going to talk about last night?' he asked, picking up the coffee pot and pouring the dark liquid into both cups. 'Milk? Sugar?'

She smiled gently. 'Milk, no sugar. Thanks.'

'I know. How absurd, to know so much about a person, yet not to know something as mundane as whether she takes sugar in her coffee.'

'I don't think you know all that much about me,' she said primly.

'I know enough. I know the important things.'

'Yes, well . . . I don't suppose we need to go into anything more.'

'Aren't we going to talk about last night?'

'I don't think so. Do you want to?'

'I mean . . .'

'No. No explanations. Certainly no apologies.'

'I wasn't going to apologise,' he said vehemently. 'Not about something that was so immensely enjoyable. If unexpected.'

He paused. Carol sat very still, wondering just how significant the pause was. She decided, after all, that she was too uncertain about her own feelings to query his.

'Did you sleep?'

'Like a log.' She smiled again. Suddenly she felt absurdly light-hearted, as if all the troubles of the world had simply fallen from her shoulders. 'Thank you.'

'Thank you,' he said gravely, his dark eyes holding hers, his expression enigmatic.

They ate in silence. It was only when they were having their second cup of coffee, that Carol asked: 'What do we do now? Do you know what time the demonstration is starting?'

'I checked the Net yesterday before I set off. Demonstrators are foregathering at ten o'clock. I suppose it'll take time before they actually get going.'

'So soon. Shouldn't we be on our way?'

'We've plenty of time. I suggest we leave your car here, get to the nearest tube station where we can park and go by underground. We could lose too much time taking the car into London, let alone having the expense of congestion charges.'

'Good thinking. I really wasn't looking forward to driving into London myself.' She considered the children's possessions in her car. 'I had to leave stuff on the back seat last night. Could we put it in your boot for safety?'

'Of course. I think we might buy a few chocolate bars, too, and a couple of bottles of water — to be self-sufficient, don't you think?'

It was going to be all right, Carol thought, smiling again. An easy camaraderie was pervading their relationship. They would do what he suggested. They would go to the Burmese embassy. They would observe, from the sidelines. They would find the children and bring them home. And afterwards? With Peter's support, she would look after the children until their parents came home. There was absolutely nothing else she need worry about.

RELEASE ALL POLITICAL HOSTAGES
SPDC CEASE DISRUPTION OF UNIVERSITIES
HONOUR THE 1990 ELECTION RESULTS
NLD AGAINST RAPE AND MURDER

The home-made banners held aloft by demonstrators flapped gently in the breeze outside the Burmese embassy watched by a handful of police who, in the main, did not seem too perturbed by the throng. Slogans against the State Police and Development Council, and for the National League for Democracy were shouted. There were a few catcalls and whistles as a curtain was twitched high above them but on the ground it was good-natured, unmenacing.

Carol tried to calculate how many were there. It was not a large gathering, though it was watched by a number of observers — sympathizers, like herself? Or were they spies for the *Tatmadaw*?

'Quite likely the Junta will know by tonight who is here,' said Peter, accurately divining her thoughts.

'They will know about the children. Do you think it is dangerous for them?'

'Who knows? Though I very much doubt if there will be any repercussions for them here. It might be another matter if they were to try to get back into Burma. Has anyone suggested family visits?'

'Not to me,' said Carol, appalled. 'How could you subject children to a prison visit? Are you suggesting you might go to Burma to visit your brother?'

Peter shook his head, grimaced and said, 'Until yesterday, last night, I had no sympathy for either of them. I still think they both behaved reprehensibly, without the slightest thought for their responsibilities as parents. But . . . '

'You think you might go to visit them all the same?'

'I think I might think about it,' he temporized.

'Look, I've seen Jess. Over there,' said Carol, pointing.

Jessica had caught sight of Carol at the same moment. She hesitated, seemed almost on the verge of flight. Then, as if she realized that flight was impossible, unless she dropped her pole which was attached to one end of a banner, she shrugged, grinned (if uncertainly) and once more joined in slogan shouting.

'There's Dan,' said Peter, unnecessarily.

Daniel waved jauntily. He, at least, was certain only that he had universal approval.

Carol and Peter waited for the best part of two hours. Gradually the observers drifted away. A few of the supporters began shaking hands, clasping others on the shoulder and preparing to disperse. Carol and Peter moved forward together.

'Did you see my banner? I made it. Last night. It's brilliant, isn't it?' Full of enthusiasm, Daniel gave one more bellow:

'*Cease brutal intimidation!*'

'I do hope you know what that means,' said Peter, drily.

' 'Course I do. It means . . . '

'You'll have to get someone else to take your banner,' interrupted Peter. 'It's time we were going.'

'Jess, I'd like to thank the people you were staying with.' Carol had approached the girl. 'Will you introduce us?'

Once again Jessica seemed to be about to flee. Then, maybe realizing that retribution wasn't going to be quite as dire as she had feared, she gave a shrug and turned to the woman who was holding the other end of her banner. 'We stayed with Kennari.'

The Burmese woman was small and slight and dressed in the traditional *longyi*, though in deference to the cooler climate she was wearing a cardigan over her blouse. Her smooth, dark hair was coiled in the nape of her neck and her light brown skin looked oiled. She was in her mid-twenties, Carol judged, very beautiful.

Carol moved to the woman's side. 'Thank you so much for looking after the children.'

'You must have been very worried. We all told Jess that it was wrong of her to have come without telling you.' Her English was excellent, her smile warm.

'I expect she thought I should have refused

permission,' Carol admitted.

'We have such a lot to thank Brian and Kimberley for. They have spent so much time raising money for us to be able to help those who succeed in getting across the border into Thailand. And now, what is happening to them in Burma ... ' Kennari shook her head. 'It is quite dreadful. We are so glad to have the opportunity to show the world that the Burmese have friends.'

'It may also have been good for Brian and Kimberley, to have it known that the children are supporting them.'

'We could not do enough to make Dan and Jess happy while they were staying with us. In honour of their parents, you understand.'

'I think Brian's brother may apply to visit them,' Carol said rashly. She was thinking how salutary it was to hear nothing but good spoken of a couple about whom her own feelings were ambivalent.

'You must make sure that Brian's brother speaks to us before he goes,' Kennari urged her.

Carol thought that Peter would have to be circumspect about that. Any suggestion that he was going to contact supporters of the NLD in Rangoon would most certainly not be helpful to Brian and Kimberley's cause, in her opinion.

'Anyway, we have to take the children home now. Thank you again for looking after them.'

'It was our pleasure. We don't often get to talk to your young people. Jess and Dan are caring and very thoughtful. You must be proud of them.' She hesitated. 'You will not scold too much?'

Carol smiled. 'I expect that I shall shout at them for causing so much worry. But, no, I won't scold too much.'

*　*　*

Chocolate bars were not going to assuage the children's hunger. They all walked in the direction of Green Park and found a restaurant where Peter, Carol and Daniel ordered steak and chips and Jess chose a vegetarian lasagne.

The children became more subdued as the meal progressed. Carol knew that she and Peter were taking a sort of sadistic pleasure in delaying the moment when explanations would be demanded but she hardened her heart. They had to learn that an escapade like this one was totally unacceptable.

Daniel broke first. 'Sorry,' he mumbled. He

put down his knife and fork. 'I guess I'm not hungry after all.'

'Is that an apology for pulling an atrocious stunt on Carol, or an apology for not finishing your steak?' asked Peter, his voice entirely neutral.

'Er . . . both.'

'Jessica?'

'Sorry, Uncle Peter. I'm going to finish my . . . Sorry.'

'Do you have any idea how frantic I was?' asked Carol. 'I was nearly out of my mind. I mean you could have been . . . '

Peter nudged Carol's foot with his own. 'What Carol means is that because she didn't know whom you were staying with, she was afraid you might be sleeping on the street.'

'As if,' said Jessica scornfully. She blushed. 'I mean, as if we'd sleep on the street. It would be too dangerous.'

'I'm glad you recognize that,' said Carol. 'So how did you contact the people you stayed with?'

'Easy,' replied Jessica proudly. 'There was a contact number. I phoned them and told them who we were. They told us where they lived and said we had to go straight there. Kennari was particular about that. They asked about money and if we knew our way round London. I said you had an A-Z. I borrowed it. I hoped you wouldn't notice it was missing. Kennari (she pronounced it KAY-nuhr-ree) was a little cross with us when she found out later that you didn't know we were coming for the demo.'

'She said we should have more respect for our elders,' said Dan, with a cheeky grin.

'Whatever,' said Jessica.

'Is that the woman I spoke to?' asked Carol. 'She was absolutely right.' She took a deep breath. 'If you pull a stunt like that again, I shall send you to your uncle. I'm not going to accept responsibility for what happens to idiots who do stupid things like running off to London. Do you both understand?'

'And if Carol gives up on you, I shall hand you over to social services,' said Peter severely. 'Now, eat.'

There was a moment's silence.

'Is that all?' asked Dan anxiously.

The three of them looked at Carol.

'I suppose so,' she agreed.

'I think I might even have suggested that you joined the demonstration with our blessing. If we had been asked in advance,' added Peter.

'Do you really mean that?' demanded Jessica.

'We do see that publicity has to be good for

your mum and dad,' said Carol. 'I've been thinking about that. You know, one of the things you must do now is to write regularly to your parents.'

'We couldn't guarantee that they will get the letters, but you should at least write.'

'I think you should both write to the Military Junta. We can find out names. I think you should send them personal letters,' said Carol unexpectedly. 'Write once a week, asking for their release. I think when you write to your parents you should also send a copy to the consul in Rangoon in case the prison authorities don't hand out mail that arrives.'

'And I will apply for a visa with permission to visit Brian and Kimberley,' declared Peter.

'Us, too?' asked Dan eagerly.

'Too expensive, and a bit upsetting,' said Peter, nevertheless managing to sound regretful. 'However, I do agree with Carol. I think we should try to gain publicity for your parents as far as we can. If nothing else, it'll make us all feel better.'

'Thanks, Uncle Peter,' said Dan. 'Er, Carol, d'you think Splodge is all right? I hope she doesn't think she's been abandoned again. You see, I didn't expect she'd be left on her own last night.'

'It's all right, Dan.' Abandoned. That was

what it was all about, wasn't it? 'I telephoned Vera when I knew we wouldn't be home. She said she'd go in and feed Splodge, but I'm sure Splodge'll be very glad to see you again.'

'Great. D'you want those chips, Carol? 'Cos if you don't, I'm still hungry.'

'Have them,' she said, 'but do leave space for an ice cream.'

She was remembering Matthew at the same age — Matthew until not so very many years past — always ravenous. Matthew and James . . .

★   ★   ★

They collected both cars and set off for South Wales, Daniel with Peter and Jessica with Carol. Jessica and Carol talked for a while, about the house where they had stayed on Saturday night and the people who lived there. Carol would have liked to know what the Burmese were doing in London — were they political refugees, were they from a tribal minority group like the Karen? — but Jessica had not thought to question them closely. Instead, the girl told Carol about the banner-making and the demonstration and how good it had felt to be doing something positive for her parents.

'That was what I wanted to do. I hated

doing nothing. When you sent us to school I felt we'd abandoned them.'

'I'm sorry, Jess. I never looked at it like that.'

'Writing to the generals'll be good. I know just what I'll say. Do you really think Uncle Peter'll go to see Mum and Dad?'

'If he says he'll do it, he probably will,' said Carol cautiously. 'But he will only be able to go if he gets a visa.'

They talked for a little longer, then Jess's eyes closed, she put her head back against the seat rest and slept. Carol was thinking that it would be late when they reached Otterhaven. Hay was another hour away. Should she offer Peter a bed for the night? (Would he accept?) He would have to sleep in Dan's room.

At least there would be no repetition of the previous night.

It was lucky that the traffic out of London was comparatively light for as images of the previous night inevitably drifted into Carol's mind, she was in danger of losing her concentration. She pushed the thoughts away then, but much later, once they were all in bed (and with Peter safely in Hay) she permitted herself to recollect what had passed between them.

All her feelings of relaxation, her conclusion that the sex had been therapeutic, evaporated. Without thought, without any feelings of remorse at the time, she had done what she most certainly would condemn in her husband. She had been unfaithful to James. Carol could not understand herself. Where were all her principles when she needed them? She longed to talk over what had happened with Marion. Marion would understand. Then, at the moment Marion was no champion of James. Carol longed for confession. She had the utmost confidence in Marion's ability to keep silent. (Did she? Would Marion be able to keep such a thing from Clive?) It was, she decided finally, something she would have to cope with on her own.

A not so very small part of her mind said that indeed the events of the night had been therapeutic. What was more, she agreed with Peter's declaration that these events, however you wanted to describe them, had also been vastly enjoyable. Which did not mean that she intended for them to be repeated. Certainly not, thought Carol. Absolutely not.

★　★　★

Carol insisted that the children should go to school as normal on the Monday. Jessica sulked and Dan obeyed leadenly, but eventually they both did as they were told. But none of them had appreciated the impact of the demonstration. It was Peter who phoned and told Carol that there were whole-page spreads in the papers about what had happened on Sunday and, though there were no pictures of the children, their presence at the demonstration was mentioned. So Carol was at least prepared when Mrs Meredith also phoned in the middle of the morning to ask to speak to her.

'The children are currently in the centre of an admiring group in the playground. Do you want me to put a stop to it, or may we use this as a lesson in the merits of democracy?'

'And also a lesson in involving parents and guardians in decision-making,' said Carol. 'Yes, of course you may, so long as you don't bring the press into it. I am sure talking about what the children did won't cause any harm. By the way, the children are going to begin bombarding the Junta with letters. It's something I should have thought of doing before but, as you may gather, all this is proving a lot more traumatic than ever I'd imagined.'

'Then,' responded Mrs Meredith, 'you might like to know that Jessica and Daniel are full of admiration for the way you handled the situation yesterday.'

★ ★ ★

If grudgingly, Jessica had to admit that both Carol and Uncle Peter had behaved with unexpected understanding. She had been prepared for endless recriminations, a grounding at the very least. It was Kennari who had brought home to her — forcefully — that her guardian (who was in that position solely because of her good nature) was entirely justified in becoming hysterical over her thoughtlessness: with visions of child abduction; rape and at the very least, the theft of everything they possessed.

'Theft of our possessions?' Jessica had attempted to pour scorn on that point. 'Well, whatever,' she had ended weakly, as she saw Kennari's expression.

Jessica had been so sure that nothing could, or would, go wrong from the moment she had contacted the group and been told that she and Dan would be more than welcome to join the demonstration. The consternation of the Burmese adults when they realized that the children had not told anyone where they were going was chastening.

Nothing had gone wrong. She had not led her brother into any danger. Good had come out of it. She really, really felt that they were doing something for mum and dad. It had never occurred to her that they should be writing to them. Jessica felt more than a little selfish because she had only concerned herself with her own feelings and worries about school and hardly at all about what her parents were going through. Even Uncle Peter seemed to have come round. Suggesting that he would apply for a visa and permission to go and see them was brilliant!

And because of that day, both she and Dan had achieved something of a cult status at school. Nobody, but nobody had gone on any type of demo. Certainly nobody had ever contemplated going to London for a demo without permission.

Jessica had the sense to realize that most people would forget what she and Dan had done within days. She hoped that one or two of the girls who were being particularly friendly would continue to be so, and accept her as one of them. She found that she was beginning to get a taste for the constant companionship of those of her own age.

★ ★ ★

Carol found a message from James in her in-box. Very briefly, it said that his plans had changed and that he would be in Sydney for a little longer than he had expected. She was aware from a postcard that he had done the tour of the Hunter Valley, looking at the vineyards. On the card James had written a cryptic *Wish You Were Here*.

She had checked her e-mails regularly but found nothing. At first she had sent a few one-line messages. Then she had decided to leave it. Now he was telling her that he'd be in touch in a little while. As assurance, it wasn't much.

So what new plans were these? Irritated, Carol wondered why James could not have told her more. She decided to call him at breakfast, before his day began. It would be good actually to hear the sound of his voice again, she thought. There were times when she missed James with a deep ache. There were also times when she never wanted to see him again! She also thought that she was far more likely to gather what James was thinking from the nuances of his voice than she would from the carefully constructed messages he was sending her (or not sending).

James, in his Sydney hotel, was about to go and eat. 'This is unexpected,' he said.

From his impatient tone, Carol knew that she had been right in assuming that his breakfast hour hadn't altered. She also sensed that her call wasn't too welcome for other, unexplained reasons.

'I wanted to hear your voice,' she said. The confession was meant to disarm him. It worked.

'It is good to hear you, too, Carol,' he said. This time he spoke more warmly.

'Are you rushing off, or do you have time to tell me what you are doing?'

'I guess I can spare a few minutes.'

Spare a few minutes. For his wife?

'That's good. E-mails can be very unsatisfactory,' she said, her own tone neutral. Not neutral enough.

'I thought I was keeping you up to date.'

'That wasn't meant as a criticism, though you haven't told me much. But it is good to talk. So, tell me, are you doing yet another coach trip?'

'You know I said I was going to have dinner with that couple I met on the train, Betty and Russ? Well, it's a fantastic coincidence, but the man Russ wanted me to meet is Oliver Knapwood. You remember Oliver?'

'Of course I do. You did some work for him about ten years ago.'

'Twelve, actually.' He began to sound enthusiastic. 'Oliver emigrated when he made his second marriage. I hadn't remembered that he'd married an Australian. Anyway, he set up a business in Sydney and is doing very well. So we were able to catch up and, you'd never believe it, he's now offered me some work.'

'Work? What sort of work?'

'The usual, of course. That is, the usual troubleshooting. That's what Oliver does. He sends consultants out all over to sort problems.'

'Don't you just have a tourist visa, James?'

'Trust you to pick on that aspect of what I want to do.'

Carol held the receiver away from her ear and stared at it. She had heard truculence this time from her husband. As if he expected her to do nothing but criticize. She put the receiver back to her ear.

'Visa, James,' she said sharply. 'You are supposed to be a tourist. Won't working jeopardize that?'

'Oliver says that doing one consultancy won't be a problem. Anyway, I don't intend to stir the waters and besides, the money'll come in very useful.'

'How long is this job?'

'As long as it takes. Probably a month to six weeks.'

Six weeks, she was thinking. Six weeks!
'Oh.'

'I told you I would be getting in touch. You see, I'm leaving the hotel. There's an apartment available in a block in Kirribilli for about what I'm paying here. It's fully furnished, in a good area, with a fantastic view of the harbour and the opera house and as the firm I'm to go to is in North Sydney it makes excellent sense for me to move out of the hotel and live the other side of the harbour. Oliver has also agreed that I should have a car. I was going to send you the address and any landline number. Um . . . Carol, it's a great apartment. As I said, fully furnished. You'd love it out here, you know. Won't you come and join me? The social life is great, too.'

'James,' she protested. 'Never mind the social aspect, whatever do you think I would do all day while you were working? In an apartment?'

'There's lots to see in Sydney. Museums and such to go to. Great shops, too. You could go on trips.'

Carol rolled her eyes. 'No garden.'

'Well, of course there's no garden. It's on the sixth floor,' he snapped. 'I take it that's a no, then?'

'You don't listen to me, do you? What would I do with the children if I came out to Australia right now?'

'The children . . . It's always the children, isn't it? Children who aren't even ours. Send them to their uncle.'

'Their uncle can't have them. He hasn't room. They would have to go into care.'

'So?'

She couldn't bear the brutality expressed in that small word. 'I don't understand you any more,' she said softly. 'What would you have felt if it had been Matthew instead of Jessica and Dan who needed the care of an adult?'

'What?' He had heard, though, because he continued, 'We would never have left Matthew in the first place.'

'That maybe so, but Brian and Kimberley can't come back to their children and I can't let them go into care.'

'I don't want to talk about this any longer, Carol. If you feel you have to do this, then of course you must. You do understand, though, that you have to take the consequences.'

'What consequences, precisely, James?'

'That I'll be here for the next six weeks, of course.'

His reply had come almost immediately but all the same, he had back tracked. She was sure of it. Why was it that she was sure James had stopped himself from saying something quite different?

12

Two mornings later Carol, having coffee with Marion, finished telling her about James's latest exploits. 'He's e-mailed me the new address and told me a little more about the job,' she said, 'but I guess that's that, for six weeks.'

Marion shook her head. 'I can't get over James. After all these years, just taking off like that. Clive and I always thought you two were the ideal couple with the perfect marriage. Now, this. It seems so callous, so single-minded.' She looked at her friend candidly. 'Though when I come to think about it, James always did come across as single-minded.'

'I wish you wouldn't speak about him in the past tense,' said Carol crossly, before she could prevent herself.

'Sorry,' said Marion at once.

'It's not as though he's dead, you know.'

Marion reached across the table and stroked Carol's hand briefly. 'Of course he's not. I didn't mean to upset you.'

'I know. I over-reacted. I seem to be doing a lot of that at the moment. As for James.

Well, he always knew what it was he wanted. That's why he is a successful business man,' said Carol, defending her husband. 'But James was never callous.'

'Maybe being callous comes with being single-minded,' said Marion cautiously.

Yet it couldn't have been planned, Carol was thinking. Surely James would never have planned one, last, glorious holiday together before he left her? The notion had sprung into her mind from nowhere. She took hold of herself. It was certainly not a thing she wanted Marion to know anything about. 'I know what you're saying, but with us, with Matthew and me, James was always kind.'

Marion was playing with her coffee spoon. 'So you don't think there is any truth in what Peter suggested?' she asked, looking up. 'That your travels — the fact that you lived together on top of each other, so to speak — were such an intense experience that James felt he needed to put space between you for a time?'

Carol had told Marion all about Peter's notion as to the cause of James's behaviour. She had told her a lot about the children's uncle. She had still not said anything about their sleeping together, allowing her friend to assume that they had occupied separate rooms on the Saturday night. It was not hard, because she had not concealed her dislike of the man at their initial meeting. Carol was sure that the last thing Marion would imagine was what had actually occurred, even though Carol had already admitted that she might have been hasty in her first assessment of Peter.

'I don't know,' she replied helplessly. 'I go over and over this impasse in my mind. What if I did go out to Australia? I'd loathe being cooped up in an apartment, however splendid the view. Simply loathe it. And as for taking trips. I ask you? Do that, without James?'

'Do you think there is any possibility that he might want to go and live in Australia, Carol?'

'I don't know.' Bewildered, and not trying to conceal it, Carol shook her head. 'Six months ago I'd have laughed at the very idea. I mean, our roots are here. Matthew is here — well, Matthew has left home, but he is in this country. Our friends are here. Uproot and emigrate to Australia? Why would we want to do that?'

'I can see that you wouldn't want to. But James has always relished a challenge, hasn't he?'

'Are you talking male menopause here? It's a bit late for that, surely. Though . . . Oh, I don't know. What am I going to do, Marion?'

'Not a lot you can do, that is until James

has come to his senses.'

Both of them looked at each other, the unspoken, what if he doesn't come to his senses, ringing loud and clear. It was Marion who looked away first.

Still toying with her coffee spoon she said, 'You know, I am amazed how easily you've managed to take up this new life of yours. Living without James and coping with the children. Not to mention putting in all those hours with the CAB.'

'Not that many,' protested Carol.

Marion shrugged. 'Go for it, girl. If James is determined to stay away, you make sure you don't lose by his decision.'

* * *

That night Carol lay in bed thinking back over their conversation. In many ways Marion had been perceptive. Of course, Carol missed James — but it was for the little things, like opening jars and fixing light bulbs now, rather than the big decisions and the important organization of the household. Come to think of it, for some years it had been Carol rather than James who had paid most of the bills at Windrush and sorted out things like the servicing of the boiler and ordering wood for the winter.

Thinking back on it, she thought that state of affairs had come about when she had decided to do voluntary work. Carol had never wanted to be the type of woman who left everything to the man of the house. James had assumed those duties when they were first married but he had not seemed to mind when, eventually, it seemed more convenient for her to manage the household finances. She knew to a penny what was in their joint account.

Carol had her own, small account into which was paid the allowance James had insisted he should give her for clothes and so on. This was also the account into which she put the money she earned from the CAB. Similarly, James had his own personal one, but she had absolutely no idea what that contained. She was beginning to suspect that James had a great deal more money at his disposal than she had ever realized. At the back of her mind was a small worry about what would happen to her financially, should James decide he wanted to stay in Australia. She was even wondering if she would have to give up this new work with the CAB in order to find a job which brought in a salary until it was time for her pension. Peter was being very generous over the children, but she thought they really needed to talk seriously about budgets and contingency funds.

The children plainly thought she had taken leave of her senses, doing work without getting paid for it. Carol shrugged inwardly. They were young. They would learn. She wondered if Kennari had mentioned anything about the help the Burmese had in London — was any of that voluntary? She thought they might talk about that some other time.

* * *

'Have you written again to your parents?' Carol asked a few days later, while they were eating their evening meal. They had both sent short letters on blue airmail forms saying they were well and promising to write longer letters later.

Dan squirmed a bit in his seat before he answered: 'It's too difficult to know what to say.'

'You don't have to say much. Think of it as a kind of diary. Tell them a bit about what you have done each time you write. It's much more important to keep the lines of communication open than to say anything meaningful each time you write.'

Now why hadn't she thought of that before, Carol thought?

'You mean, I got up. I had my breakfast. I

251

went to school. Boring,' insisted Dan.

'Yes, it would be. But, I played football. I scored . . .'

'As if,' said Jessica.

Daniel hit her on the arm.

'Daniel . . . Anyway, something on those lines. Uncle Peter is coming to lunch on Sunday. You can tell them about that.'

It was early evening. The children were in their rooms (from which no sound emanated, Carol having won that particular battle). Carol was sitting listening to Grieg, a book in her hand. She was not reading it though and her thoughts were far from the world of Salley Vickers and her Venetian angels.

Peter Pickering . . . Carol had suppressed all wayward thoughts that had come into her mind about Peter Pickering since her return to Otterhaven. After mature reflection, she had decided to consider the events of that Saturday night as an aberration. What had happened between them would never have occurred if it had not been for the stress she was under, worrying until she was almost out of her mind about what Jessica and Dan might be doing — or having done to them. Of course it would never have happened because Peter and she would never have found themselves in that situation: of having to spend the night in the same room.

Did that make of her a creature of impulse, a woman who was incapable of disciplining her passions? For it had been passionate. Ruefully she cast her mind back to the sheer enjoyment she had found in making love with Peter. That he had experienced much the same satisfaction seemed only fair. What did that make of her?

Carol was convinced that it made absolutely no difference to what she felt about James, her husband. James need never find out about Peter. She was almost sure that Peter would never tell him so what he did not know would never hurt him. Would it bother her to hurt James? Now, that was a thought. There had been times, recently, when the thought of hurting James (in a small way) seemed quite delightfully satisfactory. On the other hand, Carol did not care to believe she was petty enough to want to punish James for his neglect of her. Perverse neglect, if she wanted to put a name to it for, if anyone were being harmed by the present circumstances — if you excluded the adult Pickerings — it was she. Not James, who was thoroughly enjoying himself on the other side of the world while . . .

Having worked herself up into a rage, Carol thumped the cushion against her back. Damn James. Damn all men who could see no further than their own comfort.

The doorbell sounded. Carol went to answer it. There, on the doorstep was Matthew.

'Hi, Ma,' he said breezily, bending down to kiss the top of her head. 'Going to let me in?'

'Matthew. What are you doing here?' she asked weakly. She stepped aside to allow her tall son to enter the hall — which immediately seemed even smaller than before.

'Thought I'd come to see how you're doing.'

'You said you had things to do, people to see.'

'You are pleased to see me?'

'Of course I am.' Carol reached up to take his head between her hands and pull him down to her kiss. Matthew put his arms round her and hugged her. 'How did you get here?' she asked, when she was finally able to disengage herself from her son's fierce embrace.

'I've bought myself a car,' her son replied. 'I've found an old Spitfire.'

'Goodness. Not red, I hope.'

'Green. There wasn't a red one I could afford the insurance on,' he grinned. 'I've left it in the street. Will that be all right?'

'I think we'd better put it in the garden.

There should be room. But when you've warmed up. You haven't driven all the way from Aberdeen in one go, I trust.'

''Course I did, Ma. It doesn't take all that long.'

'Not if you break the speed limit. Coffee,' she said, changing the subject. 'Or are you hungry?'

'Could you do me some soup and a sandwich? I'll have a beer, too. If you've got one.'

'Let's go and see, mm?' Carol led the way into the kitchen. 'So, what about your friends? Did you see them?'

'I saw everyone I needed to. They were busy,' he said noncommittally. He paused, then admitted reluctantly, 'Actually, if you really want to know, Rosa and I had a bust up.'

'Oh, dear.' Carol tried hard to feel regret. Her sympathies were totally engaged in the effect this had on her son. 'Is it serious?'

'If you mean, will I forgive her for being found in our bed with a man I thought was my friend? Yes. I find I'm not that bothered, but no, I'm not taking her back. That's it, with her. He's the one who really pisses me off.'

'Matthew, I'm sorry.'

'I'm not.' He grinned, only half convincingly. 'I was getting tired of her, if you must know, though even I didn't realize it until I found her in bed with Stephen. Anyway, let's not worry about Rosa any more. I want to know about you and Dad. And I want to meet these kids.'

'I thought you might.'

'What's that supposed to mean, Ma?'

'I suppose you've been speaking to your father.'

'As a matter of fact, I have. He's very upset, you know.'

Carol adjusted the heat under the tin of soup she had opened and poured into a saucepan, then she went to the pantry for some cheese before she felt ready to reply without her anger showing. 'It probably hasn't occurred to you, then, to realize that I am pretty upset myself.'

'Dad truly wants you to join him in Australia. He can't understand why you are putting these children before him. Especially as you had such a great time travelling before you met them. He said,' Matthew ended defensively.

'I guess I'm meant to appreciate your concern,' she said drily. 'Actually, this isn't any of your business, Matt. It's between James and me. But to start with, I can't imagine anything worse than frittering away my time in Sydney while your father gets involved with a new job. Not when I could be doing something useful here, like taking care of Jess and Dan. If neither James nor you can understand this, that's your problem, not mine.'

'But you and Dad have never been separated like this before. And he doesn't see why the children are more important to you than he is. He's really distressed, Ma. I think he might do something stupid, if you don't change your mind and join him.'

'What do you mean, do something stupid?'

'Like not come back. Ever.'

'That would, of course, be his choice. Pickle with your cheese?'

'Huh? Oh, pickle, fine. Just a bit more. Thanks.'

Carol put the top slices of bread on to the two heaps of cheese and pickle to make the sandwiches which she cut into two and placed on a plate. She went to the stove, tested the soup and poured it into a mug. Then she put the plate of sandwiches and the mug of soup on to a small tray.

'Did you find the beer? Good. Let's go into the sitting-room,' she suggested. 'There's a good fire and we won't be disturbed for a while because the children are upstairs doing their homework. Oh, it is good to see you, Matthew. I've really missed you.'

The small chore of feeding her son had given Carol time to collect her thoughts.

'What's really worrying you, Matt?' she asked, when they were both sitting down.

'What? Nothing. Just you and Dad, of course. I mean . . . '

'Your father hasn't mentioned divorce to you, has he?' As she said the word, Carol realized that this was exactly what she had been fearing all along, ever since James's call.

'Divorce! God, no, Ma. I mean . . . You couldn't let it come to that, could you? It-it . . . Well, you just couldn't.'

'Darling, it wouldn't be the end of the world, you know. It wouldn't affect you at all.'

'Of course it would, Ma. Our home would be broken up. That would be just awful.'

'Matthew. You haven't lived at home for many years now. If we'd still been at Windrush, I could understand your feelings about your home being broken up, as you call it, but this is only the second time you've been to Number Fourteen. You have made your home in Aberdeen, haven't you?'

Matthew grimaced. 'Before Rosa, I might have agreed. Now? My home is still with you. With you and Dad.'

Carol sighed. 'It's a bit of a Catch 22 situation, isn't it? But on the whole I'm inclined to let James do this job and then decide for himself whether he wants to come home to me, or not. Divorce is certainly not what I want. But living in Australia was definitely not one of our options when James took early retirement.'

'Neither was looking after two children while their parents are in a foreign gaol. How long could you be responsible for them?'

'Three years, unless Kimberley is released early.'

'No wonder Dad is miserable. Ma, don't you care about him at all?'

★ ★ ★

Jessica was writing to her mother. At least, she was trying to write a letter.

'Keep it simple,' Carol had said, 'and make it interesting.'

'Better not include too much personal stuff,' Jess had been advised by Rachel.

Jessica had confessed to her friend in a text message that she didn't know what to write to her mother and had rung Rachel back after she received the text message. 'You said that you have to copy it for the consul in Rangoon. It'll be read by the prison governor and all sorts, probably. You won't want them to read stuff.'

But stuff was really what Jessica wanted to write about.

Jessica also wanted to know what her mother had been thinking of when she agreed to go to Burma with her father, taking Dan and herself with them.

Dear Mum, she began. She crossed out Mum and wrote the more formal Mother with a heavy pencil stroke because she was feeling more than a little maddened by what her parents had done. It was all right. She had also been advised to write the letter in rough first, then copy it out neatly.

Dear Mother,

I hope you are well. You always asked after the other person's well-being. She wanted to ask, Do they question you? Do you answer them? WHAT CAN YOU ANSWER THEM? Do you get hurt when you can't answer them? That was a horrible thought.

Do you get enough to eat? There was a pain in her stomach when Jessica thought about her mother being hungry. She had been told that Uncle Peter had arranged for money to be available for food for both her parents. Kennari had warned her, though, that prisoners didn't always get the extra food that had been bought for them, or any of the other things they needed, like toiletries or medicines. Or letters. It depended on the goodwill of the prison guards. So that was why they had to send copies of any letters they wrote to their parents to the consul in Rangoon. She would then take them to the prison when she went to visit. Jess thought that must be a horrible part of the job, prison visiting.

Do you speak to the other prisoners? I suppose it's difficult because of the language. Jessica wondered idly if Kimberley had been able to learn any more Burmese than the few words she and her dad had learnt before they all went to Burma. Her mother would be very lonely if she couldn't speak to anyone.

Tears sprang to her eyes. It was really, really bad, thinking about her mother being hungry and miserable in the prison where she would be for three years. And she would be without Brian.

Jessica drew a stick woman on the margin of her paper. She drew a square round the stick woman and across the square she drew bars. Prison bars. It served her right, she thought spitefully. How could her mother do such a stupid thing as demonstrate in a country like Burma and get herself arrested and sent to prison and leave her children to be looked after by someone else?

Somehow, Jessica knew she was being illogical in directing all her anger towards her mother. After all, her father had been the instigator of the family's enterprise. (Did she actually know that? In truth, Jessica couldn't say for sure.)

It was different here. Look how they'd been able to demonstrate in London and the police had been good humoured about the whole thing. Jessica had got the impression that some of them would have liked to join in. At school, Mrs Meredith had talked to them about democracy. She had explained that only in a free society was it possible for people to demonstrate without being shot at by the police or the army acting on the orders of an autocratic government. Some of the other students had been concerned. Some of them had wanted to do something about it — Jess wasn't sure they really knew what they were talking about, but it had given her a good feeling that they were on her side.

Some of the students had been turned off by the whole thing.

She returned to her letter.

Me and Dan went to London to demonstrate outside the embassy. It was brilliant. We stayed the night with . . . Jessica's pencil hovered. Of course she couldn't say anything about their Burmese friends.

She began again. *Me and Dan went to London to demonstrate. We made banners and they were great. There were hundreds of people there and they were all supporting you and Dad.* Jessica didn't think the exaggeration mattered. There had been lots there, and they had all been very sympathetic.

Carol was OK about it though we hadn't asked permission first. We got a bit of aggro, then it was all right. I think if we'd asked her, she'd have let us go to the demo.

Now she says we should write to you regularly. Uncle Peter is going to apply for a visa. If he gets it he will come and see you.

That might cheer her mother up, Jessica thought.

I hope you get this letter.

I am well and so is Dan. We go to the local school. Dad was right. The lessons are crap but Dan likes it there.

I'll write again soon.

Love from Jessica.

She read it through then she reached for the pad of airmail paper which Carol had given her for her letters.

* * *

Carol had not answered Matthew when he asked her if she no longer cared about James. She had just looked at him and Matthew, sensing that he had crossed a barrier, reddened then turned away.

In truth, Carol could not have answered her son. Not with any conviction, that is. Of course she still cared for James. Too much had happened between them for it to be otherwise. Too much water under the bridge, to coin a phrase, for her not to remember the small things that had made her so happy for so long. The way he stroked her hair before he kissed her, the way they caught each other's eyes when they were in company and someone was being particularly pompous. Then there was the fact of Matthew's existence. But it was James who had taken what she considered an arbitrary decision: to alter their plans in a way that was totally unreasonable. She still cared for James, but she could not hide her exasperation at his current behaviour.

As if they sensed that all was not quite right between Carol and her son, Dan and Jessica moved warily round him. Matthew himself, abashed by his outburst to his mother, at first insisted that Daniel should keep his room and that he would sleep in the study, but the floor space available for the camping mat and sleeping bag (which Matthew had had the presence of mind to put into the boot of his car) was not sufficient for Matthew's height. In the end it was decided that Dan should sleep on the floor and Matthew would use the single bed in that room.

'If I take away some of those boxes, there'd be room for another single bed to be put up,' said Matthew the next morning, earning a look of gratitude from his mother. 'Then it could be used by anyone else who comes to visit.'

'What will you do with the boxes?' Carol asked.

'There's not a lot in one or two of them. Some of my old sporting gear needs chucking and I've folders from school going back to the year dot which I'll never look at again. I guess a box of books could go in the attic.'

'Leave the books,' said Dan. 'That is, if you don't mind if I go through them? You've got some sporting annuals, haven't you?'

'That's right. OK. That's fine by me, then. Let's go and have a look at what I've got. You can help me do some sorting.' The two of them ambled off.

'Does Matthew come to visit often?' asked Jessica. She was a little overwhelmed by Matthew. His good looks, and height, were not what she'd expected in Carol and James's son. Not that Jessica considered herself an expert in young men. Certainly not one of the age of Matthew.

'Not now he's working,' said Carol. 'When

he comes off the oil rig he usually has a lot of catching up to do.'

'He probably wanted to look us over,' said Jessica shrewdly.

'Possibly,' admitted Carol, after a pause. The two looked at each other and grinned.

'If we behave over the weekend, do you think he'll give us a good report to James?' the girl asked naïvely.

'I expect so. Why, is it important?'

'Not to me,' Jessica shrugged. 'It might persuade James to come home and that'd be great for you.'

'Yes, it would,' said Carol. 'But I wouldn't let it bother you. James and I are old enough to sort out our own problems, you know.'

'There wouldn't be a problem, if Mum and Dad hadn't got arrested,' she said aggressively.

'Maybe not, but I don't want you getting upset about something you can't change.'

'If we weren't here, you'd go to Australia, wouldn't you, to be with James?'

'Did you hear what Matthew and I were saying last evening?'

'No. The door was closed,' Jessica pointed out. 'But it stands to reason that's why Matthew is here.'

Carol sighed, unable to refute the logic. 'Jess, I honestly don't know what James and I would be doing if you weren't here. Just promise me you won't let it bother you.'

'Whatever. Can I go into the village? I've written to Mum and I'd better post it.'

'Of course you can. Have you got money to buy a stamp?'

'I've still got some of the money Uncle Peter gave me the other day.'

'That's all right, then. Um . . . Jess, did you write to your dad as well as your mum?'

'Sort of.' There was a pause. Jess said reluctantly, 'It was difficult, writing to Dad.'

'Was it?'

'I didn't really know what to say. In the end I just copied out most of what I'd written to Mum.'

'I think that was a very good idea. I'm sure he'll be pleased to receive a letter from you, anyway. What about Dan? Has he finished his letters yet?'

'Dan wrote reams to Dad. Idiot. It took him ages to copy out for the consul. He only wrote half a page to Mum.' Most of Dan's half-page to his mother consisted of XXXs. Jess thought she wouldn't tell Carol that.

'Did he mention Splodge?' Carol asked curiously.

'He said he'd tell them about Splodge in his next letter.'

'Good thinking. It'll give him something to write about. Don't be late for lunch.'

13

After she had posted her sheaf of letters, Jessica wandered through the village. She bought some shampoo and, on impulse, a bar of Dan's favourite chocolate. Then she went into the little second-hand bookshop.

'Hello,' Philip Gerard, the proprietor, greeted her. 'May I help you, or are you coming to browse?'

'Browsing, then buying,' said Jessica gravely.

'Good. Let me know if you want any help.'

There were so many books: thick ones, thin ones, tall ones, small ones, paperbacks, hardbacks. Jessica hardly knew where to start. She took books off the shelves randomly, stroked them, opened them and ruffled the pages. She read a few lines and put them back. After a while, Philip Gerard wandered over to where she was standing, propped up against one of the tall bookcases.

'Do you have a big collection?' he asked casually.

'I did have quite a few. I had to get rid of half of them when we sold our house,' said Jessica ruefully. 'My uncle says he'll pay for me to have one book a month. I don't know where to start.'

'You must be Peter Pickering's niece. Janet, is it?'

'Jessica.'

'Hello, Jessica. I'm Philip Gerard. Did you know you have an account here?'

'Do I?'

'You and your brother certainly do. Daniel came in yesterday.'

'That doesn't sound like Dan.'

'He bought an atlas. He said he wanted to know exactly where Rangoon is and he wanted to trace the route you'd taken with your parents. I'm sorry your family is in a spot of bother. It mustn't be much fun for either of you.'

'Nor Mum and Dad.'

'Especially not them. Did you sell your books before you went to Burma?'

'Dad said they had to go to a charity shop.'

'The worst thing about deciding which book to get rid of is that about six weeks later you find out it's just the one you need to read,' said Philip. 'There is probably a law governing that, but I can't remember its name off hand.' He was thinking that if the children had sold their books instead of giving them away they'd probably have a few more pounds now to use to build up their library. Typical of the father, judging by what he'd read. Very much the single-issue fanatic.

'Read any North-American classical children's authors? L.M. Montgomery, Laura Ingalls Wilder? I've a nice copy of *Little Women* here.'

'I've seen the film,' said Jessica incautiously.

'Ah. Not quite the same thing,' said Philip, with a little laugh. 'You could try *Anne of Green Gables* for a start.'

'Whatever,' said Jessica. 'Actually, I'm more into romance,' she added shyly.

'You mean paperbacks? I only have a small collection of those.'

'I was thinking of something by Thomas Hardy.'

'Were you now? I've a copy of *The Woodlanders*. You could try that. Not too keen on Hardy myself. My partner says *Vanity Fair* is the best romance ever written.'

'Better than Jane Austen?'

'Why don't you decide for yourself. Here, take *Sense and Sensibility* as well,' he said, handing both books to the girl. 'I'll make it right with your uncle.'

'Um, if it's second-hand, can I sell it back to you, if I don't like it?'

'Cheeky girl. Well, let's decide on that, if you honestly don't get on with it. And next time I'll see if I can find you a Jacqueline Wilson suitable for a teenager.' Philip Gerard was thinking that a little light-relief wouldn't come amiss in Jessica's life, if all he had heard was true.

Jessica was about to tell him that her mum didn't approve of teenage books. Then she thought, well, if a bookseller was willing to recommend a book, neither Uncle Peter nor her mum could say too much, could they?

★　★　★

As arranged, Peter Pickering came for Sunday lunch. Carol was cooking Welsh lamb with a gooseberry sauce, new potatoes, spring greens and peas. Jessica had already prepared a spicy lentil casserole with lots of vegetables (which would reheat for another meal) and this was simmering gently on top of the stove. Carol had decided that Daniel should not be left out of the kitchen activities, and he was cutting up fresh fruit for a salad to go with meringues and crème fraîche. The meringues were shop bought, because Carol said hers stuck to the baking tray now she had no Aga.

'I'm very impressed,' said Peter, poking his head through the door. 'May I leave the wine in here?' he added, brandishing a bottle of red and one of white.

271

'There's space over there for the red,' said Jess. 'Mum usually puts white wine in the fridge.'

'Very wise,' said her uncle gravely.

'I guess you'll want to open both bottles. The corkscrew is over there. Have you met Matthew yet?'

'He opened the door for me. A very pleasant chap, I thought.'

'He's all right,' answered Jess, shrugging. 'I'd better set the table.'

Whatever else Carol was doing for the children, their parents couldn't fault her on her ability to encourage them to co-operate in family life. Maybe that had been a part of their upbringing for which his half-brother had been responsible, or even their mother. He'd found Brian difficult ever since his half-brother had left university and he'd never understood Kimberley. His own fault? If it were, it was certainly something he would have to rectify.

Peter poured wine for the three adults. He raised his eyebrows at Carol, then poured half a glass of red wine for his niece.

'Add some water if the taste is too strong. I've always held the view that a little wine drunk sociably by teenagers prevents abuse when they can drink legally.'

'Thanks, Uncle Peter,' said Jessica, gratified. This time it did not even occur to her to mention that her parents were of the opposite opinion, her father being, in any case, a beer drinker.

They sat down at the kitchen table. It was a lacquered stripped pine so Carol did not use a cloth, but she had put out her good Wedgwood china and told Jessica to use the silver cutlery. The table was oval-shaped. Matthew automatically took the seat at the head of the table and picked up the carving knife. Carol was not sure whether to be more amused or gratified by this assumption of precedence but took the seat beside him, indicating that Jess should sit next to Matthew with Peter opposite her.

Over lunch, Peter told them that his application for a visa to visit Burma had been granted.

'Already? I was sure the Junta would make difficulties,' said Carol.

'Not only that, I am assured that I will be able to see both Brian and Kimberley in prison. I get the feeling that the presence of the children at the demonstration in London wrong-footed the authorities who now feel that they have to permit me to visit. I expect there will be problems when I actually arrive in Rangoon, but at least it's a start.'

'When are you going, Uncle Peter?'

'At the end of the week, Dan.'

'Can I come, too. Please.'

'We've been through this before, old chap. Just not possible.'

'I tell you what we might do while Peter is away,' said Carol brightly. 'You still have some means of contacting Kennari, haven't you, Jess?' When the girl nodded, Carol continued, 'Perhaps we could all go to London and see her. You could get her to tell you a little more about Burma, what sort of a country it is, and so on.'

'We did see quite a bit of Burma when we were there,' pointed out Dan. He intercepted a glare from his sister and added hastily, 'Still, it's a brill idea.'

'Do you really want to get involved?' asked Matthew frostily. 'I mean, I'd have thought keeping a low profile was more sensible, Mother. You don't want to appear in public any more than is essential, do you? I mean, you could run the risk of antagonizing the Burmese to the extent that Peter could have trouble over there. Don't you agree Peter?'

Involuntarily Carol's eyes met Peter's. (Just so had she been accustomed to making a mental connection with her husband.) In Peter's eyes she caught a flash of the amused tolerance of an alpha male. He clearly

274

interpreted her son's comment as full of the bristling jealousy Carol herself saw. But knowing that the jealousy was justified only served to make her more annoyed at Matthew's antics. Carol could cheerfully have strangled her son. Why, oh why was it that two of the important men in her life were being so — bloody — awkward?

Two of the important men in her life? That statement presupposed that there was a third. Peter?

Peter read consternation in Carol's eyes. He was not yet sufficiently adept at interpreting her emotions to appreciate why this was. He assumed that she was embarrassed for her son. He did not understand that her mind had made an emotional leap and thereby given a significance to her association with him which she would need to consider afterwards.

★   ★   ★

Matthew declared that he would not stay for tea.

'Such a short visit!' exclaimed his mother. 'I thought you were not planning to return to Aberdeen for a couple of days.'

Matthew shrugged. 'I see you have plenty to occupy you and I'd like to call on Jon on

275

my way north. I guess I'll come and see you next time round. Dad might be home by then.'

'Indeed he might. I'll get another bed, too, now that you've cleared all that space. Then you'll be more comfortable.'

Matthew mumbled something which Carol deliberately ignored. She thought it probable that her son was insisting that he would not be comfortable until his father were re-installed in his proper place in his house. It crossed her mind to tell him that he should grow up. Then she concluded that preserving the peace was a mother's job, after all, and that nothing would be served by quarrelling with Matthew.

'It's been great to see you,' she emphasised. 'Thank you for coming. You know I always have found telephone calls unsatisfactory. Though a lot better than e-mails,' she added hastily. 'I can never get the nuances right in those.'

'With Dad, too?'

'Leave it, Matt.'

When he left, though, she put her arms round him to hug him. 'Take care. I do want all that is best for you, you know.'

'I know, Ma. Just, you know, think about Dad a bit more.'

'I do. Every day. I only wish . . . Oh, never mind. Just come and see me again, soon.'

Peter, who was staying for tea, suggested that he and Carol should go for a walk by the river.

'You don't want us to come, do you, Uncle Peter?' asked Dan, recoiling at the very idea.

'Not at all,' came the robust reply. 'Carol and I have things to discuss.'

'Do we?' asked Carol, not sure that she altogether liked the sound of that.

'Financial things,' said Peter firmly. 'I need to know that everything will be all right while I'm away.'

'Won't you need jabs?' asked Jessica. 'We were pin cushions before we went.'

'Actually I'm pretty much up to date. I've already started taking the malaria pills, though I do wonder whether they're strictly necessary in Rangoon, but I suppose you never know about conditions in the prison.'

There was a pause while Peter cursed himself for his lack of tact.

'I expect the consul has organized things for your mum and dad,' said Carol gently, not being in the least sure of any such thing. Something else she ought to remind Peter to do, she thought, making sure both Brian and Kimberley had the medicines they needed.

They walked along the river bank for a

while in silence, neither seeming able to begin a conversation. Someone had installed a wooden seat at a bend in the river which gave a long view upstream. With tacit agreement, they sat down on it.

It was the first time since that night in the travel lodge that they had been alone. The realization had plainly come to both of them at the same time and the silence was fraught.

'I'm sorry about Matthew,' Carol said.

'I'm sorry I caused you embarrassment at lunch.'

Both spoke together. There followed an uncomfortable pause.

'Matthew was unpardonable.'

'Your son had every right to question my presence.'

Again both spoke together.

Carol went on immediately, 'Matthew has no right to dictate who should, or should not receive my hospitality.'

'Does that include the man you took to your bed?'

They had come, inevitably to the crux of the matter.

'I thought we agreed we weren't going to mention that again. I thought we agreed it was just something that had happened, but which wasn't going to be repeated.'

'Did we, Carol? I don't exactly remember

using those words.' Peter took hold of her hand which lay on the seat between them.

She made a feeble attempt to pull away. Then her hand went limp in his. 'Well, neither do I, I suppose. Not in so many words,' she said reluctantly. 'But it was a one-off, wasn't it? I mean, it's not going to happen again. Of course it's not going to happen again. We shouldn't even be speaking about it now . . . '

'You mean we should ignore the fact that we spent a most enjoyable night together.'

'Peter . . . ' Carol protested, her whole body, becoming uncomfortably hot. She pulled her hand away, succeeding this time. Then she inched away from him until she was pressed against the armrest.

'It was a delightful occurrence, Carol. One I'm not going to forget, even if you would prefer to pretend it didn't happen.'

'That's not the point,' she said weakly. 'I'm not saying that . . . What I mean to say is, it shouldn't . . . No, I mean, it has to be embarrassing, with the children involved. It would be so much better if . . . '

'I think you're becoming a tad confused. For instance, the children have absolutely nothing to do with this.'

'Of course they have.'

'Only because we met through them. That

means I have a lot to thank them for,' he said gravely.

The seat was not large. Surreptitiously Peter had closed what space there was between them so that now his long legs were pressed against hers. Carol's hands were on her lap. As she was speaking, she was now moving them constantly, betraying her agitation, though her body remained quite rigid. Her face was turned resolutely away from him.

Peter reached across and took her hand again.

Carol sighed heavily, allowing her hand to rest in his once more. 'I have been confused since the moment James told me he wasn't coming home with me,' she confessed.

'You think I took advantage of you?'

'Yes. No. Of course you didn't take advantage of me. Not at my age. At the time I needed that physical closeness.'

'You needed James,' he said frankly.

Again there was silence between them. Carol removed her hand, took out her hanky and blew her nose. Put like that, it sounded so cold-blooded, so callous. Callous was what Marion had called James. Carol thought that it went with the territory, the state into which their relationship had deteriorated, a mentality that preferred cruelty to kindness.

'Got a cold?'

'I think it's the pollen.'

'Do you want to go back.'

'Not yet.'

'Ah. What are we going to do? May I kiss you?'

The request came abruptly. Startled, Carol turned to face Peter. He took her change of position to mean consent, and kissed her. He kissed her very thoroughly.

'Oh, dear,' said Carol afterwards.

'You didn't like that?'

'Unfortunately, I did. But,' she added hastily, 'you mustn't do it again, you know. It isn't fair.'

'I suppose not,' he agreed meekly.

His tone was far too meek, Carol was thinking. She said severely, 'Don't laugh at me!'

'My dear, I wouldn't dream of doing that.'

'You shouldn't call me your dear.'

'Would love do?'

Carol recoiled. 'Stop it, Peter. Stop making this into a kind of joke. It isn't fair.'

'Carol, I assure you that I have never been more serious in my life. I know I sounded curmudgeonly when we spoke over the phone that first time. If you knew the state of affairs between Brian and me you . . . Well, that isn't important. But, you see, I had told him, impressed on him that what he intended to do was both dangerous and totally immoral, if it involved his children. I told him I washed my hands of them all, if he did anything stupid. And then social services, or whatever they call themselves nowadays, rang me. You phoned. If I hadn't . . . I go cold when I think that if I had done as I swore I would and had nothing to do with Jess and Dan I'd never have met you.'

It was an impassioned speech. Carol felt totally incapable of replying in any way at all. She sat very still.

'You know that I've never married?'

'The children said you were a bachelor.' It emerged as a croak. She cleared her voice and began again. 'The children said . . . '

'What the children don't know is that I lived with a woman for a number of years. She was divorced but refused to marry me.'

'Lived . . . '

'Chris died of breast cancer five years ago.' It emerged coldly, without emotion.

'How sad.' Her comment was banal. All the same, Carol was aware how much it had cost Peter to utter those words. She wanted to take him in her arms to console him. She would have done if two walkers had not been coming towards them.

'It was sad. It was dreadful. That was when I moved into the flat above the bookshop. Before that we'd . . . Well, Chris had a small house on the outskirts of Hay where we lived once she and her husband had parted.'

'Did she have any children?'

'Her husband couldn't have them and refused to adopt. That was part of the reason they separated.'

Carol wanted to ask why Peter and Chris hadn't had a family. It seemed too intrusive.

'You don't ask the obvious. The answer is that almost as soon as we decided the time had come to start our family her cancer was diagnosed. She was dead within five months.'

'Appalling.' Carol squeezed his hand. 'I never intended that Matthew should be an only child. That just happened. James completely refused to consider adoption, too. Is that a male thing, not to adopt?' Was that why James was so adamantly opposed to Jess and Dan now, she asked herself? 'But at least I have Matthew.'

'And Brian and Kimberley have Jessica and Daniel. I suppose it's because the only opportunity I had to have children of my own was taken away that I feel so strongly about their irresponsibility.'

'There wasn't anyone else? Sorry. That's none of my business.'

'There hasn't been anyone else. Until you,' he said softly.

'Setting aside the fact that I'm past child-bearing age,' Carol said, equally softly, 'I am married to another man.'

'You omitted the vital word, happily.'

'Don't, Peter. Please. It's dangerous, foolish, too soon . . . Anything you like to call it,' she added emphatically. 'You wanted to talk about money? That's what you said we were coming for a walk to do.'

Peter sighed. 'Fair enough. I really don't want to press you too hard. I just need to know that you understand me. I think you should be aware that I am an opportunist. You know, a man who sees the half-full glass as the means of quenching his thirst.'

Carol gurgled. 'How refreshing. I think that for the past few years I've been more of a pessimist.'

'Then you must make a big effort to understand that it was no one-night stand. Very far from it. If your James doesn't come home soon to claim you, he . . . '

'He what, Peter?'

'No. As you say, it's too soon. Now, to financial matters. I need to know you all have enough. Until I return, that is. You see, I have no idea when I'll return.'

'You are not anticipating trouble, are you?'

'I'm glad to know you are concerned. Sorry, sorry,' he said, raising his free hand in mock surrender. 'Totally out of order.'

Carol saw the smile that lurked at the corners of his mouth and suppressed one of her own. 'Of course I'm concerned. We all are. Do you anticipate trouble?'

'No. Only delays. I think the suggestion that you visit Kennari is very apt. A little campaigning on behalf of Brian and Kimberley while I'm in Burma won't come amiss.'

They discussed practicalities for a bit: what he would tell Brian and Kimberley about the children's welfare and how Carol was coping.

'Don't mention Splodge. I have a feeling pets are a no-no. Besides, Splodge's welfare is one thing Dan feels he can write about. What are you taking out for them?'

'I've discussed that with the consul. She advised a few books which they have asked for and which aren't available in Rangoon. Medicines, of course, in case they've gone astray, and a few personal things for Kimberley.'

'Do you need help with those?' Carol asked delicately.

'I think I can manage. But, thanks, anyway.'

They discussed an account which Peter had set up in Carol's name. She objected, but reason suggested that it might be wise to accept his offer.

'I insist. Generosity with your time is one thing. It is not right that you should be out of pocket.'

Then they agreed it was time for tea. Peter's helping hand as Carol rose from the seat was far from impersonal. Nor did she seem to mind, he noticed, and they walked side by side back along the way they had come.

'You are a compassionate woman,' he said, as they reached the gate to Number Fourteen. 'I like that. It's one of the many things I like about you. And I'm sure you understand that when I get back I am going to have to return to what we were talking about before. You see, the idea of finding a woman I can care for again is so fantastic that I need you to know that I won't be able to let you go, just like that. Whether the questions with James have been resolved, or not, you and I will talk about how we feel when I come home. I just hope that by then you will feel the same way as I do.'

* * *

A wet May turned into a hot June. There were hose-pipe bans; then a wet Wimbledon.

Everyday life in Otterhaven became, if not humdrum, at least mundane.

There were daily e-mails from Peter, recounting the delays in Rangoon he had warned them about, while he waited for the evasive authorities to make good the final arrangements for him to visit Brian and Kimberley in prison. The members of the consulate were as helpful as they could be, but they were as powerless as Peter was when it came to exerting real influence. Yet, despite the trauma of the situation, he was an interesting correspondent and managed to allay the fears the children continued to harbour that something even more terrible than imprisonment had happened to their parents.

There were also occasional messages from James, who was plainly relishing his return to full-time work; who continued to express his admiration of the Australian way of life and spoke of a reunion with his wife hardly at all.

Jessica and Daniel survived end-of-term exams and began to talk about what they would do at school in September (to Carol's relief, for she feared that they would be urging her to send them elsewhere). They also began making arrangements for their visit to their new Burmese friends.

Kennari had sent them a short list of books

about Burma which she suggested they might like to read. Philip Gerard obtained these for the children — and refused to count them as their part of their monthly selection paid for by their uncle. The Burmese girl, they learnt, was a Shan, a member of a tribal group which had been dispersed decades previously and which was now present in the nations which bordered Burma, Laos, Thailand and even northern Vietnam, as well as Burma itself. The children were looking forward to their visit which was to be over a weekend.

Carol herself was not going to accompany them after all. She had decided that Jessica was responsible enough to look after her brother on the train journey and that they would feel less inhibited if she were not there.

'Are you really sure about this?' Marion Henderson asked dubiously. 'You know what they got up to last time.'

'But this time they have my permission to be there. I'm quite sure they will be looked after properly and they do deserve a little fun, poor dears. If you can call spending the weekend talking about their imprisoned parents fun,' she added.

'So what will you do while they are away?'

'Stay at home and cultivate my garden.'

'There's a John Lill concert we could go to.' Marion mentioned a nearby venue.

'Excellent. Will you get the tickets? Assuming the weather stays fine, I'll arrange a picnic for us to have first.'

The weather continued warm and dry. The smoked salmon and chilled white wine by the river were delectable, the concert both soothing and uplifting. The two friends met several acquaintances with whom they spent the interval. No one mentioned Burma or demonstrations, or errant husbands.

Marion, who was driving, dropped Carol back at home soon after 10.30 that evening.

'Thanks,' said Carol. 'That was just what I needed. I'll ring in the morning. Perhaps we could do something like that again, soon?'

As she entered the house, Carol sensed there was something wrong. Not wrong, precisely, but the house seemed different and not as she had left it. The hall light was still on, however, as was the lamp she had left lit in the sitting-room which could be seen from the front gate.

Cautiously she put down her handbag and without making a sound she took one of the walking sticks from a pottery urn which was kept by the front door for sticks and umbrellas. Then, very carefully, she opened the sitting-room door and stepped across the threshold.

14

Carol was greeted by a loud snort as James, deep asleep on the sofa, turned on to his back. She knew at once it was her husband, the sound of that exhalation, part grunt, part snore was unmistakable.

'James! What the hell are you doing here!' Carol, her heart thudding from the tension she had been under, dropped the walking stick and, arms akimbo, went to stand in front of her husband.

There was another snort as James was rudely awakened.

'Hi, Carol,' he said, and sat up and yawned, passing his hand across his face to wake himself properly. 'Where've you been?'

'I've been to a concert with Marion,' she answered shortly.

'I expected to find you at home.'

'Well, I wasn't,' she snapped. He probably hadn't intended it to sound as though he were criticising her, she conceded at once. Then, neither of them was being particularly welcoming. She bent down and picked up the stick.

'What on earth are you doing with that?' he

290

asked. 'Since when have you needed a walking stick in the house?'

'Since I thought there was a burglar in the sitting-room,' she replied tartly. 'James, you are a total fool. You frightened me half to death. Why on earth didn't you ring to tell me you were coming home? I should have stayed to welcome you, if I'd known.'

'I thought I'd surprise you,' he said sheepishly.

'You certainly did that. Have you eaten?' she enquired, the housewife's standard reaction to an unexpected visitor rescuing her from the irritation it was hard to conceal. *Visitor?*

'I could do with a sandwich, now you ask,' he replied. 'And a drink. It's a long journey from Heathrow.'

'I've got some sliced ham. Will that do? Oh, and you can pour me a white wine from the bottle in the fridge while you're at it.'

Carol was placing the ham on to buttered bread before it occurred to her that they had not yet embraced, nor even touched each other, which was interesting. She was uncertain how significant it was, but it certainly felt as though she was entertaining a mere visitor rather than her husband whom she had not seen for some time.

Sitting down across the room from her

291

husband who was now demolishing the plate of ham and mustard sandwiches, Carol regarded him closely. 'You look well,' she said. James did look well, if a little tired, though that was understandable, given the length of his journey and the time difference between Australia and the UK. He was tanned and she thought he had lost a little weight — not that he had ever carried more than a few surplus pounds occasionally.

'I am well. Got a lot to tell you, too.' He yawned again. 'But maybe not tonight. I guess I'll get a few hours sleep in before the jet-lag hits at around five. I think I'll take a bath first, though. Chuck all the clothes in the basket, huh? It's all washable.'

Carol removed the glasses and plates thoughtfully. She supposed there was no question but that they would share the double bed.

★ ★ ★

Carol woke to the smell of frying bacon. Bacon? She shot out of bed wondering what on earth was going on in her kitchen. Then she subsided weakly on to the edge of the bed. James had returned. Her mind went blank. She remained where she was for several minutes, an inadequate feeling of not knowing quite what to do next creeping over her. In the end she did the obvious: first going to the bathroom, then dressing. After that she went downstairs.

James was making toast. The frying pan was still on the hob, his empty plate in the middle of the table. Butter and honey stood next to his place. Also on the hob was the large cafetière which was less than half-full and by it was a jug of hot milk. Carol was impressed. She had never known James be so competent at breakfast time.

'A cooked breakfast,' she remarked. 'That's new.'

'I was starving.'

'Where did you get the ingredients?' Carol asked, peering at the mushrooms, two sausages, a single rasher of bacon and one slice of black pudding that lay uncooked on the work surface. 'I thought I'd only got eggs and mushrooms in the fridge. I was going to do a large supermarket shop today.'

'That's right. I went to the local one, of course. I've been up since five thirty. Couldn't wait any longer for something to eat so I got to the shop just as it was opening.'

'D'you want that rasher?'

'Not if you do, but you could cook me another sausage and the rest of the mushrooms. Shall I put some bread in the toaster for you?'

'Yes, please. I suppose you're going to finish the coffee?' When James nodded emphatically, she reached for the small pot she had taken to using herself. The children preferred orange juice for breakfast.

James munched steadily through the extra sausage and mushrooms, another piece of toast and honey and then he finished the coffee. Carol carefully removed the thin strip of fat on the bacon and ate it with dry toast. When she had finished the bacon (which was surprisingly good) she spread the remainder of her one slice of toast with a little butter and marmalade. James eventually sat back with a sigh of repletion.

'Do you always eat so well at breakfast nowadays?' she asked, coffee mug in hand.

'No. I have the usual cereal and toast. This is probably my dinner, if you think of the jet-lag.'

'Ah. Why have you come home, James?'

As she spoke, Carol went cold with a mixture of chagrin and apprehension. That was definitely not what she had intended to say.

'No, 'It's good to see you, dear', then,' he commented drily.

'Of course it's good to see you,' she cried,

still flustered, wondering if . . . 'It's just so unexpected.'

'I have things to tell you, things to organize,' he admitted then. 'I didn't think it was such a good idea to mention them on the phone — or try to e-mail you. You don't always answer my e-mails,' he added, his tone reproachful.

'I most certainly do,' protested his wife. 'Every one of them.'

James shrugged. He got up and removed his dirty plate to the dishwasher. Then he picked up the frying pan and began to wash it in the sink. Carol thought that was also a first.

'Where are the children?' he asked casually, once he had put the frying pan and the spatula on to the draining board.

'They've gone to London for the weekend.'

He sighed. 'I didn't think you'd managed to palm them off on to their uncle. Though when I couldn't see anything belonging to them in the bathroom, I did wonder. I hope you noticed that I used the other bathroom in case I disturbed you?'

'Thanks for that,' she acknowledged the courtesy. 'I took their towels to wash. Obviously they've taken the rest.'

'Obviously.'

'James, I did tell you that Peter has gone to

Rangoon to see Brian and Kimberley. I mentioned it in an e-mail a couple of weeks ago.'

'Did you? I forgot.'

There was a pause. Carol got up determinedly and went to the door, saying, 'I'll go and make the bed.'

'Do we get the Sunday papers delivered now? They hadn't arrived when I went to the shop.'

'I cancelled them. Far too much to get through in one day. Yesterday's papers are in the sitting-room, if you want to read those.'

'I've done that already. Look, Carol. I do want to talk. Don't be too long upstairs. Please.'

★ ★ ★

While she was still upstairs — clearing up and tidying the bathroom, (James hadn't changed that much), it occurred to her that she was delaying the moment. The telephone rang, interrupting her train of thought.

'I'll get that,' she called.

It was Peter. He was ringing from Rangoon. He'd no idea what the time was, he told her, and apologized for disturbing her.

'It's not a problem,' said Carol.

He told her that, amazingly, the Burmese

authorities had decided to release Kimberley immediately. They'd no idea why.

'It could have something to do with the children, PR and all that,' offered Carol. It was difficult to take in: Kimberley was to be freed. Though it hadn't happened yet.

'It hasn't happened, yet,' she said aloud.

Peter agreed. He was going to remain in Rangoon until Kimberley was out of prison, he said then. 'We'll fly home together.'

'What about Brian?' Carol asked, already knowing the answer.

Brian was to complete his sentence. There did not appear to be the slightest chance that he would be freed early.

★ ★ ★

'That was a long call,' said James, when Carol finally went downstairs. 'Marion, was it? You two always did take an age to say the simplest of things. Now, come and sit down. I want us to talk.'

Carol sat down, because once again she felt weak at the knees. 'That was Peter Pickering on the phone,' she said. 'Calling from Rangoon,' she added unnecessarily.

'You seemed to have a lot to say to each other.'

'It was what he said to me that was important.'

James raised an eyebrow and sighed, almost audibly. Carol, however, could see that he was about to erupt, so she said hastily:

'Kimberley Pickering is to be released immediately. Peter says they will fly home together. Oh, God. The children. I have to ring the children. They can't possibly know, yet. Now, where did I put that number?' She went through to the study and began hunting feverishly among papers on the desk.

This time James's sigh of frustration was meant to be heard. After a moment he got up and went through to the study himself.

'You usually put new numbers in your book,' he pointed out, mildly enough. 'Don't tell me you have broken the habit of a lifetime.'

'Of course I haven't,' said Carol impatiently, having come to the same conclusion only seconds before. 'James, I know you want to talk, but I really have to call the children first.'

Without waiting for any reaction, she punched in the number. It took time for anyone to answer, and when they did, there was a language problem. Carol concentrated on the one name she knew. 'Kennari. Kay-nuhr-ree,' she repeated. 'Jessica. Dan,' she added, urgently.

Eventually Jessica came to the phone.

'Carol? This is, like, the middle of the night?'

Carol related what Peter had only just told her. 'You might find something about it on the Net — if Kennari has means of getting it,' she said. 'I'm sure it must be true or Peter wouldn't have phoned. I mean, he wouldn't want to raise your hopes if there was the smallest suspicion that it wasn't actually going to happen. That they are going to let your mum go free. Jessica? Jess, are you still there?'

'Oh — my — God,' the girl said. There was a pause. 'Gotta go, Carol. Gotta tell Kennari and the others. Um — look, if it is true, can we stay in London for just one more day? Please?'

'You must ask only if you are sure you won't be a nuisance. And I definitely want to speak to Kennari before it is agreed. Understood?'

'Whatever.'

But this time, sullenness had been replaced by a note of positive optimism. Carol, herself, was smiling as she put down the receiver and went back into the sitting-room.

'My goodness,' she said. 'I still can't believe it.'

Remembering his own brush with the Burmese authorities, James nodded reflectively. 'I heard what you were saying. I'm sure you're right, though. No one in Rangoon would have encouraged the uncle to contact you unless they were pretty sure Kimberley is going to be freed. God, she's a lucky woman. I thought they'd both be in prison for the duration. I wonder if you are also right, that the good PR the Junta'll get from freeing Kimberley to return to her children is at the bottom of it all?'

'Well, it doesn't matter, so long as she comes home. Wow!' she exclaimed softly. 'I feel totally exhausted all of a sudden, as if I'd climbed a mountain.'

'Reaction. You'll feel better in a bit' He got up. 'Returning to what I was saying about breakfast actually being my dinner, and you being in need of a restorative, I'm having a brandy. You?'

'At this hour?'

'A medicinal brandy.'

She knew James had come home for a particular reason. She was beginning to have the glimmer of an idea as to what, exactly, that reason was. (More than a glimmer, if truth be known.) 'All right,' she agreed recklessly. She could always sleep it off in the middle of the day, she thought, as she saw the size of the brandies he had poured. They could always eat in the evening. There was a pork joint from a local farm in the fridge. James might prefer to eat in the evening, anyway.

'I'm going for Australian permanent residency, Carol,' he said, as he sat down again. 'And until that comes through, I am also applying for a business visa.'

Carol remained absolutely still.

'I'm applying . . .'

'I did hear you the first time,' she said quietly.

Whatever she had expected him to say, somehow it had not been that. But there was something missing from his declaration: something in his tone of voice. There was something he wasn't telling her, she concluded.

'Is that all?'

'What do you mean, is that all?'

'Well, for instance, why do you want Australian residence?'

He shrugged. 'For all sorts of reasons, most of which I think you know. Oliver wants me to stay on. As you, yourself, pointed out, I can't work with my tourist visa.'

'Is there someone else?'

'Why do you ask that?'

This time it was Carol who sighed deeply.

'Because it seems the most logical explanation for something that I find hard to understand.'

'But last night we slept together,' James said defensively.

'We slept in the same bed. Not together, in that way.'

'I could see the other rooms were set aside for the children. While I was waiting for you to come home, I even expected the three of you to walk in together at any moment. It didn't seem a good idea to sleep anywhere else but our bed. Your bed,' he corrected himself.

'James, I do want to hear what you have to say. Maybe you'd better begin at the beginning.'

What was the beginning? James told Carol that he hardly knew himself. He had never meant it to happen. He said that several times. Carol didn't interrupt. She was finding it difficult to piece together what was turning into a rambling account of her husband's feelings, anguishings (did he use that word?), problems, dilemmas, and all the various ills that seemed to have beset him for some considerable time.

She found it hard to remember that this was the man she had lived with for so many years. She hardly knew him. Male menopause, Carol was thinking scornfully, recalling what Marion had said to her. Then she felt mean and small. She suspected there had been many times over the recent years when she'd not been easy to live with.

'I can understand why you gave up the job here,' she said eventually. 'But why embark on a very long, intense period of travel with me, when you wanted to end our marriage? And if you weren't sure what you most desired next out of life, we could have gone on a cruise while you worked it out. Or if you had needed activity, we could have gone on an adventure holiday with a small group. Perhaps if we'd travelled with other people you wouldn't have found me so dull.'

That wasn't it, at all. She wasn't getting the point, he protested vociferously. James had never, ever, wanted to go on a cruise, of any sort. Travelling with a small group could have been equally disastrous, because they might not have got on with the others. That happened all too frequently, from what he'd heard.

'You mean, you were fairly certain I would be a civilized travelling companion? Thanks. I suppose that's something in my favour.' Her comment was loaded with sarcasm.

James's reaction was to pour another large measure of brandy for himself. He thought he'd got the wanderlust out of his system when they reached Burma, he told her as he put the cork back into the brandy bottle.

'D'you know? I was looking forward to coming home. I was,' he insisted. 'I still wasn't sure quite what I'd do with my retirement, though I had no intention of sitting on my backside for the rest of my natural. You must remember how it was when we planned the trip. We thought we'd have masses of time just to sit and absorb everything we saw on our travels. Plan ahead. I mean, plan for our return home. Though it didn't work out like that, did it? I mean, we were always so busy. It was a lot more tiring than I'd expected. Even so, I loved every minute of it, all those new sights, the smells, the people, especially the people. I was even beginning to plan the next trip. To India, as we always said we'd do. But as for ideas about how we would live in Otterhaven, they just didn't materialize at all. I realized we'd have to wait until we were actually here, in the new house, to decide what happened in the future.'

'Otterhaven. Is that what all this is about? You hate the small house, even though you insisted it was what we needed when we sold Windrush. I begin to think you even dislike Otterhaven. You want big city life.'

'Actually, you're wrong. Sydney is much

like London, in many ways; a series of suburbs. Kirribilli was interesting. Being in a high rise apartment and all that was fine for a time, though essentially you shop as if you're in a village, unless you want a huge supermarket. Where I am now, where I would want to live, would be in a suburb.'

'As I said, you dislike the small village mentality.'

He ignored that. 'I tell you, I had come to no decisions while we were travelling. Then it all went pear-shaped. Those wretched Picker-ings. They ruined everything.'

'So we're back to the same old argument,' Carol cried. 'The one we began in Bangkok. I will never understand how, bringing back two children to the UK, could ruin anything for us, let alone all those plans you hadn't made.' It was a cruel jibe, but she made it remorselessly.

'Then you're the fool, not me,' he answered bitterly. 'I could see all along that we'd be landed with them for ever. I knew their uncle would never accept responsibility once he realized there was a sucker to do his job for him.'

'Peter is no such thing!'

'Not like his brother, then.'

'Half-brother.'

That needed explanation. James's eyes

narrowed as Carol began to describe how caring Peter was; how, very much against his inclinations, he had gone out to Burma to visit Brian and Kimberley.

'He is a good man, James,' she insisted. 'Peter may have told Brian that he'd have nothing more to do with him if he and Kimberley persisted in his crazy scheme to demonstrate in Burma, but, when it came to it, when the children were left on their own, he has done his best for them.'

'With a good deal of support from you. But I can see he has convinced you,' he commented drily.

'So why you had to go to Australia to decide what you want to do for the rest of your life, just eludes me. As I see it, there must be another explanation. Along with this marvellous new job, you've found someone else. Are you seriously going to tell me I'm wrong?'

'That is what I want to talk to you about.'

Carol froze.

'I keep telling you how exciting Australia is, young, vibrant . . . '

'Brash?' Carol suggested snidely.

'Maybe that, too. But it promises so much, for anyone willing to work hard. I reckon I've got at least ten years of work left in me. That's enough time to make a pile out there.

Far more than if I'd stayed with the old firm in South Wales. So I want to start afresh. I want to buy a small place, get my residency and put down roots.'

'And naturally you aren't planning to do this alone. Are you leaving me, James?'

'I don't plan to spend the rest of my life living alone. That's certainly true. What I'd like most is for you to be with me. I've missed you, Carol. You must know that.'

'Must I? You've not been exactly fulsome in your e-mails, nor over the phone, when you've managed to find time to contact me.'

'I did keep asking you to join me,' he protested.

'Oh, please. Not again, James. I couldn't, wouldn't leave the children. But you never gave me an ultimatum, as I suppose this is what this is all about now. You never said that you intended making a new life so far away. You kept telling me that after a few more weeks you would be coming home.' Yes, she thought, he had said that, except that the initial, short visit had become an extended stay. The extended stay had itself turned into a quick job for a favour. And this was to become a lifestyle.

'Look, I don't know whether I want to end my days in Australia, or not. What I want to do, is to see how it goes for the next few years at least. Is it asking too much of you to join me? You were always up for something new. Where has your spirit of adventure gone? After all, your excuse about needing to care for the children is no longer valid, is it? Kimberley Pickering is on her way home.'

'Whatever new ventures we've contemplated have never included decamping to the other side of the world. I don't think I'm a pioneer. I think I'm just a European. What exactly have you come home to do, James?'

'There's a lot of paperwork. Tomorrow I must go to London and get it sorted. There's the money side, too.'

'You want to put this house on the market?' Carol recoiled. So James was going to take the roof over her head, should she refuse to agree to his demands.

'Certainly not. It's too good an investment. Whether you come with me, or not, we'll keep this. If you come with me, we'll rent it out. Of course, if you choose to stay, we'll have to work out just how much you'll need to live on, before your pension kicks in. I hope you do appreciate that I'd never leave you short.'

Carol admitted grudgingly that it was true. She might have harboured a few moments of doubt when she was feeling particularly pessimistic but deep down she had known the truth; whatever her husband's failings were, meanness was not one of them.

'I've got investments that'll prove to the authorities I have sufficient assets to keep me until the new work pays and the rest of the Windrush money will buy me somewhere to live. Money is not going to be a problem. You know that.'

'And if I don't come with you, who will share this Australian house with you, James? It seems to me you must have wanted to get away from me, and everything in Otterhaven, for a long time. You'd have had to face it, if we had come home together. Refusing to bring back the children with me was just an excuse.' There was scorn in her voice as she persisted with her argument which was not lost on her husband.

'All right. Having the children foisted on us was the catalyst. I could see it was an opportunity to make decisions on my own. But Carol, you have to believe me. I always intended coming home to be with you. I never intended for us to part.'

'But now you've changed your mind. There is someone else,' she repeated her accusation.

'There is a possibility. I have met someone, yes, but our relationship — '

'There is a relationship . . . '

'The relationship, such as it is, is only just beginning . . . '

'You've slept with her.' There was a subtle shift in James's manner that told Carol she was correct. She wouldn't — couldn't — condemn him. They had been apart for some time — and it really didn't matter whose fault that was. The lives of both of them had suddenly diverged, like railway lines on a plateau that paralleled each other for miles before they curved apart, to skirt a lake or a mountain range, in all probability never to converge again. The analogy made her eyes moist — or was that the brandy?

Setting aside the matter of the children, James had more or less suggested that she was perverse in refusing to go to Australia with him. There was also the matter of her own, tentative, relationship with Peter.

'I need someone in my life, Carol,' James said simply. 'It could still be you, if you come back to Australia, with me. If you come with me now neither of us would be alone. Besides, it's such a great place. Let me tell you about the country.'

James's whole attitude altered as he went on to tell her about his experiences in Australia: that the climate was great, the food

310

was plentiful and varied. 'You wouldn't believe just how varied the cuisine is.'

'I'd heard food was expensive. And it rains.'

'Yes, yes,' he agreed impatiently, 'of course it rains, but above all the life there is free and easy, and basic living is a lot cheaper than in Europe.'

'Rotten newspapers and dreadful American TV.'

'You're missing the point, Carol.'

Of course she was. 'What about your roots? Your friends?'

Then it came to her that James had very few friends. He had many acquaintances, witness his extensive Christmas card list, but how many of them were truly friends? She thought she could name three, all dating to his student days. He saw these men infrequently for none of them lived anywhere near Otterhaven. So his ties to people generally were loose. Inwardly she conceded that he would most probably gain a circle of new acquaintances, who might become friends, more easily in an Australian suburb than he would by staying in Otterhaven. For her it was very different.

'I have friends, James. I would miss Marion, for one, very much. It is never easy to find kindred spirits and it becomes harder the older you are. When you have found real friends, you should nurture them. And what about family? What about Matt, our son? How can you think of moving so far away from him?'

15

'I'm well aware that Matthew is our son, thank you, Carol.' James answered his wife frostily. 'You forget that Matt has already left home. He's in Scotland now. Who knows where he might be in eighteen months' time. The oil business is worldwide.'

'That doesn't mean he won't ever need us again. And what about grandchildren? I can't imagine how dreadful it would be, never to see them, which would happen if we were on the other side of the world. That would be awful.'

James guffawed, 'Planes, Carol. But you're jumping a long way down the line, aren't you, unless you know something about our son you've yet to tell me?'

Carol shook her head. 'Matt doesn't even have a girlfriend at the moment.' She told James about Rosa. 'Poor darling. He was being robust, but I could tell it hurt, as it does, when you lose someone you love,' she said neutrally. 'You see, he came to see me on the spur of the moment. He couldn't have done that, if I'd been in Australia.'

'What you are actually saying is that you

have no intention of uprooting yourself to please me. You won't even contemplate trying out a new way of life. You've no idea how sad that makes me.'

'Fine. Just suppose I did agree to go back with you to Australia, for a few months, just to visit, once Peter and Kimberley have returned home. After all, you have had the opportunity to see quite a lot of Australia already — and please don't tell me that it is my fault,' she snapped before he could interrupt her. 'What would happen to this — relationship of yours — that might, or might not, develop, if I were to come out?'

There was a pause. Carol knew that it was a defining moment.

'You see?' James said. 'You're playing for time. You won't come with me immediately . . . '

'I can't.'

'You won't come with me immediately. It's not reasonable to expect me to give up Fenella on the off chance that you might decide to stay with me. I want — need — more than that and she has given me every encouragement to believe she wants commitment.'

Fenella. So that was her name. Fleetingly Carol wondered how they had met, what sort of a woman she was. It was a fair bet that

Fenella was much younger. So how had it come to this? Carol wondered if she had ever truly known her husband. Yet, as Marion had pointed out, there had always been more than a streak of ruthlessness in James and perhaps she was right. She had never imagined, though, that he would be capable of exercising this ruthlessness on her.

'What are we going to do?'

★ ★ ★

When it came to it, a decision to make a clean break was far from easy. (Were marital breaks ever clean?) James said he'd take a nap to cope with the jet-lag, which Carol interpreted rightly as sleeping off the brandy. He'd use the bed in Matthew's room, he said, firmly refusing to mention its new occupier. In the afternoon he needed to go through some papers which were in their fireproof box. He'd leave for London in the morning. It transpired that he'd made appointments previously. He had a flight to Aberdeen two days later. He wanted to tell his son face to face what was planned.

At least that was brave of him, Carol conceded. James could have left it all for her to explain. He expected to fly back to Sydney within the fortnight, he told her.

'Let's leave decisions for now, Carol,' James said the following morning, as he hovered on the doorstep while the taxi driver put his bags into the car. 'Sleep on it, without the distractions of brandy fumes. If you change your mind we can still fly out together.'

And then he was gone. Once again it came to Carol, as she shut the door, that not once during those hours that they had been together had James so much as touched her, let alone embraced her.

Then, neither had she felt the need to touch James.

★ ★ ★

It was ten days after Peter's phone call from Rangoon before he and Kimberley flew out of Burma. By then, Jessica and Daniel, back home from London and their Burmese friends, were suffering such swings of raw emotion that Carol was expending all her energies in trying to distract them. Her efforts at maintaining equilibrium were not always successful.

First Jessica burst into a flood of tears because she was convinced that her mother was so desperately ill that the Military Junta did not dare allow Kimberley to fly because it would prove to the world how they treated prisoners. Daniel, though, was manically preparing welcome home banners, and planning trips round Wales with his mother in a gypsy caravan which he had seen advertised for sale in the local paper.

'She'll need plenty of peace and quiet,' he said, showing an encouraging degree of maturity.

Then Jess decided that of course the prison authorities were just being dilatory and that her mother was in perfect health, having had the benefit of all the good food supplied by her uncle's generosity. Dan, on the other hand, told Carol that he very much feared that Kimberley had been tortured to death several weeks before and that no one dared tell their uncle, who was just kicking his heels in Rangoon while the consul was trying to find out exactly what had happened to her mutilated body.

As these nightmarish possibilities changed several times a day, Carol found it all extremely taxing so that she had no time at all to think about James and the ultimatum he had issued. Even in bed, before she dropped off to an exhausted sleep, or in the middle of the night when she woke with a pounding heart — not sure whether that was on account of Kimberley or Fenella — she could only hear a refrain reverberate in her brain:

How can I leave the children? They need me more than James does. James can't love me any more. How much do I still love James?

And the days were slipping by. Carol had taken two very impersonal calls from James, concerning some papers which were being sent to her for her signature. She needed to return them by special delivery, James insisted. He said not one word about a second plane ticket. Nor did Carol mention anything more about her intentions — or lack of them — other than to tell him that there was still no positive news from Peter Pickering.

★ ★ ★

Eventually there came the long-awaited phone call from Bangkok. They had not been able to contact her from Rangoon. Now they were about to get on their last flight, Peter told Carol. They would be in Heathrow in a matter of hours. Kimberley was so looking forward to seeing Jess and Dan.

'You might want to warn the children, though,' he said guardedly. 'Kimberley's going to have an immediate check up before we leave for South Wales. She is very, very tired.'

'What does that mean?' asked Dan, disgustedly. 'Can't Mum sleep on the plane?'

'Tiredness can mean a lot of things,' said Carol, who indeed wished that Peter had been a little more specific.

'Like what? Exhaustion?'

'I don't know, Jess. I am sure your mother must be physically tired because of the journey. She is probably also mentally exhausted as well. It would be surprising if she were not. But I know you'd like to be at the airport to meet her, so we'll give ourselves plenty of time to get there. But let's sort out the beds first, shall we?'

Once again there was the problem of their sleeping arrangements. Carol had agonized over who should sleep where. Although Matthew had cleared out all the boxes of his stuff, except for the books, the room was still very cramped with just enough space for a second single bed. Carol thought that Kimberley would value privacy. She wondered if she should give up her own room — but that would mean she, herself, would have to share with Jess, which she was sure the girl would hate.

In the end, Jess said that she didn't think it was a problem. Their mum could sleep in Dan's room and he could go back to the study.

'Cool,' said Dan. His thought processes were transparent.

'So long as you promise to have the computer switched off by nine o'clock,' said Carol firmly. 'I mean it. Why don't you go and fix the welcome home banners?'

She did wish that Peter had said a little more about Kimberley's state of health. Still, the joy of having their mother home with them would help the children get over the debilitated presence Carol feared Kimberley would reveal.

Someone had arranged for them to meet away from the general throng at Heathrow. Peter told Carol afterwards that this was because of the inevitable presence of the press, clamouring for pictures and interviews, which Kimberley was in no fit state to give.

Peter first hugged Jess and Dan. Then he hugged Carol, holding her tightly for a fraction longer than was socially justified. 'How I have missed you!' He said it so quietly she doubted anyone else had heard. 'You look lovely, so good, so normal. I am immensely glad to have you here, beside me.' His relief was palpable.

'You look well.' How inadequate that sounded. In contrast to Kimberley, Peter was tanned and fit. She was very conscious that she could not take her eyes from him, any more than he seemed able to leave her side. Electricity fizzed between them to such an extent that she was sure the others must feel it, too.

But Kimberley was too dazed and the children were in too fraught a state to notice anything that did not pertain to their mother, for they were shocked to the core. It was sadly all too evident that Kimberley was a shadow of her former self. Also, Kimberley would not even kiss her children or allow them to come too close.

'Not until I've had a course of antibiotics and been smothered again with cream to cure the scabies,' she told them, with a wan smile. Scabies, chest and ear infections; Kimberley, who had never been overweight in her life, had also lost a stone and a half.

'What's wrong, Mum? Why are you like this?' Jess wailed.

'Burmese prisons aren't quite like the ones in this country, dear. I suppose I was a fool not to have thought of that before . . . ' Her voice tailed off. Then she said more brightly, 'There was this disgusting curry every day.'

'But you like curry, Mum.'

'There are curries and curries, Dan. Even when I was starving, I could hardly get this one down. It's no wonder I lost weight.'

Food, books, toiletries, medicines had all

been withheld or been given out just before the consul made one of her regular visits. Kimberley had received no letters directly from home and her only news had come from the copies of those letters which the children had sent to the consulate.

'Did they hurt you, Mum?' Daniel whispered, wide-eyed.

'No, my darling,' she reassured him.

(Was she telling the truth, Carol wondered? If not, it was a kind lie told to permit her children to sleep at nights.)

'I was kept in solitary confinement. I only saw my guards and an occasional prisoner who was cleaning the yard. On the whole they were quite kind. Burmese people are basically kind, you know. It's just the Junta, the effect of the power of authority which makes people do bad things. Julie Deane, the consul, who was permitted to visit me monthly, says it's the same with your father. And no, I haven't seen Brian since we were sentenced and taken to prison, though you must ask your uncle to tell you about his visit. He and Julie were allowed to see Brian just the once.'

A cursory check up had proved that Kimberley was well enough to go home. Peter promised the doctor she had seen that he would take his sister-in-law to hospital for further tests the following day. A short press conference was arranged — at which the children demanded to be present, though they promised to be silent.

Peter read from a prepared statement. In it Kimberley thanked the prison governor for his compassion in setting her free early so that she might take care of her children. She hoped her husband would be the recipient of similar care.

All mention of the Junta, the position of 'The Lady, Aung San Suu Kyi', and other injustices were omitted because, for once, Kimberley had agreed that she should not be confrontational. Carol could sense that inwardly this opponent of the Junta was seething. But now was not the time for protest. Pictures were taken and while the cameras were rolling the still silent Dan whipped out a small placard which he held in front of him. It said simply:

Free My Dad

No one had the heart to upbraid him.

Carol had been very quiet from the moment of Peter's embrace. His presence, along with his touch, suddenly clarified all the doubts and uncertainties that had beset her. It was not so much that she knew what would happen to her in the future, for that was scary, unknown territory, it was more that she knew what she could not do, which was to embark on a new life thousands of miles away.

'I just have to make a telephone call,' she told everyone, as they were gathering up their things for the journey to Otterhaven.

She contacted James on his mobile phone. 'Kimberley and Peter are back,' she said. 'We're on our way home to Otterhaven.'

There was a pause. 'So?' asked James guardedly, on whom her use of the word 'home' was not lost.

At that moment Carol's certainty that what she was doing was absolutely right, was sustained. 'Don't worry, James. I'm not ringing to ask you to get a ticket for me on your plane. And it's not just because Kimberley is in a bad way and will need care for a time.'

'I assume it's because of Peter Pickering,' James said abruptly.

'No. It's not.'

'I don't believe you. It would have been more honest if you had told me about him when I was baring my soul to you about Fenella.'

'You don't go in for soul-baring, James. And in any case, I have made no commitment to Peter.' There was no point in maintaining that Peter did not figure somewhere in her life. Carol thought miserably of the old-fashioned virtues of love and loyalty and her heart almost broke that they — she — had failed to uphold them. For a moment her resolve wavered.

'I can hear in your voice that this man matters to you, though. Far more than I do, anyway.'

'It wasn't meant to be like this, was it?'

'I guess not. No, of course it wasn't. I never imagined we would part. Not after all those years together. Sometimes, though, you come to a crossroads and just know the path you have chosen is the right one for you. Mine is no longer in this country.' The words 'Or with you' sounded unspoken between them. There was finality in his voice.

'For the moment my commitments are to Kimberley's family,' Carol replied, unwilling herself to put into words these new thoughts and emotions that were still so raw, so novel in her own mind. 'It may, or may not, apply to Peter. But, yes, it does mean that it looks as though we have both moved on.'

'That's what I told Matt.'

'You actually told him we were separating!'

'Perhaps I know you better than you know yourself. Don't fret. He's not going to do anything stupid as a result.'

'I should think not.'

'Carol, I must go. We'll need to stay in touch. At least until the financial side has been settled.'

'Of course.' There was little more to be said. How did you end a relationship that had seemed to be rock solid but the rock of which had eroded over the years to become sand?

★ ★ ★

It was several days later. Kimberley Pickering, who had been kept in hospital overnight after her second lot of tests, was pill-popping several times a day, but already she was looking a great deal better and sounding more like her old self. Jess and Dan had stopped shadowing her every move and were beginning to revert to their normal, vocal, contempt for each other to the extent that Carol was becoming decidedly frazzled over how much authority it was now permitted her to exercise over them.

Peter had come and gone regularly between Otterhaven and Hay, though there had been little time for them to do more than snatch a few unsatisfactory moments together. The first day after Kimberley's return he had told Carol firmly that there were decisions that had to be made.

'But do you mind if I set things in order

326

before we all talk about what happens next? You see, we know things can't go on like this. Living arrangements, for a start. I have tried to talk to Kimberley about it.' That conversation had been unproductive. 'Then there is the matter of your husband and when you are to join him.'

'Not going to happen, Peter,' she replied. His eyebrows shot up. 'James and I are separating,' she added casually, as though that was one decision that had come about without any trauma.

Peter looked decidedly shaken. 'Is this . . . '

She knew he wanted to ask if this decision was because of him. Because she wasn't quite sure what his reaction was likely to be she went on hastily. 'No. I find that it doesn't actually have anything to do with you, or Kimberley, or the children. This is something that has become inevitable.' It was true. Carol understood that, now. Even if she had never met Peter Pickering, she and James were bound to have separated. 'And before you suggest that I am being very brave about the whole matter,' she went on determinedly, 'let me assure you that our parting is mostly to do with the fact that I don't in the least want to leave Otterhaven for the New World where James wants to build a new life, and it also has a little to do with James's having found a new woman with whom to share this new life. I may have been made redundant, so to speak, I am not in the least unhappy about it.'

'Oh.' He rallied. 'Right. Well then . . . '

'Why don't we have that conference on Sunday, after lunch?'

★   ★   ★

They had finished eating and the dishes were in the dish-washer. Over coffee Kimberley said:

'Thanks are inadequate, aren't they, Carol. I mean, you had every right to ignore my request for you to look after my children. James was also quite within reason not to want to have anything to do with us. That is what I should have done, given the same circumstances.'

'Mum . . . ' protested Jess.

'I mean, if I had been in Carol's place.'

'Mum, you must have known we would be left on our own. How could you just dump Dan and me for a political cause?'

Carol heard the outrage in Jessica's voice, saw the anger expressed in the way she was holding her body rigid. She had enormous sympathy for the girl's reaction. It had been a most appallingly irresponsible act on the part of two adults who should have thought

328

carefully about the consequences of their naïve actions before ever they reached Burma.

'I don't believe your mother truly understood what the likely outcome was going to be,' Peter said mildly.

'We talked about it. Of course we did,' insisted Kimberley. 'Brian knew we would be arrested. He thought he might have to serve a few months in prison. And he was prepared for that. He-we were both convinced that I would be released just because Jess and Dan were with us. We never dreamt that the Junta would do what they did. You must believe me.'

'I'm sure they do.' Carol could also see that Kimberley was becoming upset. She might be well on the way to a physical recovery, it was clear that her mental resources were still fragile.

Jessica glared mutinously at her mother and Dan moved closer to his sister.

Peter interrupted before feelings became overheated. 'I think we could argue about the rights and wrongs of what has happened for a long time and still get nowhere. What we need to do is look to the future.'

'Which is what I have been considering,' Kimberley continued. 'You might like to know that I have applied for a Burmese visa.

When it comes through, I intend to fly out. Once I'm back in Rangoon, I shall look for a small house to rent where I can live until Brian is freed. I shall keep myself by teaching English. I very much hope that Jess and Dan will come with me.'

'No way!'

'You have to be joking!' Both children spoke at once.

'Kimberley, Brian will come out of this. It will take time, but he will come home. You need to conserve your strength. Take proper stock of all your futures.'

How unexpected that Peter had been the stalwart in all this, Carol was thinking. When it really counted, he was so much kinder to the weak than James.

Kimberley shook her head stubbornly. 'My mind is quite made up. I can live very simply there and that is what I intend to do, but I would much prefer it to be with my children.'

'Do you honestly believe that the Junta will permit you to enter the country again? And as for taking the children with you, that is an outrageous suggestion. Where would they go to school? It's a well-known fact that the education system in Burma has been shot to pieces by the Junta.' Peter sounded utterly appalled.

'I shall teach them myself, as I've always done.'

'We don't want to go to Burma, Mum,' objected Dan. 'We want to stay here and go to school. There's this boy in Otterhaven whose father takes him fishing. They said I could go with them next week when he has a few days off.'

'I'm glad that you have found at least one friend here,' Peter smiled at his nephew. 'I was hoping that we could find the three of you a small house nearby. The family can't impose on Carol for longer than is strictly necessary. So having a real friend, Dan, will be much nicer for you next term when you go back to school. You see, Kimberley, Burma, for them, is totally out of the question as I am sure you will agree, once you are feeling better.'

There was steel in his voice, this time, which was not lost on the women. So Peter also had his ruthless streak, Carol was thinking with considerable approval, for she supported him entirely. She wondered fleetingly just how long Kimberley would do as she was bidden, but that was a problem Peter could deal with.

'We're going back to school in Monmouth? That's great. I'll definitely get into the footie team next year.'

331

'How do you feel about it, Jess?' Peter asked.

'Whatever,' shrugged Jessica. Then she smiled.

'You are both doing so well here and Jess has her exams next year so it would be too disruptive for you to move schools, especially to be home-taught in Burma. So it looks as though anything more than an annual visit to Brian in Rangoon is quite out of the question, Kimberley. But I promise you that I will help you to see him. And though Brian will come home, it looks as though it could be several years before that happens. So you might as well be near enough for me to visit for the time being. I suggest we look at the new development on the other side of the village. Then you'd be able to visit Carol when you like. When she invites you, that is. Carol, as Kimberley says, we can't thank you enough for what you have done for this family, but it is time for you to reclaim your life and for us to take over our own.'

It was a long speech. It was also made with conviction. But, reclaim her life, thought Carol? In spite of her declaration that her separation from James was inevitable, the realization that she was going to emerge from this totally alone came to her compellingly.

Her heart quailed. That was going to need a fortitude she was not sure she possessed.

★ ★ ★

Since Otterhaven was not one of those sprawling villages with one central street, the new housing development chosen by the Pickerings was no more than a seven minute walk from Number Fourteen. In the end, they found a three-bedroomed semi-detached house which had been acquired as Buy-to-Let. The market having become saturated with these, the owner was only too pleased to have found tenants for an initial six-month period at a reasonable rent with the option of extending the tenancy, should they desire it.

'It is to be hoped that they do settle,' said Peter to Carol, when she went to view it. 'The house is very convenient and it should be easy enough for Kimberley to run.'

The move took place in the middle of August. A van brought the family's stored belongings from Woking, but there were certain acquisitions to make. Considering that the children had arrived in Otterhaven with one small bag between them, it was amazing just how much had to be transported to the new house when they actually left, Splodge and her possessions taking up half a carload. Dan had worried about his mother's acceptance of the cat, but as with so many things, Kimberley scarcely took any notice.

'Just don't let her out for a couple of days,' advised Carol, as she carried a bag of dried cat food into the new kitchen, 'and I'm sure she won't stray.' Splodge was so much Dan's pet that she was fairly sure the animal would settle without any trouble.

'It'll be great here, won't it, Carol?' Dan enthused. 'I mean, I'll miss you. Miss you nagging about homework, I mean,' he added cheekily.

'I never nagged,' Carol protested. Dan grinned and she ruffled his hair affectionately. 'Come and see me sometimes, won't you. After school, perhaps?'

'If you keep the cake tin going, I certainly will. Mum doesn't . . . Well, I guess I might.'

'Good. That's settled, then. Jess, too, tell her. And I'm sure I'll see you all, and Uncle Peter, occasionally.'

'It'll seem strange, living here with Mum but not Dad.'

'Don't forget to keep writing those letters to him. He'd be devastated if the consul never brought him any. I should think your mum would write to him, too, if you suggested it.'

'I guess.' But Dan looked a little doubtful.

It was difficult to persuade Kimberley to be interested in anything. Then, considering what she had been through, no one could be anything but sympathetic. As her health improved, so would her mental well-being. That was what they all told each other.

16

It was the second evening after the Pickerings had left Number Fourteen for their rented house. Between them, Vera and Carol had done a massive laundry; the beds were freshly made-up, everything was spotless, and all evidence of the upheaval of the past months had been eradicated. All that was left was the cookery book which belonged to Jessica and which Carol made a mental note to return.

Carol had cooked herself a lamb chop and made a salad, which she had then eaten in the garden with a glass of red wine. Now, in the still evening of a very warm day she sat back in the lounger, gazing around the garden, her arms listlessly by her side. She had managed to keep the grass more or less under control but the edges needed trimming and weeds abounded in the borders. But somehow it all seemed such an effort.

She realized that for the first time in more weeks than she could count easily, she had absolutely nothing to do. There were no children over whom she should be concerned: had they finished their homework, who was Jess phoning, had Dan found out anything more about his father on the Net (horrors, had he discovered a chat room)? There wasn't even Kimberley to consider. There was no James she should be e-mailing with a query about his well-being.

Life, a large black hole of it, loomed in front of her and she had absolutely no idea how it would absorb her.

There came the click of the garden gate followed by a scrunch of gravel. Peter Pickering was walking up the garden path.

'I rang the bell but when there was no answer I thought I'd come round the back way in case you were out here. It's too fine an evening to be indoors.'

'Oh. I'm sorry, I didn't hear a thing.'

'No matter,' he said easily. 'Got another of these?' He indicated the lounger.

'There's one just inside the shed.' Carol gestured towards the wooden shed, partly covered with jasmine, the fragrance of which was perfuming the evening air. She found she did not even have the energy to get up from her own chair to fetch one for her guest. She scarcely had the will to wonder why he was there at all.

However, when Peter was sitting beside her, she asked him anxiously, 'Nothing's wrong, is it? They have all settled into the house? I thought you had to go back to Hay tonight.'

'They are doing very well, all things considered. Jessica sent her mother to bed immediately we had eaten and Kimberley went without a murmur. I am very impressed with those children. The influence you have exerted on them has been quite extraordinary.'

'Nothing to do with me, I assure you. If they weren't basically nice kids, nothing I could have done for them would have made the slightest difference.'

'I shan't argue,' he said amicably. 'I didn't come here to argue with you, Carol.'

'Why did you come here?'

'Well, now that I've settled Kimberley and the children for the time being, I thought the moment had come for me to do something for myself. So I came to see you. I find that I cannot be too harsh about Brian, nor can I feel anything but pity for Kimberley. If they had never gone to Burma I would not have met you. And that, as I think I mentioned before, would have been an enormous tragedy. You see, whatever happens between us now, even if you send me back to Hay telling me that you have had it up to here with the Pickerings who, what with one thing and another have ruined your life, I know that my life has been enriched immeasurably by just knowing you. I think that maybe I should have left it a few days before saying any of this. But I didn't.' He shrugged and sat back.

Carol remained silent until her breathing had returned to normal. Good, for some reason, had come from unspeakably sad events. At least, it was so for her. She turned her head towards him and her smile was sweet. 'I don't think I said it at the time. But, welcome home, Peter.'

★ ★ ★

Late summer came and went; autumn arrived, wet and windy, and the leaves changed their colour. From a tired green they became firstly yellow and then a fiery bronze heralding the demise of the year.

Bizarrely, Carol continued to feel as though she were living in limbo. Welcoming Peter home had resulted in a new, intense relationship. Yet Carol was uncertain where it would lead. At her age? Peter was altogether less emotional, less exhausting than James. Yet along with the passion (immediate, thrilling,) there was comradeship between them and shared laughter, which itself was new and exhilarating.

They lay against the pillows one afternoon

in the wide double bed which just fitted into the bedroom. They were holding hands. Mugs of tea were on the bedside cabinets. Peter had come over from Hay, having closed the bookshop for the day.

He said, 'You are the most comfortable woman I've ever known.'

She considered that. What would she have preferred to be called, stimulating, exciting?

She sat up and thumped him lightly on his smooth chest where only a few grey hairs sprouted. 'Twenty — ten years ago, I'd have been offended by that remark. Walked out, at the very least.'

'And now?'

She laughed softly. 'I'd better be flattered,' she said. 'Comfortably flattered.'

★　★　★

As Dan had promised, he came to visit her after school at least once a week. She was very touched, feeling that a boy of his age surely had friends to see, things to do, which should not include visiting an elderly woman. Then she thought that maybe his visit to her meant that his arrival home was delayed (a delay that might be put down by way of an excuse to a charitable impulse), for his relations with his mother were ambivalent, to say the least.

Jessica rarely visited. Dan dropped the odd hint of a group of girls who were always huddled in a corner, giggling. Carol thought that this was entirely healthy, given that for most of her adolescence so far Jessica had only had one friend of her own age to support her. There was even talk of a boy called Tim, who was said to fancy her.

'Yuk,' said Dan to Carol. 'As if.'

'It's good to have friends,' Carol said circumspectly. 'But do tell Jess that I would like to know if she has tried that recipe for the Mexican croustade which she said she thought sounded yummy.'

'I am so, like, bored with vegetables,' complained Dan, munching a large slice of fruit cake.

'I thought your mum cooked meat for you.'

'Mum isn't in to much cooking,' said Dan. 'If Jess cooks, it's never meat, and I'm not much good at it. Besides,' he hesitated. 'Mum says meat is too expensive.' He reddened. 'I don't think I'm supposed to tell you that.'

'I shan't repeat it,' said Carol, wondering if she had the right to betray Dan by mentioning to Peter that the family finances seemed a bit stretched.

'I guess that's OK, then,' he answered

graciously. 'I say, is there any more of that cake?'

'If I'd known you were that hungry, you could have had a sausage sandwich first. I've two cold sausages in the fridge.'

'Oh, yes,' he said eagerly. 'Sweet and sour, you know. You are great, Carol.'

'And you are a shameless flatterer,' she grinned in reply. 'Pass me over the tomato sauce, please.'

★　★　★

Later, Marion called round. 'Have you heard the news? Johnny Covington collapsed this morning.' Johnny had taken over Carol's work at the CAB when she went travelling with James.

'Goodness! Is he all right?' asked Carol anxiously. 'I always thought Johnny was the epitome of good health. You know, played golf regularly; gardened. Poor Cindy. She must be very worried.'

'I guess we'll hear soon enough. Seen much of Peter recently?' Marion asked innocently. She had met Peter one evening when she called unexpectedly and found him there. Over a prolonged drink, Marion had formed an excellent opinion of him — which view she impressed on Carol frequently. 'You don't

342

want that one to disappear, you know.'

'I only know you talk a lot of rot on occasions,' Carol glared.

Marion merely gave her a superior smile.

Johnny made an excellent recovery but Cindy demanded that her husband curtail his interests. Sandy Williams called Carol, who had half expected to be approached. 'You will do it, won't you? We have a whole list of cases piled up and I'm getting desperate.'

'Of course I'll come in. Hey, starting tomorrow?'

It seemed godsent, if you could call the ill-health of someone else such a thing. Carol felt renewed energy surge through her. At least work would take her mind off other things that seemed to be stagnating in her life.

For Peter was suddenly proving elusive. They saw each other at least once a week. Peter came over to Otterhaven every Sunday and the Pickerings always asked Carol to join them for lunch — which, in any case, was cooked by him, for Kimberley still seemed unable to cope and Peter said it was unfair to expect Jessica to provide a meal for five, whether it contained meat or not. So he would arrive in sufficient time to put the joint in the oven (which he brought with him), and leave the children to prepare the vegetables while he strolled round to Number Fourteen to fetch Carol.

There was usually an evening in the week when Peter also came over — though he rarely stayed the night, insisting that he needed to return to Hay to be ready for the morning rush. They would cook together, eat their meal, engage in conversation, sometimes watch television. It was almost like being in a marriage of many years' standing. Though as running a secondhand bookshop seemed an unlikely source of early morning 'rush', Carol was left perplexed as to how Peter actually saw their relationship, other than as an outlet for occasional passion. She knew that what she felt for Peter was special, though she found it difficult to tell the man so, since he was so reticent about his own feelings. Peter, taking over from where James had hardly been for some years should have been wonderful. His sudden ambivalence was unnerving.

Then James communicated with her at last. This time it was through a firm of solicitors in Sydney.

Since his departure, there had been virtually no news of her husband. Indeed, Carol's main source of information was Matthew. She was so relieved that father and son were able to maintain some contact. She was also greatly reassured that the break in his parents' marriage had not turned Matthew against his mother. Apparently James was still enthralled with Australia. His new job was proving lucrative as well as inspirational (James's description). He was becoming increasingly besotted with Fenella.

This, alone, ought to have alerted Carol to the news that her husband wanted a divorce.

Well, of course he did, she acknowledged after the first, foolish feelings of outrage and despondency. Such an immature reaction, she also recognized, once she had had time to consider the matter objectively. James would never return to the UK. She still had not the slightest wish even to visit the Antipodes. James had never cared to fend for himself. That was why she had been so astounded when he had proved capable of cooking his own breakfast. James also liked the company of other people. While not being wholeheartedly gregarious, he could be the life and soul of a party (and become morose on returning home). He did not like being excluded from the social scene for long. No wonder he had latched on to Fenella so quickly.

That was a bitchy thought, Carol accepted. For all she knew, Fenella might be James's soul mate in a way she had never been. Of course he had the right to want a divorce.

'So how do you feel now?' Peter asked two evenings later when, over their meal, she had told him. It was a Saturday night and Peter was intending to stay with Carol.

'It is so stupid. I can't make up my mind whether I am bitter, angry, relieved, happy, or just resigned.'

He looked at her strangely for a moment. 'Bitter? As in you want him back?'

'Of course not! That is the very last thing I want. I think I am just so dismayed that I failed to keep our relationship going.'

'It takes two to . . . '

'Tango? I know, Peter. If Matthew had been younger I might even have gone out to Australia to try again. But as he's an adult . . . ' she shrugged. 'Matthew says he's been invited to spend Christmas with his father. He says he'll definitely go, but that he can't see himself ever wanting to live there. I think he means it, which has to be a relief. I couldn't imagine losing them both,' she ended unguardedly.

'Even though the decision to divorce came from James and not you?'

'Is that important?'

'I did wonder. I thought the reason you were hesitant about committing to me was because you couldn't make up your mind whether or not to divorce James.'

She was looking at him with utter bewilderment.

'What do you mean, that I am hesitant about committing?'

'You come to bed with me. You have never yet said that you love me.' His voice was harsh. 'You know how I feel about you.'

'I thought . . . I was sure you . . . This is utterly idiotic.'

'Is it? You are angry about James. You feel bitter. That doesn't sound as though you have much room for positive feelings about me, does it?' Suddenly he threw down his napkin and got to his feet. 'Thank you for the meal. I don't think I shall be staying the night, after all.'

'Peter . . . '

'We shall, naturally, expect you for lunch tomorrow. The children would be very upset if you were not there. I guess it's not too late for me to use Kimberley's sofa bed tonight.'

She was still sitting there, her fork in her hand, total amazement in her eyes, when the front door closed firmly behind him.

'But you haven't had any pudding . . . ' The words emerged as a soft cry of protest. She doubted if she had ever felt as low as she did just then.

She looked at the food which was slowly congealing on her plate. She got up from the table and scraped what was left into the bin. She couldn't even remember, at that moment, what the meal had consisted of. She looked at the fruit tart which was keeping warm on the stove and she pushed the dish to one side; contemplated coffee. She went back to the table and refilled her glass. Full.

It was only nine thirty. The evening stretched ahead. Empty.

Yes, she would consult Polly Firmer, or someone who knew about divorce. She would do that on Monday. That would settle the matter of James. And what of Peter?

The phone rang. There seemed to be a commotion down the other end of the line. She was quite unable to hear who was ringing her. She almost put the receiver down. Something stopped her.

'Carol. Carol!' The urgent voice at the other end was Peter's. There was the distinct sound of a door slamming. Then there was silence. 'Carol, are you still there?'

Into the silence, she said, 'Peter?'

'We have a crisis. I don't know what to do. Carol. Please, would you come round? Now? I know I . . .'

She said immediately, 'I'll come straight away. Don't waste time trying to tell me over the phone. I'll be as quick as I can.'

She looked at the wine glass. It was still

half-full. To hell with it, she thought. Dutch courage to cope with a crisis. So? She finished the glass. Then she changed her shoes, put on a coat, picked up her handbag, checking to see that she had her keys. Then she pulled the front door behind her.

★ ★ ★

The new house — which had no name and was in fact Number Fifty Seven — was still in uproar when Carol rang the bell. So much of an uproar that she had to ring three times before anyone came to open it. It was a wonder that none of the neighbours were hovering, consumed with curiosity, she was thinking.

'Thank God!' Peter almost pulled her into the tiny hallway.

Upstairs, Jessica could be heard screaming hysterically. Carol could just about make out the words: 'Cow! I never, ever want to see her again!' They were repeated, variously.

Carol looked at Peter questioningly. He shook his head, but he took her coat, draping it over the banisters. He was quite pale, she noticed. Her heart smote her. First the row with her, now a full-scale tantrum from Jessica. Poor man.

Dan emerged from the sitting-room. His

hair was ruffled as if he had been burrowing into the cushions and his face was flushed from crying. He was clutching Splodge in his arms. The cat had burrowed her head into the boy's neck and her tail was twitching uneasily.

'Hi, Dan. Splodge looks a bit unsettled,' Carol said cautiously.

'Mum's done a runner,' Dan said. Then he turned and went back into the sitting-room. The two in the hall heard the TV being switched on and the volume turned up.

'Come into the kitchen. Carol,' Peter said urgently, when they were in the family kitchen with the door closed, 'about this evening.'

Carol shook her head. 'That's not important now. Peter, tell me what's happened.'

'It's true, what Dan said. Kimberley has gone. She's flying to Thailand at this moment.'

The door opened and Jess came in. She looked dreadful, her hair a mess, her face blotchy. She was clutching a handkerchief. Instinctively Carol went to her and put her arms round the girl, hugging her, then gently stroking her back. There was a moment of resistance, then Jess relaxed against Carol, pressing her face against Carol's neck as if she had always wanted the comfort offered.

They had all been worried about Kimberley. But the scabies had gone and the doctor said there was nothing wrong with her that time wouldn't heal. Gradually she was putting back the weight she had lost. It was also a fact, however, that she had no energy at all. She got up late, drank several cups of coffee for breakfast, then she went back to bed for an hour or so. Dutifully she ate what her daughter put before her at teatime. Then Kimberley went to bed early. Jessica did the washing and the ironing. Daniel dusted when he knew Carol was coming for Sunday lunch.

'I didn't know that,' said Carol, aghast. 'I would have come round more often, but Kimberley never seemed to want me here. Jess, you should have told me.'

'Not your fault, Carol,' said Jess hardly. 'Mum said we ought to cope on our own. You heard her say she wanted to go back. She kept on at me and Dan, begging us to go back to Burma with her.'

'I thought she'd given up that notion,' Carol said.

Jessica shrugged. 'I didn't say anything, I mean — for fuck's sake — d'you think they'd let any of us into their manky country again? I told Mum she had to get real. I thought she'd gone off the idea, too.'

Carol winced at the language, shot a

warning glance at Peter who she was sure would erupt. He merely shook his head.

Kimberley had not gone off the idea. She had been saving their money for a ticket to Thailand. She was sure there were no prohibitions against her entry there. She intended to make her way to the border with Burma. Once there and to keep herself, she was going to offer to teach English at one of the refugee camps. She thought that from there she would have the best chance to enter Burma. In the meantime she would try to get word to Brian to let him know that she was waiting for his release.

'She's going to The Friendship House. That place we told you about. The settlement on the Thai/Burma borders run by friends of Burmese refugees. They were the people Brian met up with at the pagoda. The man you saw him talking to. Brian had money with him to give them which had been raised in London.'

'How do you know all this?' Carol asked weakly.

'Kimberley phoned from Heathrow. Just before she boarded the plane,' said Peter.

'Couldn't she have been stopped?'

'How? Mum's done nothing illegal,' commented Jess.

'Except abandon us. Again,' said Dan, who

had crept into the kitchen while Jess and his uncle were explaining matters to Carol.

'Mum said as we weren't coming with her we'd be better off with Uncle Peter. I hate her, Carol. I hate her,' Jess yelled, and burst into tears again.

'But what are we going to do without her?'

'We'll manage, Dan, won't we, Carol?' Peter said huskily.

'Anyway, Carol's a lot better cook than Mum', said Dan brightly. 'She even cooks beef.' His voice tailed away.

'Of course we'll manage,' said Carol firmly. 'You'll see, but I suppose there's nothing we can do until tomorrow. I think we should all go to bed, don't you? Talk again, then.'

'And that's just what we'll do. At least no sofa bed for me,' said Peter thankfully, 'I'll sleep in Kimberley's bed.'

'See you tomorrow, Carol?' asked Dan anxiously. 'Um, you know,' his voice wobbled. 'Actually I could do with some help with my English.'

'We'll do it tomorrow morning.'

★ ★ ★

By rights, she ought to be half-tight, Carol thought as she strode steadily home, having first accepted another glass of wine then

353

declined Peter's offer to accompany her back. She knew very well that the children would have been on tenterhooks until he walked in through the door again. Shock had sobered her. Talk tomorrow; decide tomorrow. But in reality there was nothing to talk about, or to decide. It was just as well that their beds were made up with clean sheets, she was thinking, as she let herself in through her own front door. This time she really was in it for the long haul, for there was no possibility of her being able to leave those children on their own. As for what Peter would do, or say, well that was for him to make up his own mind about.

As she made her own preparations for bed, Carol found that she was smiling and her heart, which had felt so leaden, if not totally at ease, was infinitely lighter.

★ ★ ★

Carol went round early to the Pickerings' house. Jessica was still in bed and Dan was struggling with his homework. Uncle Peter, he told her, had said there was someone he had to see and that he was bringing back a chicken for lunch.

'Chicken for lunch? Great,' said Carol.

'Shall I peel the potatoes while you finish that?'

'Can't,' said Dan briefly. 'Don't understand it.'

'Let's have a look at it, then.'

Carol got him sorted out, then she peeled the potatoes and did some sprouts. There were frozen peas to go with the sprouts and a ready meal for Jessica. She combined the ingredients for a steamed ginger pudding and put the oven on to heat.

Peter came in around eleven o'clock, bearing the chicken and a bottle of wine. Carol was aware that immediately the door opened Dan expelled a long breath. She shut a cupboard door with more force than it needed. Wretched parents, she was thinking! How could they damage their children so.

When they had put the chicken in the oven, Peter put his arm round Carol's waist and when she turned in surprise, he kissed her. It was the first time he had been demonstrative in front of either of the children.

Dan actually chuckled. When Jessica came down he said: 'Guess what? Uncle Peter's getting soppy over Carol. How gross is that?'

'Whatever,' said his sister lightly. 'What am I eating for lunch?'

'Bought vegetarian cottage pie. Not a lot of

choice, I'm afraid. Not all that much food in the house,' said Carol carefully.

'Mum didn't spend much on food,' Jessica pointed out.

'Nor on anything else. I have to take the term's chess club money to school tomorrow,' said Dan.

Peter raised his eyebrows, but only said to remind him after lunch. 'I've something to tell you all while we're eating.'

'So have I,' said Carol. 'In fact, as there's an hour to go before we eat, I think I'll tell you now. You see, everything is ready for you at home, so you'd better pack a bag each and then you can come back with me this afternoon.'

'Do you mean that?'

'Of course I do, Jessica. Peter will need to return to Hay and you certainly can't stay here on your own. Besides, you won't believe how much I've missed you both. And Splodge, too.'

'Mum didn't like Splodge. I saw her kicking her once.'

'I daresay she tripped,' suggested Carol.

'But what if Mum wants to ring home?' Jessica asked, belying her determination never to speak to her mother again.

'She knows Peter's number. And mine,' said Carol. What the children did not have was a means of communicating with their mother, she was thinking, her blood threatening to boil again. 'By the way, did you write to your father this weekend? No? Then, why don't you do that this afternoon? But, perhaps better not mention where your mother could be. You don't want to alert the Burmese authorities that she might be trying to enter the country illegally.'

'Good thinking,' said Peter. 'I'd better tell you my news, now. I'm buying Philip Gerard's bookshop.'

It needed explanation. Quite by coincidence, Peter had met Philip Gerard in the street in Otterhaven some weeks previously. Gerard had told Peter that he and his partner, who wasn't a well man, had decided that they would give up the shop, and take early retirement. They had found a country cottage and intended living there together in peace and quiet.

'He asked me if I knew of anyone who might like to buy the bookshop as a going concern. The timing is fantastic.'

'You'd run both shops, Uncle Peter?'

'No, Jess. I've told Philip Gerard that I'll buy from him at the market rate. I'll sell my own business and come and live in Otterhaven.'

'Live with us?'

'I was hoping you'd all come and live with me. You see, Gerard's bookshop is about the same size as mine, but as the building is on three floors, there are four bedrooms. Masses of space. And a garden,' he added, looking at Carol.

'A garden,' she said feebly.

'It's not a mansion, but it could become a home.'

'Come on, Dan,' said Jess determinedly, getting up. 'I think Uncle Peter is about to propose to Carol, and I really, really don't want to hear this.'

Muttering inaudibly, Dan followed her.

'She really, really doesn't want to hear this; or she really, really doesn't want to know anything about this, do you think?' Peter asked anxiously.

She could not prevent the gurgle of laughter at the look on his face. 'I think she's just being a teenager. Oh, Peter, are you sure?'

'About marrying you? I have never been so sure in my life.'

A surge of untrammelled relief and joy went through her but still Carol persisted. It seemed imperative to be certain that this man was not changing his life for a whim. 'I didn't mean that. I meant, are you sure you want to sell your bookshop in Hay and come and live in Otterhaven?'

'I'd sooner have my stock than Gerard's, but I imagine that can be rectified. As for the house, of course it's much more suitable for a family than my two rooms. And I can see that I'm going to have that family whether I like it or not.'

'Will you mind so dreadfully?'

'How can you ask? Finding myself with a family after so long, after thinking it would never happen, is overwhelming, but in the nicest possible way. Surrogate, borrowed, that doesn't matter in the slightest. It will give me a happiness I never expected to come my way. Except . . . '

'Except what?'

'That I'm not going to have the luck to convince you how much I want this. I gather, you won't be accepting my proposal. Commit to me, live with me, marry me once you are free. All of these — any of these — so long as you don't give up on me.'

'Peter, I'm sorry about last night. I was thinking aloud. I was thinking about my life with James as having been a total failure. Which it wasn't, and I'm not going to go in for regrets because we produced Matthew,' she said firmly. 'I never meant you to feel I wasn't ready for commitment. I love you, very much, but I think I was just scared of saying more than you wanted to hear. Particularly because of James.'

So then he kissed her.

'Do you know the best part about this unforeseen family of ours?' Peter said, as he gazed deep into her clear eyes. 'One of these days we shall be able to give them back to their parents, all well-brought up and educated. And then, my dearest, then I shall have you all to myself. Bliss.'

And with that, Carol couldn't have agreed more.

ACKNOWLEDGEMENTS

Burma is a beautiful country. It is also suffering under a brutal regime. For a comprehensive study of what it means to be Burmese today read *The Heart Must Break: The Fight for Democracy and Truth in Burma* by James Mawdsley, published by Century, 2001. *Twilight Over Burma: My Life as a Shan Princess* by Inge Sargent, published by the University of Hawaii Press, 1994, tells of the military coup from the perspective of the then ruling class. George Orwell's *Burmese Days*, Penguin Books, 1934, shows how little some things have changed.

All the characters (except living, political figures) are fictional. So far as I know, there is no Friendship House — though there may be something like it, somewhere.

My thanks go to Sue Dent, Manager of the Monmouth Citizens' Advice Bureau, for explaining their valuable work to me. Any misinterpretations are mine alone. My thanks also go to the editorial team at Robert Hale to whose careful editing I am once again indebted. Thanks to the staff of Monmouth

Library who are always friendly and helpful; to Mary Newman, and as always to my husband, Eric, who showed me Pagan from the basket of a balloon.

We do hope that you have enjoyed reading this large print book.

Did you know that all of our titles are available for purchase?

We publish a wide range of high quality large print books including:
Romances, Mysteries, Classics
General Fiction
Non Fiction and Westerns

Special interest titles available in large print are:
The Little Oxford Dictionary
Music Book
Song Book
Hymn Book
Service Book

Also available from us courtesy of Oxford University Press:
Young Readers' Dictionary
(large print edition)
Young Readers' Thesaurus
(large print edition)

For further information or a free brochure, please contact us at:
Ulverscroft Large Print Books Ltd.,
The Green, Bradgate Road, Anstey,
Leicester, LE7 7FU, England.
Tel: (00 44) 0116 236 4325
Fax: (00 44) 0116 234 0205

Other titles published by
The House of Ulverscroft:

THE GIRL WHO DISAPPEARED

A.V. Denham

Fifty-one-year-old Hetty is an unmarried schoolteacher who has lived with her mother all her life. On her mother's death she is liberated and finds herself wooed by Clive and the widowed artist Tom, father of one of her students, Megan. Megan's friends, Jit and Balbiro, are Sikh cousins who are facing arranged marriages. While Jit agrees and accepts her fate, Balbiro rebels against her family's choice and disappears. But, as Hetty and Jit both learn to manipulate events to their own advantage, the true horror of Balbiro's situation is revealed.

SEEDS OF DESTRUCTION

A.V. Denham

When Joe set up separate homes with Amanda and Sara he sowed the seeds of destruction. Living with each of them for half the week, he used his deceased Aunt Ethel as an alibi for spending so much time away from his families — But the domestic calm becomes threatened, especially when Amanda's son, Simon, meets Harriet, the daughter of Sara — As the two women discover Joe's deception, they must sort out their lives. Would it all prove too much for Joe? Could living as one family solve their problems? Can there ever be an acceptable resolution?

THE STONE BOAT

A.V. Denham

Three men, Oliver, Philip and Bill, and two women, Ella and Rebecca, decide to walk the Camino, one of the world's great pilgrimages. They all come from very different backgrounds, but are drawn together by their need to move forward. For example, Rebecca is haunted by the sudden death of her children, and Oliver is recovering from a brain tumour. As Santiago de Compostela draws ever nearer, the pilgrims' various reasons for undertaking the strenuous walk are revealed, and the travellers learn a great deal not only about their companions, but also about themselves.

THE DANGEROUS SPORTS EUTHANASIA SOCIETY

Christine Coleman

After her escape from an old people's home where her son, Jack, and his new partner have placed her, Agnes's quest to find her grandchildren is complicated by unexpected encounters. These new friends include: Joe, the helpful lorry driver; Molly, the garrulous hotel-owner; Gazza, the student; and Felix, the retired barrister's clerk, whom Agnes pulls back from attempted suicide. Hoping to rekindle Felix's desire to live, she invents the Dangerous Sports Euthanasia Society, but soon fears that this falsehood, having acquired a momentum of its own, will end in tragedy.

THE TOWN WITH NO TWIN

Barry Pilton

Abernant is an idyllic rural town . . . except for the simmering hatreds, crooked politics and sexual debauchery. The mayoress, to elevate her social status, commissions a statue for the town. But the local sculptor is a drunk, who loves to shock. Duly shocked is the butcher, who has a vendetta with the deli owner, who in turn hates the mayoress. The statue's prospects seem dodgy. Meanwhile, the commodore has hired out his mansion to a film company, which has been less than honest about their plans. Watching all this is *The Mid-Walian*, a newspaper with a desperate need to increase its sales . . .

NWA

Please return / renew by date shown.
You can renew at:
norlink.norfolk.gov.uk
or by telephone: 0844 800 8003
Please have your library card & PIN ready.

26 MAY 09
5·8·15

NORFOLK LIBRARY ROTATION
AND INFORMATION SERVICE

NORFOLK ITEM

30129 052 877 751